Story Overview

Historian and ancestry website owner, Cassie first became interested in her long lost Broun clan when she realized life was about to change forever. Faced with possible blindness, she seeks out her Scottish bloodline only to discover there is so much more to it than she could have anticipated. Not only will she find answers to her questions but a doorway into the distant past via a Claddagh ring.

Betrothed since birth to a lass he has never met, Chieftain Logan MacLomain thought the unending tie between his clan and the Brouns was long past. Never was he more wrong. When Cassie appears in a skirmish on the border of his clan's land, all his noble intentions are put to the test. To desire her is wrong but still he seeks her out every chance he gets. Just a glimpse of her passing smile brightens the honorable yet lonely path he must see through.

Everything changes for Cassie and Logan the day war ravages a nearby village and a young king's fate is put at risk. Scotland's future hangs in the balance as denied love blossoms and four MacLomain warriors band together to save all that might soon be lost. Set to avenge the harm done, Logan embarks on a quest with Cassie that will take them both down a road fraught with risk, heartache and the beginning of an end they never saw coming.

Series Overview

There is a little-known part of history that celebrates four mystical men, Scottish warriors all, who would do anything to protect a wee bairn. It is a tale born of passion, magic, adventure and even time-travel. A tale of a band of warriors who sacrificed everything to keep safe the future of Scotland. Not only did they strive to see their beloved clan not lost to the past but were determined to see a great Scotsman rise up. A powerful man who would someday rule well his country and see that her heart was not lost... Here's to Roibert a Briuis, best known as Robert the Bruce, King of the Scots, one of the most famous warriors of his generation in the Wars of Scottish Independence.

Quest of a Scottish Warrior
The MacLomain Series-Later Years
Book One

By

Sky Purington

Dedication

This is dedicated to author Sharon A. Donovan. Succeeding in life despite eventual blindness, her love for painting turned to the beautiful masterpieces she created when writing. An inspiration to us all, I will never forget you, my friend.

1957-2012

"May the wearer of the Claddagh find love, friendship and loyalty." ~From The Claddagh Ring by Sharon A. Donovan

Visit her website, www.sharondonovan.blogspot.com to learn more about Sharon's memorable books.

Edited by *Cathy McElhaney*
Cover Art by *Tamra Westberry*

Published in the United States of America

Prologue

11 July, 1274

Turnberry Castle
The Coast of Kirkoswald Paris
Just North of Ayrshire, Scotland

"BE BORN ALREADY my wee bairn," Sir Robert VI de Brus muttered and waved over another mug of whisky.

Logan remained silent by his side as the new Norman ruler scanned his surroundings with bleary eyes. Most if not all had their heads down and were likely wishing they could leave as Marjorie, Countess of Carrick, released another blood-curdling scream.

"Too long this takes," Robert slurred, worry in his voice. "Hours now."

"Aye, m'laird," Logan said. "Dinnae fret. Countess Marjorie is a strong lass."

Theirs was an interesting tale what with the Countess holding Robert captive until he agreed to marry her. He had only come to deliver news that her late husband had been killed in battle, yet it seemed the lass was taken by his good looks. Either way, they had found love despite their unusual beginning and were now getting ready to welcome their second child.

Robert chugged down his newly delivered whisky then sighed. Minutes later, Logan breathed a sigh of relief when the man's chin rested on his chest and a loud snore erupted.

He flinched as the Countess released another mournful wail.

Something was wrong.

When an old woman came to the door of the Countess's chambers and nodded at him, Logan flicked his wrist and strode her way. By the time he entered, none save the woman who called him over knew he had been there. And certainly no one would ever know he'd entered this room. In fact, nobody save the Countess would ever know he had even been in this castle to begin with.

"Logan," she whimpered and squeezed his hand.

Soaked in sweat, she lay in a large four poster bed with a thin blanket covering her.

"Shh, m'lady, all will be well." He placed a soothing hand against her clammy forehead, speaking to her even as he chanted within his mind. "We will get yer bairn safely into this world."

The Countess tried to nod but was far too weak. No matter, the more he chanted, the easier things became for her. His eyes locked with the old woman's. She nodded and readied herself for delivery.

Not long after, Marjorie released another long wail then slumped back.

At first there was only silence.

A heartstopping quiet as everything hung in the balance.

Had the child survived?

Moments later he released a thankful breath when a cry rent the air. The baby lived. After she washed and swaddled the babe, the old woman placed him in the Countess's waiting arms. Marjorie murmured a soft greeting to her newborn son. "Welcome, my wee one. Welcome, *Roibert a Briuis*. Might ye be a strong and noble lad."

Logan kissed both her and the bairn on the forehead before he left.

May this be the beginning of a very short quest but somehow he sensed it would not be.

After all, a great man had just been born.

Robert the Bruce, future King of Scotland.

Chapter One

Salem, New Hampshire
2015

CASSIE TURNED DOWN the music as she took exit two off of Route 93. "I thought this trip would take less time, but I guess I was wrong."

"I told you it was a hike from Winter Harbor to Salem." Nicole snorted. "I'm surprised your old clunker made it."

"Shh, quiet." Cassie patted the steering wheel of her '87 Chevy Chevette, winked then popped a piece of gum in her mouth. "My baby might hear you." She nodded at her cell phone. "Damn thing. You need to restart it then get the GPS working again. Meanwhile, I'll pull over and gas up."

"Uh huh," Nicole said absently as she eyed the map on her lap.

Cassie shook her head, hopped out and stretched. It was still hard to believe that she was finally going to meet another long lost Broun relative. Then again, she was sort of surprised it took this long. She had already connected with three others years ago through her ancestry website. Jacqueline, Erin, and Nicole. Since then, they had become fast friends. It helped that they all lived in New England. Cassie in upstate Maine, Erin in Southern Vermont and Jacqueline and Nicole in Massachusetts.

Nicole cranked down the window. "Just got a text from Sean. He's standing by to FaceTime."

"Nice. Let him know we're close."

Sean O'Conner, or better yet the bookstore he now owned, was the reason she had discovered there were more Brouns in the area. The family name had popped up in an archive associated with his store so she wasted no time heading that way. As it turned out, the people working at the store knew nothing about it.

Not about to give up so easily, Cassie researched the name of the current owner and she and Nicole went directly to his house in Winter Harbor. Surprisingly enough, Sean was a tall, good-looking fishing boat captain around their age. Nicole, firecracker that she was, fell hard for him in under a minute.

They explained why they were there and though he seemed hesitant at first, they tossed back a few beers and he shared why the name Broun was affiliated with his bookstore. He had come by the store through a woman named Cadence who, as it turned out, was related to the Brouns. He had no idea what became of Cadence but gave them her sister, Leslie's name. Leslie currently resided in North Salem, New Hampshire.

If all that good luck wasn't enough, he was also in possession of a manuscript that apparently revolved around several Broun cousins. They were able to leaf through it briefly. Titled *The MacLomain Series: Next Generation*, it was about Broun women who traveled back in time to medieval Scotland. Better yet, a clan called the MacLomains. It was pretty fantastical with wizards and dragon-shifters, but intriguing nonetheless.

After they left, Cassie immediately contacted Leslie and told her about the Broun Society she had started on her website and how much she and her three friends would like to meet her. Though Leslie said no at first, she ended up calling back the next day. Not only did she insist they visit but that they stay at her house. No need to rent a room at a motel.

So here they were.

Almost.

Jaqueline and Erin would join them in a few days.

Though Sean wouldn't let them take the manuscript to Leslie, he said he would show it to her via FaceTime.

"I could *so* use an iced coffee," Nicole chimed through the window.

Cassie put the gas nozzle back on its hook and shut the tank lid. "You got it, sweetie."

Minutes later, Chai tea in hand, she navigated down Rt. 97. Nicole sipped her iced coffee and eyed Cassie's cell. "I'd really like to ask Sean out."

"I bet you would." Cassie shook her head. "Let it go. Long distance relationships never work out."

"He's so hot, though." Nicole pouted. "Coulda been cast in the movie, *The Perfect Storm*, that one."

"Yeah, if Clooney didn't land the part." Cassie eyed Nicole. "Did you get the GPS going? I don't hear anything."

"Right, hang on." Within seconds, Google Maps was once more talking to them.

"I still can't believe this place is so close to America's Stonehenge," Cassie said. "We'll definitely have to swing by there before we leave."

Nicole nodded. "Not really my bag but I'm on board if that's what you wanna do, my friend."

Thankfully, it was only another ten minutes or so before they turned off onto a dirt road. They passed a small, ranch-style house, but the GPS told them to keep going.

"Oh wow," Cassie said as they came to the end. A large, freshly painted barn was on the left and on the right, a quaint Colonial overshadowed by an ancient, gnarly oak tree. Autumn was peaking, swathing the land in bright orange, red and yellow.

"Yeah, no kidding *wow*," Nicole said. "Nothing like pulling your way-past-being-on-its-last-leg car up next to a brand new luxury sports car. Look at that beauty!"

"Sure, gorgeous," Cassie murmured, not paying attention to the other car. Something about this place felt so familiar, as though she had been here before. A golden colored horse with a reddish blond tail and mane trotted out of the forest.

"What the?" she whispered. With small braids interwoven into his long, black hair, a man turned the steed in their direction. Startlingly handsome, he wore a blue and green plaid, a dark tunic, and black boots.

"Dear God, look at him," Nicole said.

"I am." She glanced at her friend. "What's with the Scottish getup though?"

"Huh?" Nicole's dark red brows slammed together. "Since when are jeans and a t-shirt Scottish?"

Cassie's eyes flew back to the man. She blinked several times. What the *hell*? Gone was the Scotsman and even the horse she had seen. In his place, another man altogether…and another horse. Not to say this one wasn't a fine specimen as well.

Nicole was out of the car before Cassie opened her door. By the time she joined her friend, he was swinging off his horse and smiling

13

at them. "You must be the Brouns who contacted Leslie," he said in greeting. "Welcome, lasses. I'm Bradon."

It was the first time she had ever seen Nicole's jaw drop and her friend speechless. Cassie didn't much blame her. He was pretty hot with his tall, muscular frame and brilliant emerald green eyes. Then there was the thick Scottish burr. That alone could make a woman weak in the knees. Yet she was less interested in his astounding looks and kick-ass accent than she was the fact he was *Scottish* when she had clearly just seen an entirely different Scotsman trot out of the woods.

Cassie gave Nicole a 'snap out of it' pat on her shoulder and shook Bradon's hand. "Nice to meet you. I'm Cassie." She nodded at her awe-struck friend. "And this is Nicole."

Nicole's eyes were wide as she shook his hand. "Nicole. Never Nikkie or Nics or any other variation."

Bradon quirked the corner of his lip. "Nice to meet you, *Nicole*."

Cassie did her best not to chuckle. Nicole was the least uptight of them all but when it came to her name, watch out.

"Ah, you made it."

They turned to the tall, black-haired woman heading their way. Beautiful, her olive-toned skin made her pale green eyes pop. "I'm Leslie." They didn't have a chance to respond before she held out a hand to Cassie. "You must be Cassie."

"I am." She shook her hand; overly aware of the sharp assessment Leslie gave them both as she greeted Nicole. This was a woman that could sum up exactly who a person was in five seconds flat. "I take it you already met my husband."

Nicole blinked a little too rapidly, her eyes struggling to stay off of Bradon.

"We did." Cassie looked around. "This place is gorgeous. Thanks so much for having us."

"Of course. Our pleasure." Leslie chuckled and took Bradon's hand as they headed for the house, tossing over her shoulder, "No worries, Nicole. You can check him out all you want, honey. I don't blame you in the least."

Some women might have been embarrassed by the comment, but Nicole only smiled broadly. "If you insist."

Cassie frowned at Nicole, but it seemed she had nothing to worry about because Leslie only laughed as she escorted them in and winked at Bradon. "Looks like the Broun streak of being over honest that affected me wasn't a one-time deal, eh?"

"Och, my lass, there's not another quite like you. Never has been. Never will be," he murmured and pulled her into his arms.

It didn't seem to bother them in the least that they had just welcomed perfect strangers into their home. No, the two kissed one another long enough that even Nicole had the good grace to look away.

The house was nice. Perhaps around three hundred years old, it had been updated and decorated tastefully.

Leslie eventually and very reluctantly tore herself away from Bradon and led them into the kitchen. "Long drive for you ladies. You thirsty?"

"Sure, thanks," Nicole said.

"Name your poison." Leslie urged them to sit at the kitchen table. "Coffee. Tea. Beer."

Bradon pulled a bottle out of the cabinet and thumped it down on the counter, eying them both. "Or whisky?"

Leslie gave him an odd, fleeting look.

"I just had coffee so I'm good with beer, thanks," Nicole said.

Cassie eyed the bottle and though she'd never once tried whisky she suddenly had an unexplainable craving. Her eyes met Bradon's. "I'll try some of that if you don't mind."

"Not at all." He pulled out a few small glasses and poured before handing her one. Leslie grabbed Nicole a beer then sat down with them at the table.

Cassie sniffed the liquor then took a tiny sip. It burned like hell going down. Eyes watering, she looked at Bradon. "Maybe an ice cube. Seems like it might be better chilled."

"Nay, lass." He eyed her almost as oddly as Leslie had him when he offered the liquor to begin with. "It's best enjoyed as it is. Chilling a good whisky takes from the flavor."

"Enough with whisky." Leslie's eyes locked with Cassie's. "Let's chat about what brought you here to begin with."

"Right. Yeah." Cassie nodded. "Of course." She fished her phone out of her purse as she again explained everything she had told Leslie over the phone. "And there's this manuscript." Eyebrows arched at Leslie, she said, "Sean's waiting to show it to you if you're cool with that."

"Absolutely." Leslie nodded at the phone. "Let's go live."

"Great." When Cassie got Sean on FaceTime, Nicole scooted over and waved into the phone. "Hey there, stranger."

Sean grinned and nodded. "Hey, Nicole."

Then he said hello to Leslie and Bradon when they introduced themselves.

"Thanks again for doing this," Cassie said.

"No prob." He released the kickstand on his iPhone and held up the Next Generation manuscript, explaining, "This was left in your sister's former bookstore, Leslie. I did a deeper search after the girls left. Not sure how it leaked onto the net but somehow a record of not only the Broun name but the existence of this manuscript is in a database for anyone searching out the Scottish Broun clan." He kept flipping the pages. "Seems you can pull it up if you're researching the MacLomain clan too. Leads right to my bookstore."

Bradon made a strange sound but buried it in a shot of whisky.

Cassie watched both Leslie and Bradon's reaction closely. Besides the weird grunt from Bradon, neither was overly responsive. If anything, Leslie was playing it too cool, her expression unwavering.

"Funny thing." Sean set aside the manuscript. "You and your husband are mentioned in this…quite a bit."

"My cousin, McKayla wrote that." Leslie's tone was fairly curt. "Not only is it copyrighted but under contract with a publishing house."

Sean held up his hands and shook his head. "I'm not interested in cashing in on this thing." His expression remained unreadable. "I showed you this to help out Cassie and Nicole. They're interested in their heritage and I get that. Listen, now that I have confirmation that this belongs to you give me an address and I'll mail you the manuscript."

Leslie's eyes narrowed. "How do I know you won't copy it first?"

"All right, lass." Before Leslie could say another word, Bradon took the phone from her and left the room.

Leslie scowled. Brows knitted together, she put on black-rimmed chic eyeglasses and turned on her tablet. Fingers flitting over the surface, she peered at the screen. "Who is this guy Sean again?"

"He's really nice. A fishing boat—" Nicole started.

"We just met him and he's been nothing but helpful," Cassie cut in, frowning at Leslie. "My apologies if all of this, us, and Sean, is too much. That wasn't my intention when I sought you out. I just really wanted to make contact with more Brouns. Sean was an innocent and remarkably helpful bystander."

"Innocent bystander," Leslie murmured, eyes scanning the tablet. "Those don't exist in my world."

Cassie put a hand over Leslie's wrist, stopping her short. "But they do in mine and I'm asking you to respect that."

When Leslie's incredulous eyes rose to hers, Cassie continued. "Please. History is everything to me. My family heritage more so." She shook her head. "And you are part of my heritage. A person I've only just met but share blood with. That's not only intense but very important to me."

Leslie eyed her for a long, uncomfortable moment before she said, "You do realize that your blood is far removed from mine? And I can't imagine there's much Broun in you. But, as it turns out, I guess there's enough."

What a bizarre thing to say. Cassie banked her rising aggravation at Leslie's somewhat callous declaration. "How could you possibly know that?"

Leslie removed her glasses and pinched the bridge of her nose, whispering, "Because you couldn't *possibly* be here otherwise." She shook her head. "You're just enough Broun to slip through the cracks. Like a sixth or seventh cousin removed."

"What*ever*." Nicole stood and shook her head, eyes on Cassie. "Let's scoot, girl. I love that you brought us Brouns together, and I'm all about what you have to offer." She shot Leslie a less-than-impressed look. "But apparently she's *not*. We don't deserve this elitist bullshit."

Leslie arched a disgruntled brow at Nicole. "Hell, we really are related, aren't we."

Bradon returned and handed the phone to Cassie. "Please dinnae leave. It's been a while since Leslie has…reconnected with blood."

17

"Too long," Leslie muttered under her breath. Then she motioned with her hand at Nicole. "Sit. Bear with me. This is just a lot to take in is all."

Sean hung up and Cassie couldn't help but wonder what he and Bradon talked about.

"Yeah, all right." Nicole sank back into her chair and took a swig of beer. As a general rule of thumb, her friend was quick to forgive unless she was truly pissed off.

"*What* is a lot to take in?" Cassie asked Leslie in response to her statement. "I'm a little unclear why us showing up and wanting to connect with our lineage is getting such a strong reaction."

"I'm ordering take-out," Bradon said, obviously trying to ease the tension. "What would you like?"

Leslie's eyes caught Cassie's, a little lost, before she snapped out of it and looked between her and Nicole. "Again, I'm sorry if I've been weird. Just overtired. What do you guys like? Chinese? Pizza? Name it, we'll get it."

"I'm fine with anything," Cassie murmured.

"Total Chinese girl here," Nicole volunteered, clearly moving past her previous discontent.

"Chinese it is then," Bradon said.

Cassie grabbed her purse. "Let me give you some money."

"It's on us." Bradon winked. "Anything for a Broun." Then he left the room.

"So now that we've met," Cassie continued, eyes on Leslie. "We'd love to know anything you might be able to share about our lineage."

Leslie shut off the tablet and crossed her arms over her chest. "I don't know a whole lot save the history of this house and my connection to it."

Cassie got the feeling that Leslie was being deliberately vague. Even so, this was more than she expected. "We'd love to hear anything at all."

Leslie hesitated, eyes flickering between them before they landed on Nicole. "You too?"

"Yeah." A strange look passed over Nicole's face. "Definitely."

A long bout of silence passed as Leslie considered them before she nodded and continued. "I can't speak for the history of this house beforehand, but the first Brouns of importance lived here in the early eighteenth century. Rumor has it they were witches. After that, history is a little fuzzy until my cousin, Caitlin moved in. Since then this house has always welcomed Brouns."

Cassie felt like she had been doused with ice water. *Witches?*

Nicole outright laughed. "You're screwing with us about the witches part, right?"

"I'm not screwing with you in the least," Leslie said dryly. Her eyes swung to Cassie. "You're a historian right?"

"Yes," she said slowly.

"And a bit more too, huh?"

Forget being doused with ice water, it shot straight through her veins. "Not sure what you're getting at."

"Why are you so drawn to the Brouns when you're at least ten other nationalities," Leslie said.

"How do you know that?"

Leslie ignored her question. "You can't stay away from Scottish history can you?"

"Actually, I'm drawn to all history out of the United Kingdom. English, Welsh, Irish." When she tried to say Scottish, her throat closed and she shook her head.

Leslie leaned forward, eyes narrowed. "And Scottish. Most especially Scottish I'll bet."

Cassie tried to swallow but ended up coughing instead. To clear her throat, she shot back the whisky and closed her eyes.

"Damn," Leslie muttered.

"What's going on?" Nicole said. "What am I missing?"

Cassie eyed Leslie, who now wore a speculative look. "Good question. What are we missing?"

"Well, I suppose we outta find out." Leslie stood. "C'mon, let me give you a tour of the house before the food gets here."

This was getting odder and odder. How would a tour of the house further explain things? Yet the minute they entered the living room, her eyes went to the framed pictures on the mantle above the fireplace. One picture, in particular, drew her instantly.

"Oh my God," Cassie murmured, chills racing through her as she walked over to it. "Who is this?"

"That's my cousin, Caitlin," Leslie said softly.

"No, I mean who is the guy she's with?" She shook her head. "He looks so much like…"

"So much like who?" Leslie said when Cassie trailed off.

Cassie frowned. "It was a long drive. I must be overtired."

"While you might be overtired, I suspect whatever you were going to say has nothing to do with exhaustion." Leslie held out the picture. "Here. Hold it."

Suddenly wary, feeling like she was standing on the precipice of something larger than she could comprehend, she shook her head. "I don't think that's such a great idea."

"You need to, Cassie," Nicole murmured.

She glanced at her friend. Nicole's eyes seemed a little distant, as though she was not quite here. "Why?"

Nicole cocked her head. "Why what?"

"You just said I need to hold the picture."

"No, I didn't." Nicole's eyes were clear again. She shook her head. "I think you're definitely wiped, hon."

Leslie kept holding it out. "Please. I insist."

Not wanting to be rude when Leslie was gracious enough to invite them to stay, Cassie pushed past her uneasiness and took it. First her eyes locked on the man's face but were soon ensnared by the young child sitting on his lap. For a split second, she could have sworn his eyes glowed. But she must have been mistaken because when she blinked there was no glow.

"The man in the picture is Caitlin's husband, Ferchar," Leslie said softly. "But I'll bet you're far more interested in the child."

Her eyes shot to Leslie. "Why would you say that?"

"Because he's a cute wee bairn, aye?" Bradon said as he entered and set down more drinks.

Nicole grinned as she eyed the picture. "He really is. Check out those blue eyes!" She shook her head. "Looks like he inherited them from his smokin' hot Dad, huh?"

"The child's name is Logan." Leslie urged them to sit as Bradon lit a fire. "He was born in this house."

Cassie sipped her whisky and kept starting at the picture, whispering, "Logan."

She was getting that same sense of familiarity she had when they pulled up in front of the house.

"Logan MacLomain," Bradon said with pride. "A good lad. I miss him."

"Me too," Leslie murmured, eyes still on Cassie. "You recognized Ferchar though. Why is that?"

MacLomain? This was getting more and more crazy. Cassie managed to pull her eyes from Logan. "Like I said. Just overtired."

"Humor me," Leslie said. "Please."

"Yeah, I'm curious too." Nicole's pale cedar eyes went from the picture to Cassie's face.

"Okay, fine." She glanced between Leslie and Bradon. "This is gonna sound totally out there but...well, when we first pulled into the driveway I didn't see Bradon coming out of the woods on a horse but another guy entirely."

Cassie explained his attire and features. How much he looked like Ferchar. "He could've stepped right out of *Braveheart*." She shook her head. "Then there was the horse. Really beautiful."

Silence settled over the room and she didn't miss the strange look that passed between their hosts before Leslie said, "It sounds to me like you've got a touch of the Broun gift."

"Broun gift?"

"Yup," Leslie said matter-of-factly. "Witchcraft."

Oh *yay*. "You're kidding me, right?"

"Nay," Bradon piped up. "My lass doesnae kid."

"I do on occasion," Leslie defended.

He grinned and shook his head. "Nay."

Leslie's eyes swung to Cassie. "Have you ever ridden a horse?"

"I'd rather hear about witchcraft," Nicole interrupted.

"I'm all set with the witchcraft thing." Cassie was just fine steering clear of that subject. "As to riding a horse? No, never."

"Hmm." Leslie considered her then looked at Bradon. "Looks like you better get busy teaching her."

"I dinnae think there will be much time for that," he murmured.

Leslie arched a brow. "That fast then?"

"Excuse me but what're you two talking about?" Cassie asked, fairly alarmed at this point.

Leslie stood. "Join us, ladies. We want to show you something."

"Okay." Cassie and Nicole followed them. For some reason, the closer she got to the barn, the less and less concerned she became with the bizarre conversation they'd just had. The smell of fresh hay met them at the door. At least seven stalls lined either side.

Cassie and Nicole stopped short when yet another tall, gorgeous guy emerged from one of the stalls. Like Bradon, he had to be around six-foot-five. With shoulder length black hair streaked with dark mahogany highlights, his startling silver-hued blue eyes swept over them with interest.

Bradon nodded at him and made introductions. "This is Darach. He helps me with the horses on occasion."

"Greetings, lasses." Darach cracked a smile that had Nicole leaning against Cassie, no doubt trying to stay on her feet. "'Tis a fine day to meet more wee bonnie Brouns."

"Holy accent," Nicole murmured as she gawked at him.

Cassie narrowed her eyes. Too thick of an accent. She was more than familiar with a Scottish brogue, but his was not only tricky to understand but…old fashioned sounding?

"Though he's taken clan Hamilton's name, like Ferchar and even Bradon, Darach is a MacLomain," Leslie said.

"Really?" Cassie's eyes went from Darach to Bradon. "Both of you are MacLomains then?"

"Aye." Bradon urged them to follow him. "The Brouns and MacLomains cannae get enough of one another."

"So it seems." Cassie eyed the stalls. "You have quite a few horses, don't you?"

"They do." Darach strolled alongside, eyes roaming over her with appreciation. "Four excluding Bradon's. All save his are thoroughbred females we speculate were donated by family."

Speculate? They didn't know for sure? But it was none of her business so she left it alone.

If Cassie wasn't getting such an edgy feeling the closer they came to the last stall, she would probably be blushing like mad. It was pretty intense having a guy like this checking her out. And he was definitely making a project of it.

"Oh, *look*," Nicole murmured, stopping at a stall.

Cassie eyed the chestnut horse with a dark auburn tail and mane Nicole was admiring. "She's beautiful." She eyed her friend. "In fact, you'd look great on her." A grin crept onto her face "Similar coloring."

Nicole shook her head. "I don't do horses but something about this one just, I dunno…draws me."

"Erin would think she'd died and gone to Heaven here," Cassie mentioned. Erin was the only one out of the four of them who actually owned a horse.

Darach rested a well-muscled arm on the stall, eyes torn between Cassie and the horse as he spoke to Nicole. "Her name is Vika. It means, 'from the creek' in Scotland."

"Why was she named that?" Nicole said.

He shrugged. "'Tis hard to know, but I'm sure there's a good story behind it."

Bradon made another one of his indiscernible sounds and urged Cassie to keep following. As she continued, the feeling of trepidation only increased. By the time she got to the beginning of the last stall on the right, it was nearly impossible to put one foot in front of the other.

Somehow she just *knew* what she was going to see.

Darach wrapped a gentle but supportive hand around her upper arm. "Are you well, lass?"

A little lightheaded, she was grateful for the gesture as her eyes locked with those of the horse in the stall. Just as she thought.

It was the one she had seen the mystery Scotsman riding when they first arrived.

Chapter Two

"THAT HORSE IS called Athdara," Darach said. "It means, 'from the oak ford'."

"Wow, she's beautiful." Nicole's eyes flickered between Athdara and Cassie. "And look at that, she has the same gorgeous strawberry blond hair as you!"

Tiny tingles raced over Cassie's skin as she whispered, "Just like Vika had the same hair color as you."

"Ceud mìle fàilte."

Shivers raced up her spine and Cassie jumped at the masculine whisper in her ear. Yet when she looked over her shoulder, no one was nearly close enough to have said it. Jesus, was she losing it? Because if she wasn't mistaken, the words were Scottish Gaelic.

"Athdara is the same horse you saw earlier, isn't it Cassie?" Leslie said softly.

"Yeah," she whispered and blinked several times when her vision blurred and dimmed. She'd had laser eye surgery a few weeks ago and she was starting to think they had done something wrong. "I need to go get my glasses."

Nicole put a concerned hand on her shoulder. "Are you having problems with your eyes again, Cassie?"

"I guess," she muttered and gripped the edge of the stall. "Or maybe the whisky's just catching up with me."

Cassie yelped with surprise when Darach scooped her up and headed for the exit.

"This is *so* not necessary," she said, embarrassed. "I'm good."

"Nay," he said. "You are not."

"I really am," she argued. But he would hear none of it and the next thing she knew, he laid her down on the living room couch, propped a pillow beneath her head and covered her with a throw blanket.

In little time, Nicole was putting Cassie's glasses on her and Leslie was urging her to drink some water. Bradon stoked the fire as Darach crouched, eying her with concern.

Cassie adjusted her glasses. "God, I hate these things."

Darach cocked his head. "Nay, lass, 'tis good when glass can make such bonnie eyes even bigger."

Now that was a new take on the boggle-eyed affect her bifocals had. "Um, thanks…I guess. Not actually glass though but a form of plastic."

"Cassie has advanced macular degeneration," Nicole said. "And just had laser surgery so she could at least see clearly while she still has time…"

Nicole stopped talking when Cassie directed a heavy frown her way.

Leslie sat on the edge of the couch and took Cassie's hand. "I'm not going to tell you I'm sorry because I know that's the last thing you want to hear but…" She squeezed her hand. "You've come to the right place because though your eyes might be weak there are parts of you that are so much stronger than you think."

"I know," Cassie said, because she did. Long ago, she had mentally prepared herself for what lay ahead. "I might be going blind, but I've still got intelligence and a positive attitude on my side."

"'Tis good that," Bradon said with a level of pride she didn't expect. He headed for the foyer when someone knocked on the front door.

Darach grinned and nodded with approval. "You are *every* bit a Broun, Cassie."

"He's right," Leslie agreed. "You are. One who deserves the truth." She twisted her lips. "A truth I would have been inclined to give once your other two friends arrived, but I don't think we have that kind of time."

When Cassie tried to sit up, Darach shook his head and gently pushed her back down. Though she scowled, she didn't fight him. "What truth? And what do you mean we don't have time?"

Bradon came in with a bag full of Chinese boxes and chopsticks. "Why don't we eat first?"

Cassie shook her head. "No. Please, just tell me."

Leslie nodded and gave Bradon a look before she turned her attention to Cassie. "As I hinted at earlier, we Brouns inherited a gift, better yet, witchcraft. It means that we possess something a little extra special. Sometimes it's a small thing, sometimes it's big, but it's always important and an intricate part of who we are."

"So you're saying we're all witches?" Nicole said around a mouthful of what Cassie suspected was pork fried rice.

"That's exactly what I'm saying." Leslie kept her eyes on Cassie. "And I'm guessing you can often see things much clearer than most despite your eye condition."

Cassie swallowed hard. *This* was the number one reason she had been so eager to search out her Broun heritage to begin with. But she wasn't quite ready to share as much. "Not sure what you're talking about."

"No, I wouldn't imagine you're ready to admit it yet," Leslie said. "Either way, here's the long and short of it. I'm a witch as are my cousins, all of whom currently reside in medieval Scotland." She nodded at Bradon. "He's from there." Then she nodded at Darach. "And so is he."

Nicole froze with chopsticks halfway to her mouth. Cassie stiffened as Leslie's eyes returned to her and she continued. "I'm not sure how thoroughly either of you read Sean's manuscript about the Next Generation, but that story definitely revolved around me and my cousins' tales. And yes, the Highlanders you read about, even the ones in this room, are wizards."

Wide-eyed, Cassie's gaze went from Bradon to Darach, who was smiling broadly as though immensely pleased with what Leslie had said.

"But you don't need to worry about me and Bradon's story." Leslie's eyes went to Darach. "But likely his." Then her eyes shot to Cassie. "Not for you though I don't think. Darach that is." Then she shook her head. "But then this end of things is sorta new to me."

"You can be for me, Darach," Nicole volunteered then shot him a wink when he grinned at her.

The glasses were starting to make things blurry at this point, so Cassie yanked them off, glad that the room was bright and clear again as she eyed Leslie. "So let me get this straight. You were actually part of the Next Generation story that's set to hit bookstores soon?" She cleared her throat. "A story about time-travel between the twenty-first century and medieval Scotland? Something that couldn't possibly exist in real life?"

"But does," Leslie assured. "And I suspect you and your friends are gonna find that out soon enough, but at least you'll go into it with a bit of knowledge under your belt."

Cassie's stomach flipped and she shook her head. "This isn't what I was looking for when I came here."

"Not intentionally," Leslie said. "But I'd guarantee something inside of you was seeking this out. In fact, when the horses showed up a few days ago, Bradon said I needed to call you back."

"Horses?" she said weakly, already knowing the answer.

Leslie nodded. "All four of them. Gifts we're assuming are from the medieval MacLomains. Gifts that were not for Bradon and me."

"What are the odds?" Nicole looked at Cassie, awed. "Considering how there are four of us Brouns coming here."

Cassie pinched the bridge of her nose when pressure built in her forehead. "I know."

Compassion flickered in Leslie's eyes. "I get how overwhelming this is. I also get that you'll likely not believe a word I'm saying until you've lived it. I sure as hell didn't."

Cassie ran the tip of her forefinger back and forth over her lower lip as she contemplated.

Nicole kept eating and shrugged. "My Nana was a tea leaf reader, the real thing, so I'm not that surprised to hear I'm a witch." She shook her head, still eying Darach. "But what's the point of traveling that far back in time?" Her eyes shot from Bradon to Leslie. "Is it all for the romance? No offense but that seems like an awful long way to go to hook up with a guy." Then she arched a brow at Cassie. "Makes Winter Harbor, Maine look a whole lot less long distance, doesn't it?"

Leave it to Nicole to take this all in stride. Cassie gestured at Leslie and Bradon. "Assuming they're from different centuries, do they look like they're living in a long distance relationship to you?"

Nicole took a swig of beer, released a dainty burp and shrugged. "True enough."

Darach chuckled as his eyes went from Nicole to Cassie. "She's a free spirit, aye?"

"To say the least." Cassie shot Nicole a little grin. "But she is who she is and we love her for it."

"Back at ya, girl," Nicole said and worked her chopsticks like a pro as she kept at her food.

Cassie met Leslie's eyes. "I get that you think we're witches and that the guys are *wizards* but what else exactly are you trying to tell us? That we're going to be traveling back in time to medieval Scotland?"

She ignored the thrill of the idea because honestly, it was only thrilling to think about, *not* actually do. That thought scared the heck out of her. Some things were better left to the imagination. Yet she knew it wasn't precisely her imagination at work when she saw the Scotsman on the horse, Athdara.

"I'm trying to tell you that there is an unending tie between the Broun and MacLomain clans, whether it's in the medieval period or here," Leslie said. "I'm trying to tell you that it's time you and your friends become very open-minded because there's a good chance things are gonna get real crazy real soon."

"I just came here to connect with relatives." Cassie tried to keep her voice level. "Nothing more."

"And you will," Bradon assured, offering her a box of Chinese food. "You'll find a family you never could have anticipated."

Cassie shook her head. "No thanks, I'm not hungry." Her eyes darted between the men before they landed on the picture of Ferchar, Caitlin, and Logan. Shoot, had Logan's eyes just glowed again? She tore her gaze away. "If Athdara really exists then who is the guy I saw riding her?"

Leslie glanced from the picture to Cassie. "Do you really need to ask?"

"It can't be Logan." She shook her head and breathed deeply through her nostrils. "He's just a little kid."

"He was," Darach said. "But time passes differently back home than it does here. Much faster. Now he's a few winters older than me."

"But you're what, in your mid-twenties?"

"I'm twenty-six winters. Logan is five winters older."

So Logan had about six years on her?

Cassie's eyes again flickered to the child in the picture. *"Really?"*

"Yes, really," Leslie said. "Caitlin, Ferchar, and Logan moved to medieval Scotland about a year and a half ago, but it's been over twenty-five years in their time. The theory is that the past is trying to catch up with the future, that's why it works like that. Faster and faster as time goes by it seems."

When Cassie heard the sadness in Leslie's voice, she said, "So your cousins have aged that much and you're still only a year and a half older than you were when they left?"

Leslie nodded. "Yeah. My cousins and my sister are now in their fifties."

"I'm so sorry," Cassie murmured.

"No need to be sorry." Leslie sat up a little straighter, renewed strength in her voice. "I chose my path and have seen them on and off through their lives. Now I'm glad I decided to stay here because someone needed to be around for you and your friends." Bradon was right there to squeeze his wife's hand, their eyes meeting one another's. "And I wasn't alone, not even for a minute, to face all this."

"Nay, lass," Bradon said, lowering enough to kiss the back of Leslie's hand.

Tender as the exchange was, Cassie felt like she was in way over her head and had officially hit information overload. "Listen, I'm super wiped. Totally in need of a clear head. Any chance I can lay down for a few hours somewhere?"

"Of course. Honestly, I'm surprised you didn't ask ten minutes ago." Leslie stood. "I have guest rooms set up for you and your friends."

Nicole set aside her food. "I'll come with you, Cassie."

"No." Cassie shook her head. "No need. Hang out. Learn all you can, okay?"

"Are you sure because I don't mind staying with you until you crash."

"Positive." Cassie smiled at Darach. "Keep an eye on her?"

He surprised her when he kissed her forehead and murmured, "'Twould be my pleasure. If you need me, lass, think it and I will be there."

Think it? Now didn't that sound a bit magical. A blush warmed her cheeks. These Scotsmen weren't just delicious but dashing. "Thank you."

Cassie grabbed her duffle bag from the car then Leslie led her to a room at the top of the stairs. With cream colored walls and flowing silk curtains, it was elegant and warm. "This was Caitlin's room when she lived here. She would want you to enjoy it."

Right, Caitlin was Logan's mother. "Great. Thanks so much."

"No need to thank me." Leslie set a glass of water on the bedside table.

Cassie's eyes fell to the little wooden box carved with Celtic symbols beside it. Propped open, three gold Claddagh rings glittered from within.

"Ah, yes." Sadness flickered in Leslie's eyes as she looked at the box. "Caitlin still wears hers, but two of those belonged to Broun women who lived in this house during the eighteenth century."

"What about the third?"

Leslie shook her head. "Not sure but rumor has it the third was once worn by a druidess. Like the others, the story goes that is was created by a Celtic god named Fionn Mac Cumhail then given to an Irish goddess named Brigit."

"Oh, wow," Cassie whispered. Her eyes went to Leslie's hand. "I see you wear one too."

Leslie nodded. "All the Broun cousins do now."

Before Cassie could continue questioning her, Leslie said, "Listen, I'm sorry about how snippy I was when you arrived. I meant no harm. Just overprotective of my family I guess."

Cassie was about to respond, but Leslie took her hands and shook her head. "No, really, I can be a total bitch on occasion. Just habit I suppose." She pressed her lips together. "It was a whirlwind at the beginning of last year and now I'm on the opposite end of the stick. That's big and I'm gonna try my hardest not to screw it up, okay?"

"Sure, okay." Cassie squeezed her hands. "But as far as I'm concerned you haven't screwed up anything. You've just given me a lot of info and I seriously need to assimilate."

"Assimilate?"

"Sorry, I'm a bit of a Matrix fan."

"Matrix?"

"You've never watched the movie, *The Matrix*?"

Leslie shook her head, totally confused.

"With Keanu Reeves?"

Leslie shrugged, still baffled.

"Oh, dear God." Cassie pulled her in for a hug on that one. "Life really *is* rough if you haven't watched *The Matrix*." She frowned as she held Leslie at arm's length. "Epic sci-fi movie, came out in '99. Ringing any bells?"

Leslie shook her head. "No time travel involved?"

"No." Cassie arched her brows. "*But*, there was a definite sense of not living in reality. That there was a whole lot more out there you didn't know about."

Leslie chuckled and shrugged. "Then I guess it's safe to say you entered a little bit of a matrix the minute you contacted me."

Cassie nodded. "So it seems."

"I'm putting your eyeglasses right here." Leslie set them on the table next to the water. "If you need anything at all, please let me know."

"You got it." Cassie worked at a smile. "Again, thanks so much for letting us stay here."

"No problem." Leslie smiled then left.

Cassie stared after her, almost wary to look around…to be part of this place. When cold wind whistled through the partially open window, she went to shut it but stopped. Instead, she opened it and touched the spindling oak branch beyond.

Like earlier, tiny tingles covered her body and for a second she swore she saw the oak from afar with a sweeping castle behind it. When she squinted, Cassie realized that it wasn't the same oak, but a much larger one covered in green leaves. When she pulled her hand back sharply, everything returned to normal and autumn leaves once more blew in the wind.

She blinked in disbelief and shut the window, more inclined to think this had to do with vision issues than anything else. Right? Because everything Leslie said couldn't possibly be true. Could it?

Exhausted, she threw on some sweats and an oversized t-shirt then crawled into bed. She should brush her teeth, wash her face, *something*, but she figured she would cat-nap then rejoin everyone. It was the least she could do considering Leslie and Bradon's hospitality.

That was the last thought she had before she rolled over and thumped to the floor.

Huh?

Sitting up, discombobulated, she looked around. Shoot, she had fallen out of bed. That was a first. Her eyes shot to the digital clock on the table. It was a little past midnight. Untwisting from the blankets, she wiped an unfortunate bit of drool from the corner of her mouth and stumbled to her feet

Everything was pitch-black but the barn.

Her eyes narrowed as Athdara trotted out of the dark into the building. Uh oh. Why was she running free? Did anyone know? Sliding on sneakers, Cassie headed downstairs. The house was dark. At this hour, it was safe to assume everyone was sleeping. So she headed for the barn. Wind gusted and the doors banged off the outside walls. A single, glass enclosed lantern swung lazily between stalls halfway down.

"Darach? Bradon?" she called. "*Anyone?*"

The lantern swung so wildly she swore it would drop and catch the hay on fire. That alone had her rushing forward. Yet by the time she got to it the lamp had stopped swinging. It was perfectly still. As if it had never moved to begin with. Still, she touched it just to reassure herself.

And saw the ring.

When the *hell* had she put on one of the Claddagh rings?

"Oh no." She tried to pull it off, but it wouldn't budge. Squinting, she eyed the stone nestled in the middle of a handheld heart. Clear, it almost looked like a dull diamond. Now she wished she had pressed for more answers about these things.

Athdara was staring over the stall, eyes wild, nostrils flaring.

Disregarding the ring, Cassie leaned against the opposite stall and breathed a sigh of relief as she eyed Athdara's stall. Strange that it was locked. "You're safe. That's good."

The horse eyed her for a few seconds before it huffed and backed away. Convinced Athdara was okay, she headed toward the exit but stopped short when a whinny rang out and a loud thunk pounded behind her.

Turning slowly, her eyes locked with Athdara's. Head over the stall door, the horse's nostrils again flared and she released a mighty neigh.

"Sorry." Cassie shook her head. "I'll go get someone who can take care of you."

Completely weirded out, she headed for the house but stopped again when a loud bang echoed behind her. By the time she turned, Athdara was trotting up behind her. Within a foot, she stopped, sunk to one knee and lowered her head.

Surprisingly enough, she wore a saddle.

"Oh, hell," Cassie whispered. All she could think was that this big horse was loose and she didn't know how to get her back into her stall. So she started making motions toward the barn. "Go back, girl. There, where you came from. *Please.*"

Athdara kept her head lowered and a steady eye on Cassie.

She gestured at the barn. "Go on now. Get to where it's safe, all right?"

But no, the horse wasn't budging.

So now she could do one of two things. Head into the house to get someone and hope Athdara didn't run off *or* she could try to walk her back to the barn. Not particularly frightened by the horse but well aware that she was clueless about how to handle one, she figured the most logical thing to do was to go get help. Then again, would she ever forgive herself if the horse took off and got hurt?

Decision made, she slowly came alongside Athdara, murmuring over and over, "It's okay, girl. I won't hurt you."

The horse made no movement, but Cassie sensed rather than saw that Athdara continued to watch her closely. She ran her hand carefully over the horse's mane until she had a firm hand on the leather strap attached to the bridle. Eyes closed, she inhaled sharply when heat rushed over her. It almost felt like she stood in a fiery hot wind. One the horse clearly felt as well because her eyes grew a little wild and she neighed.

A strong sense of 'fight or flight' seized hold and while Cassie briefly contemplated running away from the horse, she did not want to leave Athdara alone. Unlike anyone with half a wit that knew nothing about horses would do, she followed an overwhelming impulse.

She put her foot in the stirrup, grabbed the reins and swung up into the saddle.

Thank God she had seen Erin do this before and that Athdara was kneeling or she was pretty sure she would have fallen off onto her ass. Holding tight, she released a small squeal when the horse swiftly came to her feet and started trotting toward the forest.

"Oh no, no, no, no." Cassie pulled on the reins to no avail. If anything, she seemed to be egging on the blasted horse because Athdara was already heading into the woods. *Shoot* was it dark. What the heck was she thinking? That she would hop on and steer the horse into the barn like an old pro?

Head lowered, she closed her eyes and tried to regroup…tried to remain calm. Maybe if she said nothing and made no movements, the horse would stop. Yeah, right. Figure the odds. Opening her eyes, she frowned. Why did it almost seem like it was getting light out. Foggy, yes, but still far lighter than it had been moments before. Had she looked at the clock right? Maybe it hadn't been midnight after all.

Still, it was getting light far too quickly.

Not that she was complaining.

At first.

Until a strange sound rent the air, almost like a thwap, thwap, thwap before a solid thump sounded against a nearby tree. Cassie narrowed then widened her eyes when she caught sight of what it was. An axe? Thankfully, or not, Athdara had things figured out because she bolted forward. Luckily, Cassie had a death grip on her mane or things could have gone really bad. As it was, she was pretty sure she would be suffering from whiplash later.

Thighs clamped tight, she ducked low against the horse and tried to make out what was happening around her. It was beyond her wildest imagination. Horses were everywhere and weapons sailed through the air.

Arrows, axes, sometimes swords.

But that wasn't the truly nutso part.

No, that would be the men riding the horses. Some wore kilts, others trousers, but nearly all were long-haired and pretty damn scary. *All* were speaking another language. An older version of Scots Gaelic she would say. If all of the above wasn't daunting enough, Cassie was trying to figure out if these guys were aiming at her or each other.

If she wasn't mistaken, she was simply caught in the crossfire though some seemed to be catching on that she was there. The ones in the blue plaids seemed surprised. The ones in the dingy, hard-to-tell-what-color-they-were plaids seemed to see her as an opportunity because one steered his horse up alongside Athdara. Terrified, Cassie tried to bat him away while holding on but, unfortunately, that was a *big* mistake.

She would never know how he managed it so quickly, but the man scooped an arm around her waist and hauled her onto his lap. Scared shitless, she was torn between holding on tight and shoving

35

the smelly bastard away. What fresh hell had she been thrust into? Was she having some sort of nightmare her foolish mind hadn't awoken from?

Meanwhile, men were sword fighting from horseback while arrows whizzed by. As far as she could tell the grungy plaids were losing and the blue plaids were winning. Though she intended to shut her eyes to the horror, she became morbidly fascinated.

Or maybe she was just in shock.

Because she could have sworn she was screaming though nothing came from her mouth. Did it?

She became vaguely aware of the horses riding on either side as they sped through the forest. More so, she became aware of the men riding them. Both wore blue plaids. The one on her left was a ferocious bit of work with black hair and what appeared to be equally black eyes. He steered his massive steed in such a way that it was slowing down the horse of the grungy guy holding her. It was the man on the right, however, that grabbed her attention. With blue-black hair and pale blue eyes, he was every inch the man who had ridden Athdara when she first arrived at the Colonial.

There could be no doubt.

He was Logan MacLomain.

All grown up.

Logan released arrows so quickly she couldn't begin to count how many men were falling. Dagger suddenly in hand, he winked at her seconds before the man holding her cried out in pain.

After that, it was all a blur.

Screams of anguish. Blood. The clang of swords. The whiz of arrows. Yet somehow in the midst of it all she was pulled from the grungy guy's arms into Logan's then plunked in front of her newfound hero. His strong arm wrapped around her waist as he spurred the horse into a run.

Cassie wasn't sure what to think never mind do but decided it best to hold on tight and pray they made it to safety. Then again, she got the sense she had found safety the minute Logan pulled her onto his horse. Even so, he was a complete stranger and she was pretty sure based on the numbness settling over her that she was *definitely* in shock.

Maybe that was a good place to be for now.

There was no telling how long they rode before his horse slowed and the forest fell silent around them. Minutes, hours, days? Everything felt disjointed. Even—no big surprise—her eyesight. Unless Leslie and Bradon were having a good laugh at her expense and staging some sort of reenactment, she knew she wasn't in New Hampshire anymore. Could not possibly be. But had she really traveled back in time as it was promised she might? Hell and damnation, *no*. This had to be a nightmare...right?

"Is the horse I was riding okay?" she rasped.

"The horse is safe. You will soon be reunited."

Lost, trying to make sense of things, she barely processed that they had stopped until Logan swung down and pulled Cassie off the horse. She tried to urge him to put her down, but nothing seemed to be working quite right, especially her vocal chords.

"All is well, lass," he murmured, his deep words rumbling like a freight train through her body, the roll of his r's soothing when he said, "'Tis a thing you've been through. Rest, 'twill be all right."

Though her vision blurred, she could make out the stubble on his strong jaw and the width of his broad shoulders. She felt the heat of his body and smelled the tempting muskiness of his skin. A masculine scent mixed with sinful spices. Inhaling deeply, she closed her eyes and rested her head against his hard chest.

Again it might have been moments or hours before she felt cool water against her lips, cheeks, forehead, and neck. Both relieved and alarmed, her eyes shot open. This time her vision wasn't blurry but crisp. The lethargy she felt earlier seemed to have vanished and she was very much aware of what was going on around her.

The leaves overhead were no longer bursting with autumn colors but green and mixed with far more pine trees. For a split second, Cassie almost thought she was back in Maine until her eyes locked with *his*.

Their eyes held—more like hers drowned—as she gazed into what she initially thought were simply pale blue eyes. Sure they were gorgeous, you-want-to-study-them-for-hours blue, but more. Seen up close with sunlight shining down, it was clear that tiny golden flecks not only swam in them but formed a thin layer around the blue.

Mystical eyes.

Eyes that already owned her until he spoke and sent her into sheer panic.

"Ceud mìle fàilte. Welcome…" His hand lingered on her cheek. "To medieval Scotland."

Chapter Three

Cowal, Scotland
1281

"M-MEDIEVAL SCOTLAND?" CASSIE pushed past her lips, surprised she was able to say as much. The man just about had her tongue tied he was so handsome. If handsome was the right word for it. More like super-gorgeous, I can't believe I'm sitting on his lap good looking. One eye-roll down his muscled, slightly scarred chest had her nerves raw with unexpected desire.

He tilted up her chin until her adventurous eyes had no choice but to connect with his. "Aye, medieval Scotland. A place exactly seven hundred and thirty-four years in your past." His thumb made a slow sweep over her chin as if to comfort. "Do you ken, lass?"

Not, "Are you serious?" or "You're outta your mind!" popped from her mouth but, "Shouldn't you say 'ye' not 'you'?"

His lips twitched in what she guessed was repressed amusement. "'Tis a way we MacLomains sometimes speak when with our futuristic Brouns. A way to make it a wee bit easier to follow."

"*Your* Brouns," she whispered. Stop gawking, she preached to herself but was pretty sure she was doing just that. Was she scared witless that he was right and she had traveled back in time? God, yeah. But something about sitting on his lap with his blue-eyed gaze on her made everything seem all right.

His eyes softened as they roamed her face. Seconds later he clenched his jaw as if upset with himself and sat up straighter. He didn't set her aside, but she sensed that was out of obligation to her welfare more than anything else.

"Aye, our Brouns," he said. "Did Leslie not tell you of all you might expect here?"

"Um..." Hell, Cassie, untwist your tongue and sound halfway intelligent. "She did." More words needed. Keep talking because you definitely need answers. Move past the distraction of sitting on his hot-ass lap. "Leslie explained as much as she could, but there's still a lot hanging."

She sputtered the word 'hanging' because there was certainly something hanging between his legs based on his...

As if he sensed her thoughts and was disgruntled by them, Logan swiftly lifted Cassie to her feet. Though he didn't let her go, he certainly put some distance between them. "Are you well enough to stand without assistance, lass?"

Confused, she nodded. The pressure of his hands lessened a fraction, as though he didn't quite believe her. After he eyed her with concern for another moment, he moved away. Unexpected coolness flooded around her that had nothing to do with the temperature of the air.

"I wet your cheeks," he murmured, crouching in front of a stream. "But you should do so again, aye?"

Cassie put a hand to her cheek. Of course, he had dampened her face. Less interested in wetting her cheeks but definitely thirsty, she crouched and scooped some water into her mouth as he splashed some over his head.

"I'm Cassandra, by the way," she murmured. "But everyone calls me Cassie."

"I know." He nodded. "I'm Logan."

"I know."

They stared at one another for a long moment before he resumed splashing water over himself.

"How do you know my name?" she finally asked.

"Your horse, Athdara told me."

"My horse?" She shook her head. "No, she's not mine...and she told you my name?"

"Aye." He cocked a brow. "Did Leslie not tell you I'm a wizard?"

"Ah, right, that," Cassie trailed off as she stared at the water. "Gotta say, the concept's a lot to swallow. Just like the fact that you're supposedly from the twenty-first century."

Logan nodded and stood, holding out a hand to help her stand. "Aye, 'twould be but 'tis the truth. I was born and raised in New Hampshire for three winters."

When she stood, her breath caught as she looked up and up at him. He was as tall as Darach and Bradon. And oh let the mighty Lord keep her on her feet, he was built like Legolas from *Lord of the*

Rings but buffer. Yes, she and Nicole were movie junkies but still, it provided for good comparisons.

"Who is Legolas?"

Oh, darn, had she said that thought out loud? A little sheepish, she replied. "Just a fictional character. Well, an actor based on a fictional character from a book." She watched him, gauging just how insane he thought her. "He was an elf that could shoot arrows like they were going out of style." She made a gesture toward the woods and skirted around the truth. "I saw a glimpse of what you could do with a bow and arrow earlier. Pretty impressive."

His expression grew dark as they walked toward his horse. "Are you comparing me to an *elf*?"

Cassie flinched. "No...not really."

He arched a brow.

She offered a weak shrug and a forgive-me face. "I guess a little bit, but in a good way." Then she rambled as she had a tendency to do when nervous. "I mean look at you. You were fighting with a bow and arrow and still came off as masculine."

Oh, shoot, *that* didn't come out right at all.

He crossed his arms over his chest and scowled at her.

"What I mean is that Legolas was hot in his elfish way just like you're hot in your...wizardly Scottish...way," she rambled like a damn fool.

Logan's brows and lips were lowered now.

Detour time. Fast. Regrettably, her words were a weak squeak as she peered up at him. "Thank you for saving me?"

A little smirk crawled onto his face. "'Twas my pleasure, lass."

"*So*, no hard feelings over the elf thing?"

Logan swung onto his horse, held out his hand and winked. "'Tis no hardship to be compared to an elf. They are a noble creature."

Like they *really* existed? But she wasn't above leaving good enough alone. Sort of. As he swung her up, she said, "Then why let me get all anxious about comparing you to one?"

He turned his steed into the forest. "Honestly?"

She glanced over her shoulder at him. "Yeah, honestly."

His eyes held hers, something indefinable flickering in them. "'Tis amusing to watch you get flustered."

"Is it?" She turned forward, not miffed in the least but using it as an excuse to keep her eyes off of his sumptuous lips.

"Might I ask you something?" he said a few moments later as they made their way through the forest.

"Sure, I guess." She tried to ignore the feeling of his strong body at her back and joked, "I'm at your mercy after all."

"My mercy?" There was an edge of humor to his voice. "Nay, lass. You are at no one's mercy so long as you're with the MacLomain clan." Before she could respond, he continued. "My question is, do you often compare those you just met to characters in a book or movie?"

Cassie chuckled. "Sorry, bad habit of mine. My friends and I sort of formed a movie/song/book club as a way to help us bond over the years and we tend to compare things to them on occasion. Or people in this case."

What she would not tell him was that they had a very specific reason for doing so. One that would hopefully help each of them cope with what lay ahead. Because they were all facing something pretty big. In Cassie's case, it was looming blindness.

Logan remained quiet for a few minutes and she got the impression that he was mulling over what she had said. That he was the sort of guy who thought things through before speaking.

"I'm not as in touch with the twenty-first century lately as I should be, but I remember Disney...and *Handy Manny* from my childhood," he finally said.

Warmth curled around her heart. Was he trying to lessen her tension or was he sincerely just touching base with his youth? She quirked a lip at him over her shoulder. "Really? What was your favorite Disney movie? And did you learn any Spanish from Handy?"

"I liked *How to Train Your Dragon* and *Frozen* wasnae so bad." He shrugged. "Good movie about women defending women."

"Sisters," she said. "And *How to Train Your Dragon* was by DreamWorks, not Disney...not that it really matters."

Seriously, Cassie. He's a medieval Scotsman, not a movie connoisseur. She figured she would leave his lack of response about Handy alone.

"Speaking of sisters." His eyes met hers. "Do you have one? Or a brother?"

"Nope." She shook her head. "So weird to think you were only two when *Frozen* came out in *2013*." She turned back to the forest. "Most kids don't remember being that young."

"Most kids aren't wizards," he said.

"Right." Too curious, she asked, "Do you have a brother or sister?"

"Nay, I am the only bairn born to my parents."

She thought he sounded a little bummed so asked, "Is that a good thing?"

"'Tis not a bad thing." He paused. "But I would have liked a brother or sister." Before she could feel too bad for him, he said, "Yet I have my kin and they are verra much my family."

"So you're happy?"

"Aye, happy enough."

Feeling safe and remarkably comfortable with him considering how little they knew about one another, she again looked over her shoulder. "Just happy enough?"

As if they hadn't just met, he answered candidly. "Verra happy with my kin but eager to take a wif and have some wee bairns."

"Wif?"

"Bride?

"Ah. *Wife*." She turned her focus ahead. "No luck with that yet, eh?" And because she couldn't leave good enough alone. "I'm surprised."

"Why?"

Oh jeez. *Because you're hot as hell.* But she couldn't say that. Instead, she firmly inserted her foot in her blasted mouth. "Well, you're not getting any younger, right?"

A little rumble came from Logan's chest, but he didn't *quite* chuckle. Then he went still and she felt his upcoming response almost like she could feel the wind move a building when nobody else could.

"Nay, I'm not getting any younger. But it matters naught because I am pledged for betrothal."

His words weren't just a breeze against the walls of a rhetorical building but more like a gale force wind against the cardboard walls of…what? Not her heart. Definitely not that. Way, way, too soon. No, something different but noticeable and cringe-worthy. "Nice."

Nice? The word hung between them like a chilled Jello mold left unattended under a hot sun. Not pretty.

"We were pledged to one another at birth," he finally continued. "But have yet to meet."

"Oh," she murmured, feeling a little sorry for him. "So an arranged marriage?"

"Aye, to strengthen our clans." He surprised her with his next question. "What of you, lass? Are you betrothed or pledged to be?"

"*Definitely* not." She shook her head. "Way too young for that level of commitment."

Again, Logan waited several long moments before he murmured, "I see you wear a Claddagh ring. Did you put it on or did it appear on your finger?"

Shivers rippled over her. Odd question. Then again, there *was* that whole wizard thing. She debated telling him the truth because she didn't want to sound insane. "It appeared there...or I did it in my sleep. Not sure."

"So you saw the ring prior to sleeping?"

"Yeah, Leslie had them in a box by the bed," she said. "Three of them."

She could hear the frown in his voice. "And how many of these Broun friends do you have?"

She glanced over her shoulder. "Lots of questions."

His disgruntled eyes met hers. "'Tis important."

"Why?" Uncomfortable, she looked at the ring. "What's the story with these?"

The pines were thinning but still spread far and wide as streaks of sunlight cut through the forest. "There have been several Claddagh rings over the years. The ones from my generation, often referred to as the Next Generation, helped Brouns travel through time. They also warm when their true love is near." He cleared his throat. "Then there are the original Claddagh rings, those created when a couple came together beneath an oak. Overseen by the god Fionn Mac Cumhail, they each had a gem at their center. The gem matched the wizard's eyes that the Broun lass was meant for. It glowed. That ring you wear is one of the originals."

Cassie grew tenser as he spoke. "So these Claddagh rings... bring love together?"

"Aye, always. A MacLomain and a Broun," he murmured. "It can be no other way."

Holy heck. About the last thing she was looking for was *romance*. Best to steer clear of that for now. "Leslie told me one of the rings was supposedly worn by a druidess."

"Aye, 'tis a part of the tale not often shared," he said. "I'm surprised to know it actually exists."

Cassie kept eying her ring nervously and whispered, "Is it *this* one?"

"I dinnae ken," he said softly. "I only know that what you wear is one of the originals."

"But it's just a clear stone." She peeked over her shoulder at him. "Not a gem at all and certainly not something that would match an eye color."

Especially not yours.

Now she needed to get *that* thought out of her head immediately. He was taken. Even if he wasn't, this was medieval Scotland! And she wasn't on the market for a guy. If anything, her next focus was preparing for a new lifestyle...in the twenty-first century of course.

"'Twas once a gem." His eyes fell to hers. "My guess is that 'twill once more become a gem when it finds your true love."

She tore her eyes from his, far too aware of his proximity. "I like to think I'm my own true love. Best to depend on myself. I don't need a man."

Yet even as she said the words she sometimes wondered how much she really believed them. Still, they sounded confident and that's what she was going for.

"'Tis good that you love yourself, lass. 'Tis an admirable quality." His voice lowered. "But because you wear that ring there is room in your heart for another. And the ring will find him for you."

Though tempted to see the expression on his face, she was feeling a little too aware that *he* had been the first Scotsman to interact with her here. Not to mention he was the first one she saw when she pulled into Leslie and Bradon's driveway. Then there was that whole thing about his eyes glowing in the picture. But she wasn't about to share any of that right now, if at all. Even if he weren't engaged, she would not want him to know.

She was about to respond when another horse trotted through the woods and came alongside. It was the Scotsman who had ridden on her left-hand side when the grungy warrior had her. With dark features, she thought him striking in an intense, masculine sort of way. His muscles were slightly bulkier than Logan's, but she suspected their towering frames were similar. While at first she thought his eyes were nearly black she realized they were an unusual shade of dark blue.

"All the bloody bastards have been killed, my Laird," he grunted, his eyes on her though he clearly spoke to Logan. "Some were taken prisoner. 'Twill be good to have at them later, aye?"

Logan was the *laird*? Well, didn't that just take the cake.

The men leaned over and clasped hands briefly before Logan made introductions. "Cassie, this is Niall, son to Malcolm MacLomain and his Broun from the future, Cadence."

"'Tis good to meet you, Cassie." Niall nodded. "Welcome."

Ah, Cadence, Leslie's sister. It was so strange meeting medieval Scotsmen with mothers from the future. She nodded as well. "Nice to meet you too, Niall."

She didn't miss the way Niall's eyes flickered over her ring with interest.

"So you are a Broun?" he said.

Again, she heard the frown in Logan's voice when he said, "You know she is."

"Just making conversation." Niall quirked his lip at her. "'Twill be good to have another bonnie Broun aboot."

"Aboot?"

"About," Logan said. "'Tis not always easy to lessen our accent."

He was actually *lessening* his accent right now? "You were speaking Gaelic when I arrived, right?"

"Aye," Logan said. "A form of it."

"'Tis a good time that you came," Niall said to her. "'Twill be much celebration with the summer solstice. And more than usual because of the battling."

"Will Darach be here?" She didn't mean to sound slightly desperate but like her he had just been in the twenty-first century. For some reason having him here now might make all of this seem less insane.

46

Niall's brows arched. "You've met Darach?"

Cassie nodded. "In the twenty-first century."

She was not quite sure what to make of Niall's expression when he looked at Logan. "'Twas little doubt his Da made sure his bairn met her first, aye?"

"Och, mayhap," Logan said. "But 'tis difficult for Darach to stay in one place too long. He's restless. 'Tis doubtful Laird Grant had much to do with it considering he wants his son to settle down and become chieftain of the Hamiltons."

Cassie was about to speak, but the words died on her lips as they left the forest behind. The panoramic view was something out of a historic painting. Beyond a wide, sprawling field speckled with wildflowers and a glorious oak tree was a beautiful castle surrounded on three sides by a sparkling blue loch back-dropped by mountains. *Stunning.*

"Welcome to the MacLomain castle," Logan said close enough to her ear to make both chills and heat simultaneously rush through her.

"It's unbelievable," she murmured. It was the same one she had seen when she touched the oak in New Hampshire. Cassie took in the multiple wall walks and towers, the double moats and portcullises. It was every historian's dream come true, especially one with a love for Scotland. "This is yours?"

A logical question considering he was laird.

"Nay, the castle belongs to the clan." Logan urged the horse forward. "'Tis but my privilege to oversee its people right now."

Only then did she realize that a small band of warriors on horseback had fanned out behind them. Niall's eyes met hers. "*They* protect the castle's chieftain." He grinned at Logan. "Who is determined to be at the heart of every battle he can find."

"I didn't see them earlier," she said, eyeing the ferocious-looking men.

"They're verra good at remaining unseen when they wish it," Logan muttered.

"We live in perilous times." Niall shook his head. "Enemies everywhere now, even on our own land."

"There has always been that, cousin." Logan slowed his horse the closer they got to the glorious oak tree. She had never seen one like it. Towering, twisting, it was easily twice as tall as the oaks back home. Its base alone had to be as wide as a California redwood. A man stood beneath it, but it was hard to make him out.

"Come, let's walk now, lass." Logan swung off and pulled her down. Cassie nearly stopped breathing when his hands hesitated a moment longer than necessary on her waist. Their eyes met and her breath caught. His grip tightened a fraction before he pulled away.

Niall swung down as well. "I'll join you."

"Of course you will," Logan muttered then made a slight clicking sound. In response, the horses took off for the castle.

It was more than intimidating walking between two Highlanders. She didn't come across guys like this at home. Or should she say such tall, well-built men. Though surprisingly at ease with Logan, Niall freaked her out a little. He seemed so fierce, his dark eyes constantly scanning their surroundings as though waiting for someone to jump out at them. But maybe he was doing the same thing as the men behind them and protecting his chieftain. Yet she surmised it had more to do with his nature than anything else.

The man who had been standing beneath the tree headed their way. It wasn't long before she could make out his features better. Surprisingly handsome for his age which she guessed was mid-forties, he had gray-flecked brownish black hair and pale bluish gray eyes. He didn't bother with the men but strode up to her, lowered his head then brushed his lips across the back of her hand.

"Welcome, Cassie," he rumbled, the look in his eyes kind as his gaze flickered from her ring to her eyes. "I am Grant Hamilton. A MacLomain by birth."

Cassie blinked several times and tried to focus on his face as colors suddenly swirled around him. There was something very different about this man.

He squeezed her hand gently and shook his head. "Dinnae worry, lass, 'twill pass. You but see my magic."

"Come again?" she managed. She had no sooner said it before the colors faded and his face became clearer.

Grant held out the crook of his elbow. "Walk with me?"

Cassie didn't realize what she was doing until she looked at Logan in question. Was she asking his permission? Apparently so because he nodded. Though slightly frustrated with herself, she supposed it made sense since he *had* technically saved her. And he *was* laird of the castle despite how humble he seemed to be about it.

Laird of the castle. What a hoot! In a good way…well, unbelievable way. She was still sort of wondering when she was going to wake up from this dream.

"'Tis a lot, this, aye?" Grant said as they walked.

"More than you can imagine," she admitted, the rest of her words sputtering out as she eyed him and his name truly sunk in. *Grant.* That was familiar. Too familiar. Her eyes widened as she thought about the snippets she had read from Sean's manuscript about the Next Generation. "You're not the Grant MacLomain from…" How to phrase this?

"Aye, lassie." His eyes twinkled. "I am Grant from Sean's manuscript."

"You know who Sean is?" She shook her head. "A fisherman from twenty-first century Maine?"

"I do," he acknowledged. "We met briefly, but he wouldnae remember me."

"You've been to the—" Her mouth snapped shut. It wasn't all that unbelievable that he had been to the future considering that was where she last saw Darach. Regardless, what a concept.

"Aye, I've visited the future." His eyes met hers. "It warms my heart more Brouns are arriving. I wasnae entirely sure if the connection betwixt our clans would continue."

"Our clans?" Ah, yes. She was a Broun. "You know I'm only a little bit Broun right?" Her eyes again widened at the castle looming in the distance. "It seems almost…I dunno, wrong that I'm here considering."

"Nay, lass." Grant's voice was warm. "If you are here then 'tis meant to be and you are special indeed."

"Special?" she murmured, uncomfortable with the word because it cut too close to home.

"Aye." He nodded at the castle. "'Tis a great thing to be meant for all this." Then he made a small motion with his head toward the men walking behind them. "'Tis an even greater thing to be meant for the MacLomain warriors who will see Scotland through to glory."

Well, when you put it like that. She shook her head at her lackluster thoughts. "How are they going to see Scotland through to glory?"

Cassie couldn't help but touch the trunk of the massive oak as they passed it. Not only warmth but a tremendous amount of peace passed through her. Then she stopped short as something altogether different blew through her.

Looking up, she blinked as her vision once more blurred.

Then sharpened.

For a terrifying moment, Cassie swore she saw a massive, winged creature hovering above the highest branch, its cat-like eyes staring down at her.

"Dinnae fear, lass," Grant murmured. "You but see the tree's memories. There is nothing there but the wind and sky."

"The tree's memories?" she whispered as whatever she had seen vanished and there remained nothing but sunlit leaves twisting in the wind. "How is that even possible?"

"'Tis part of your gift." He squeezed her hand. "To see things others cannae. Ghosts of the past and future. Memories that span in both directions."

"I see. Well, you know what I mean. Not literally." The truth was whatever this weird gift was it had been happening more and more frequently over the past year or so. "I've gotta admit, it's pretty creepy."

"Magic can seem that way on occasion," he acknowledged as they started walking again. Now they were behind Logan and Niall. "If you get the chance, you should speak with Rònan MacLeod when he arrives later. 'Tis a tree he well knows as his Ma was at the root of its birth."

Didn't that sound intriguing. "Who's Rònan MacLeod?"

"He is cousin to Logan, Niall and Darach," Grant said. "The lads have been close since they were wee bairns."

"Darach's super sweet." Cassie grinned. "He looks a lot like you."

"Aye." She could see the pride in Grant's eyes. "But he's got his mother's personality." He chuckled. "'Tis likely a blessing."

"So his mother is a Broun from the future too?"

Grant nodded. "All of the lads save Ronan have mothers from the future. 'Tis likely the reason they've all remained close…for the most part."

"For the most part?"

"Aye." Grant shrugged. "Like any young lad, they fight over the lassies on occasion. Niall and Rònan mostly. 'Tis good they dinnae reside in the same castle."

"No doubt." Her eyes roamed over the men, mostly Logan. She couldn't seem to help herself. Though she knew she should just leave it alone, Cassie said, "So when is Logan supposed to be married?"

Grant almost seemed reluctant to say, "In a few days' time."

A few *days*?

"Ah," she said, inwardly cursing because it almost sounded like she was disappointed. She tried to cover it up by focusing on the positive. "So I'm just in time to see a medieval Scottish wedding. That's pretty cool."

"Aye." Grant nodded. "And 'twill be a grand affair in that 'tis the Laird marrying."

"He seems young to be the laird."

"'Tis a good age," Grant said. "He's old enough to have learned much and young enough to still have a sharp mind and a strong body."

Cassie swallowed, trying hard to pull her eyes away from that strong body. "Shouldn't his father still be laird though?"

"Ferchar was laird a verra long time ago. Since then it has gone from Colin, who had no sons, to Malcolm. 'Twas the clan's choice when he stepped down to make Logan Chieftain."

Cassie frowned as they drew closer to the first drawbridge. "Isn't Niall Malcolm's son? Shouldn't he be laird then?"

"Nay, 'twas something he had no interest in," Grant said. "At least not at the time and I dinnae think so much now. He'd rather be battling and chasing the lasses."

She eyed him. "I hear you want Darach to become laird of your clan."

"Aye," Grant muttered. "I need to be available to travel more often and dinnae want to spend my later years still ruling the Hamiltons. Like the MacLomains, they need young blood."

"You still look pretty young." Smiling, she stared up at the first portcullis as they walked beneath.

"Och, I'm past my fiftieth winter." Grant shook his head. "Young enough but beyond the age of wanting to oversee a clan. 'Tis a lot of work."

"I can imagine," she murmured, taking in all the activity around her. The clothing was amazing...or should she say ancient. This was truly unbelievable. "I think I'm dressed all wrong. Aren't people gonna wonder?"

It seemed they already were based on the endless looks she was receiving.

"This clan knows well of its connection with the Brouns from the future." Grant stopped as Logan and Niall joined them. "But we will get a change of clothes for you. I will send my daughter Lair to help."

"Chieftain Grant and I must see to some business." Logan shot Niall a distrustful look. "Niall will show you around the castle, Cassie."

Niall? When her eyes met his, Logan's cousin chuckled. "I willnae bite, lass." Then the corner of his lip hitched. "Quite yet."

Cassie might have grinned if she wasn't so busy being intimidated. These men were *huge*. The top of her head barely came to their shoulders.

"Oh, ye dinnae want this one showing ye around, lass. Allow me the pleasure," a woman declared upon greeting as she swung down from her horse. With long, thick brown hair and feminine yet strong features, it was clear she liked battling. "I am Machara, daughter of Colin and McKayla MacLomain."

Machara's narrowed eyes went to Logan. "She who should rightfully be ruling this clan."

Chapter Four

LOGAN WASN'T SURE which choice was more unfavorable, Niall or Machara showing Cassie around. If he had his way, he would do it himself. Regrettably, there were things to see to.

Still, he wanted nothing more than to stay near Cassie.

Since the moment he pulled her onto his horse and felt her soft curves against him, he wanted to keep her by his side. He'd never had such a strong reaction to a lass and was still trying to figure out a way to set aside his attraction.

His eyes kept drifting to her bonnie hair. Long and wavy, it shimmered an eye-catching shade of reddish blond. And those eyes, like the shallowest part of a loch caught in sunlight. A rare shade of pale sea green that could enchant in an instant. Her features were delicate, her mouth a perfect little bow. Then there was her body...*bloody hell.*

He scowled when his groin tightened. The best thing he could do right now was put some distance between them. But he knew Niall was just as attracted to her, so he was forced to make an unfortunate decision. "Cassie, allow Machara to show you around." He eyed his cousin. "She will see that you're shown to a chamber and provided clothing."

Though she responded to Logan, Machara kept her focus on Cassie. "Aye, m'laird. I will see her well cared for."

While there might be bad blood between him and his cousin, Logan knew Machara would treat Cassie well enough. No doubt, with more tact than Niall would. Like Rònan, Niall would seize every opportunity to try to get beneath the lass's skirt...once she was wearing one.

Rònan. Logan almost groaned. It was unfortunate he was arriving today because he was almost more aggressive than Niall when he saw something he wanted. Or *someone* in this case. And he knew Rònan would want Cassie. Hell, he suspected most of his clansmen would. Yet Rònan fell into a different category. Not only was he more arrogant now that he had become chieftain of the MacLeods, but he shared his mother's dragon blood. A MacLomain Viking bloodline that made him more dominant than most.

"I don't mind hanging around until you're available, Grant." Cassie's wide eyes went to Logan, her voice clearly struggling to stay level. "Or you."

"Nay, lass." Machara wrapped elbows with her, voice warming considerably now that she wasn't addressing Logan. "I'll not hear of it. 'Tis good for those of us with futuristic Broun blood to get to know one another better, aye?"

"Sure...yeah, okay." Cassie straightened her shoulders, chin suddenly thrust forward with determination as she walked off with Machara.

Like Logan, Niall's eyes were locked on Cassie's arse. As much as they could make out of it beneath her bulky shirt that is.

"All right, lads," Grant said. "'Tis never a good thing to gawk at our Brouns when they first arrive. These twenty-first century lasses tend to have as much bite as yer Scotswomen. 'Tis wise to respect them, aye?"

"Aye," Logan agreed but he wasn't above keeping a wandering eye on Cassie as she vanished into the courtyard.

"Bloody hell." Niall shook his head as he muttered, "She didnae need Machara showing her around. What fun is there in that?" He frowned at Logan. "Ye cannae have her so ye might as well let me have a go."

Logan hid the discontent Niall's words caused him because he was absolutely right. He could *not* have her. Nor should he *want* her. But he did. More than he expected.

"Ye've plenty of lasses to keep ye entertained." Logan nodded toward the castle. "Why not go find some now to keep yer mind off the new lass whilst I speak with Laird Hamilton."

Niall muttered a healthy stream of curses as he strode off. Logan could only hope it wasn't to take over for Machara. Because though he had given an order, he and his cousin were like brothers. As such, Niall tended to do whatever pleased him.

Alone at last with Grant, Logan was eager for some answers. "Did ye know Cassie was coming? That more Brouns were coming?" His eyes narrowed on the arch-wizard as they entered the busy courtyard. "Better yet, did ye know the original rings have returned? How is that possible when two of them are buried with their previous owners?"

"'Tis not for me to say if I knew they were coming." Grant shrugged. "As to the rings, ye know as well as I that they've powerful magic about them. If they're meant to bring more love together, then they will find their way onto the next finger whether or not they were buried."

"Och, yer as vague as Adlin ever was," Logan grumbled.

Grant grinned. "He *was* my mentor after all."

"I miss him," Logan murmured. Though he was but a wee bairn when Adlin lived in the twenty-first century, the former arch-wizard and patriarch of the MacLomains made sure Logan remembered him. For hours and hours, the old wizard would sit next to his love, Mildred and rock him on the bench swing out front. And though Logan was only a newborn, every soft word Adlin spoke stayed with him. The endless stories about the MacLomain clan and their great adventures.

"Aye, I miss him too." But Grant always had a twinkle in his eyes when he spoke of Adlin. As if even though the wizard was long gone, he still managed to see him on occasion. Then again, Grant was almost as powerful as Adlin had been so it wouldn't surprise him in the least.

"And what of the horse Athdara? Cassie's horse?" Logan said. "I sense great destiny about her but like you, she was rather cryptic about divulging much information."

"I cannae say much about her save she's a bonnie beast, aye?"

Logan cast Grant a wry glance. "There isnae much point in asking ye anything, is there?"

"I can tell ye that the horse is bonded strongly with Cassie and 'twill protect her well."

"Will she need such protection then?" Logan murmured.

"It cannae be any other way since she is here at such a time," Grant said gravely. "'Tis telling that Cassie arrives when too soon the wee Bruce might be needing ye and yer cousins."

Though he did not want to ask, he had to. "So there cannae be any doubt that she is meant for one of my cousins, aye?"

"That they descend directly from the Next Generation of MacLomains, nay, there cannae be," Grant said softly.

Logan gave a curt nod and pushed aside emotion. He reminded himself that there was no fault in being attracted to Cassie, but it was important that he focus on his bride to be. It was unfair to her that his thoughts be consumed by another. Especially someone he had only just met. No, it was best that he focused on who was coming.

The future Lady of MacLomain castle.

Aline MacLauchlin.

A lass he had never met though he'd tried time and time again. Rumor had it she possessed old fashioned values and thought it would bring bad luck to see him before their wedding day. He had always been of the opposite mind. He would have liked to get to know her and mayhap become friends first. His cousins speculated she must be long in the tooth as even they hadn't been able to catch a glimpse of her, but Logan wasn't worried. A lass didn't need to be overly bonnie to make a good bride. Her character meant far more to him.

While he still had plenty of questions for Grant, the opportunity was taken away as several people approached him needing one thing or another. Hours passed by too fast and though he looked, he didn't see Cassie again. Nor did he see Machara or even Niall. The eve fell swiftly and the clan grew boisterous as bonfires were lit. By the time he bathed and rejoined the festivities, the pipes were trilling and the food was laid.

Logan had just made it to the entrance of the castle when he spotted Cassie in the courtyard below. His breath caught. Dressed in a simple, but stunning green dress, thick reddish golden hair haloed her face as she smiled at those around her. The tension she seemed to have felt earlier was gone and she started laughing at something someone said. Then her eyes locked with his and her laughter slowly faded.

But not her smile.

He had never felt the effects of a smile so strongly. As if it had been designed just for him. Warmth uncurled in his chest and though he meant to look away, he couldn't help but smile in return.

"Och, cousin." Niall swung an arm around Logan's shoulders and shook his head. "'Tis too bad that yer meant for another, aye?"

Logan shrugged away and started down the stairs. "And well I remember it, friend."

"Do ye now?" Niall joined him. "Because I havnae seen ye look at a lass quite like ye are our new Broun."

"I'm just keeping an eye on our new guest." Logan arched a brow at Niall. "So that she doesnae suffer any unwanted advances from my kinsmen."

Niall snorted. "'Tis already far too late for that, my Laird. But dinnae worry, I'll make sure she's well-protected."

They had just reached the bottom of the stairs when horse's hooves thundered over the drawbridge. Hoots and hollers rang out as a small band of MacLeod's rode into the courtyard led by their laird.

Rònan MacLeod.

"Laird MacLomain. Niall," Rònan roared as he whipped a dagger. Logan didn't focus on the weapon but caught it by instinct before it passed between their heads.

Niall patted Logan on the shoulder and released a hearty laugh. "*Now* the fun truly begins."

Rònan swung off his horse, kissed a few lasses then strode their way. The men embraced, clapping one another on the back before the MacLeod issued a wolfish grin. "'Tis good to be amongst my brethren again." He eyed them as he swigged from a skin. "How fare ye?" Then he leaned a little closer. "And why was my dragon blood stirring as I arrived? Has it to do with the new bonnie wee lass that smells of arousal?"

Logan shook his head and Niall kept chuckling as he responded. "Does she then? 'Tis not a gift of we wizards to smell such a thing."

"Well, 'tis good then that ye have me around, aye?" Rònan winked, his voice curious. "Who is she then? If ye dinnae tell me straight away, I'll carry her off and find out in the best way possible."

"Then ye truly dinnae know?" Logan asked, trying not to bristle.

Rònan cocked his head, sharp eyes narrowing on Logan. "Ye'd see an arrow shot in my arse if I carried her off, wouldn't ye?"

"Only if he wishes his betrothed to shoot an arrow at his cock," Niall said. "Assuming she ever gets around to seeing the poor withered thing beforehand."

Logan ignored Niall and spoke to Rònan. "Ye willnae carry her anywhere. She's a Broun from the future and I'll see her respected."

Rònan's brows shot up and he mouthed, "See her respected?"

It was always an event dealing with Rònan and Niall when they were set to celebrate together. Though he was close to all three men, these two had similar spirits and enjoyed causing havoc where

Logan and Darach tended to get on better. He had never quite understood why when he was devoted to the responsibility of leading a clan and Darach did his best to avoid it.

Logan clapped Rònan on the shoulder in passing and headed for Cassie. True to form, his cousins fell in beside him. Her eyes widened the closer they got and he couldn't help but wonder…why was she aroused? Better yet, *who* was she aroused by?

He was about to make introductions when Rònan sunk to one knee in front of her and kissed the back of her hand, lips lingering overly long. Then, still holding her hand, he swiftly stood, using his towering height to his advantage. "I am Rònan MacLeod. Welcome, lass. 'Tis always good to see another Broun from the future. Especially one as ravishing as ye."

"T-thank you. I think," she stammered. Rònan could overwhelm the highest mountain in Scotland so Logan gave her credit for not stumbling back a step or two.

"You *think*?" Rònan said, perplexed.

Her brows drew together. "I think I'm not so sure I want you to find me ravishing."

Logan buried a chuckle in his chest. Now *those* were words his cousin had surely never heard.

Rònan contemplated her for a long moment before he grinned. "Ye know the best way to get me is to push me away, lass."

"Not me," Niall kicked in. "Say the word and I'm yours."

Her eyes flickered between Rònan and Niall. "Actually, I'm not really on the market right now."

"Market?" Niall said.

"It means she isnae interested in a lad's attention," Logan said.

"Nay." Rònan quirked his lips at her. "Now that isnae true at all. She's interested. 'Tis just a matter of finding out where the interest lies."

Something stirred inside Logan. Yes, continued curiosity about her earlier arousal but more than that. A sense of wanting, no *needing* to protect her from divulging anything she wasn't ready to share. "Cassie just traveled back over seven centuries in time. Dinnae make her feel uncomfortable, cousin."

"Cassie," Rònan murmured. His hungry gaze traveled the length of her. "'Tis a bonnie name." He offered her the eyes that had most lasses falling at his feet. "My apologies if I made ye feel uncomfortable. 'Tis only my fondest wish to make ye feel as *comfortable* as possible."

"Good. Glad to hear it." She nodded then looked at Logan. "Right now that means I need to talk to you...alone."

Ronan arched an amused brow at Logan but stepped back graciously when Logan wasted no time leading her away from his cousins. He nodded his thanks when a servant handed him two skins of whisky, one of which he handed to Cassie. "I'm sorry, lass. 'Tis no easy thing meeting Ronan...or Niall."

"Definitely not," she agreed and sniffed at the contents of her skin before taking a small sip. "Oh, this tastes just like the whisky Bradon let me try."

The tricky Scotsman was likely preparing her for this jaunt back in time. Though his cousins were his lifeblood, he would always feel a special bond with those who, like him, had been part of the Next Generation.

Logan led her around the bonfire toward the drawbridge. "What would you like to speak with me about?"

Cassie offered him a guilty grin. "Sorry, that was just a ruse to escape your cousins. It's gonna take a bit to get used to them I think."

"I ken but 'twill get easier with time." Logan couldn't stop a smile as he steered her closer lest the crowd separate them. "They are good men and willnae do anything that makes you uncomfortable."

"They sorta already have by being *them*." She chuckled. "If you know what I mean."

He did but still fished for a little something more. "And I dinnae make you feel uncomfortable?"

"You know you don't," she murmured, her eyes sparkling in the torchlight as they met his. "I tend to think you make a habit of trying to make people, especially women, feel as comfortable as possible."

"I dinnae see why it should be any other way," he replied, eyes flickering over the way her skirts dusted the wooden planks of the bridge. Though he knew her legs were slender, he wondered if they were as silky smooth as her face. Snapping his eyes ahead, it took more will-power than he expected not to look at her like his cousins just had. "Though 'tis not the way of my clan to do such, please let me know if any make untoward advances."

"You got it." She took another small sip. "Sorry if I dragged you away from your lairdly duties."

"Making sure you're settling in well *is* part of my lairdly duties."

"About that. How long do you think I'll be here? Better yet, how do I get home?"

Yet more questions he had for Grant. Ones he realized he did not really want answers to. "I dinnae know but will try to find out." His eyes met hers. "How are you? Was Machara helpful? All of this must be frightening but know that no harm will come to you and that you're safe."

"I know," she murmured, eyes scanning their surroundings. "At least I think I know." Her eyes met his again. "Machara was surprisingly great even though she scared the crap out of me initially. Oddly enough, once we left you, she simmered down and got a whole lot more girly. As much as I think the woman is capable, that is."

Girly? Machara? "Though we were close when younger, she hasn't forgiven me for becoming laird when she was daughter to Colin, one of our former chieftains."

"Hmm, I sort of get that." She shook her head. "It can't be easy living in an age where men rule all and women get little say."

"Our lasses get plenty of say," he defended. "We have a great deal of respect for all in our clan, lads and lasses alike. 'Twas verra likely Machara would have been given the clan had she been ready."

"How was she not ready? She seems so passionate about it." She cocked her head. "And would your clan *really* have made a woman chieftain?"

"Aye, the MacLomains dinnae think like most clans. Likely because we're so connected to the future." He steered her to the right when a rowdy group of bairns rushed by. "Back when I became Laird, Machara was of a more reckless nature. She tended to rush into things before thinking them through. She's changed some since, but the clan remains of the mind she makes a better warrior than a leader."

"Niall said earlier that you're quick to rush into battle," she pointed out. "So what makes you so different?"

"Patience," he said. "That which Machara still works toward."

"Will she ever get a chance to become Laird again?"

"Mayhap." He took her hand as they crossed the second bridge. The crowd was thickening as people went between the bonfires. Many nodded and clapped him on the shoulder in passing. "Things can change quickly in this day and age. 'Tis verra possible I could die tomorrow in battle then there is always the chance the clan will choose Machara to lead."

Logan knew he should release her small, soft hand. Hell, he probably shouldn't be walking with her at all considering his betrothal. But he could not seem to stop.

"Well, I hope you don't die tomorrow," she said softly. "Or anytime soon for that matter."

"None of us wishes to die lass but 'tis not something we worry over. When 'tis our time 'tis our time. Meanwhile, we do what we can to keep our clan safe in a country that is slowly slipping away."

Logan hadn't meant to say so much, to express his never-ending worries, but he felt a level of comfort with her that he experienced with few. He was about to say more, to steer the conversation away from such heaviness, when a rowdy band of warriors flew over the bridge. Determined to keep her out of harm's way, he pushed her against one of the stone barriers below the second portcullis and protected her with his body.

He didn't realize how close he had come until her back met the stone and she gasped against his chest. Everything in him screamed to step away the minute the men passed but the air suddenly heated and all he was aware of was *her*. She smelled of the petunia's his Ma used to grow outside the house in New Hampshire. A scent that had lulled him to sleep many a night.

Then he became aware of everything else, as though every tiny thing sharpened his senses. How small and vulnerable her curves felt against him. The way her fingers fluttered up his chest as though she wasn't sure if she should be touching him. The way her breath caught then slowly released.

They went still at the same time.

He had no choice. Arousal blew through him so quickly, he nearly ground against her. Her breathing switched pace and while he figured she would push him away, she pressed closer. Wind blew off the loch and swooped over the moat, blowing her hair across his forearm. He closed his eyes and bent his head, inhaling deeply, breathing in her scent while mesmerized by her velvety hair brushing over his skin.

"There you are!" Grant broke through the bliss he was fast sinking into and he pulled away quickly.

Cassie blinked several times, her eyes a little glazed before they swung to Grant. "Athdara!"

Grant smiled at the horse by his side. "I thought you might like to see her again so I brought her out to graze in the field."

Logan didn't miss the look Grant shot him as Cassie joined her horse. It was a stern look meant to remind him that *he* was not meant for a Broun lass but for his betrothed. Logan nodded, frustrated by his own behavior. Though he hadn't done anything inappropriate, he had wanted to and God knows his desire for Cassie had likely been clear to all. Even so, when Grant urged Cassie to take the line and lead Athdara on, Logan joined them instead of returning to his cousins. In truth, he should be visiting with Rònan and welcoming the MacLeod's.

"She's so beautiful," Cassie said to Grant, her eyes almost childlike as she led the horse.

"Aye, she is." Grant smiled. "When you're ready you can release her line. She will follow you anywhere, lass."

"Really?" Cassie shook her head. "Why?"

"Because she's your friend," Logan said softly, admiring her alongside Athdara. They were well suited to one another.

"When will she hear my thoughts?"

Logan smiled at Athdara's voice in his head and responded in kind. *"When the time is right."*

He was still trying to figure out exactly *who* the horse was. Her voice was soothing and peaceful within his mind, like trickling water in a stream.

"Ye desire Cassie," Athdara said.

" 'Tis safe to say most lads do," he responded.

The horse gave no response but seemed quite pleased with the way Cassie released the line and eyed her fondly. "Okay, Athdara, don't run off now. All right, girl?"

"She needs to stop speaking to me as if I am a dog."

"She knows nothing of horses," Logan assured. *"Give her time."*

"Dogs are noble creatures too," Grant cut into their thoughts. *"Never forget it."*

"Look, she's actually staying with me," Cassie exclaimed, grinning at Logan.

Captivated by the happiness on her face, he tried to respond but could not find the words.

"And she will," Grant said, covering for him. "Athdara recognizes a good friend when she sees one."

Cassie shook her head and kept smiling, her attention solely focused on Athdara. "Awesome."

"Go. Walk with her." Logan nodded toward the field. "I'll be at the bonfire if you care to join me after. Have no worries over Athdara. She will always find her way back to the stables."

Her brows perked. "Really?"

He smiled. "Really."

Cassie's eyes held his for a moment before she nodded and walked away with her newfound friend.

Grant said nothing at first as they headed for the fire. Logan greeted many along the way but when he was at last alone with the arch-wizard, he murmured, "I know I cannae have her."

"'Tis a thing to want someone we cannae have." Grant's eyes met his. "'Tis more of a thing to walk away from something that could have been ours."

"Something that I dinnae believe is part of your tale," Logan murmured, disappointed in himself the moment he said it. Regardless, he knew Grant's love story and walking away from desire was not part of it.

"Ye think I cannae relate, but ye forget that I was imprisoned fourteen winters when a bairn," Grant said. "Ye forget that my want had nothing to do with love of a lass at first but love for my kin." Grant's frown humbled Logan. "And ye forget that I walked away from my clan and seemingly betrayed them so that I might ultimately save them."

Before Logan could speak, Grant shook his head sharply. "Ye must always think of yer clan first and foremost, lad. The love of a lass truly meant for ye will find its way to ye no matter what. Meanwhile, ye cannae put at risk yer integrity or yer promise to yer blood, to the *MacLomains*, do ye ken?"

Logan took a shallow swig from his skin. Even drinking was not something he could overly indulge in. But that was part of his commitment to this clan, as was what Grant implied. And he was right. The moment he became chieftain he took an oath to defend and protect the MacLomains always.

"I will see through my betrothal," he said softly. "Have no worries."

"I dinnae doubt ye will, laddie." Grant squeezed his shoulder. "No doubt at all."

Logan's eyes drifted to the fire and while he tried to focus on Grant's words and how important they were, his thoughts kept wandering to Cassie. How was she faring with Athdara? Were they connecting? He wished he was walking with them and helping her learn more about the beautiful horse that was hers. He already craved her smiles when Athdara warmed her heart. He already craved the sound of her laughter when she realized the horse really was her friend.

Then there were the other thoughts.

Or better yet, just the one.

He wished they were back on the bridge and her body was still pressed against his.

Be better, think better, he said to himself. Yet a small smile came to his lips and his eyes were ensnared when long hours later, or maybe minutes, Cassie and Athdara reappeared. As her eyes met his and a wide smile blossomed on her face, he knew he was doomed. Aye, he was used to women smiling at him, even desiring him, but he wasn't used to the simple friendship he saw in her eyes. The *want* of a woman who looked at him because she missed him, because she was glad to lay eyes on him again.

Everything inside let go and muscles he didn't know were knotted released.

Was this love?

No, far too soon for that. Then again, he knew nothing of love. What did it feel like, look like? He had no way of knowing save what he saw betwixt his parents. What he *did* know was what he felt beneath the portcullis with Cassie was far beyond anything he'd ever experienced. Maybe it was nothing. Maybe it was something. Either way, they had formed some sort of connection and it felt like a lifeline.

One he was not allowed.

Cassie was about to speak when a voice boomed, "It took longer than I expected but bloody hell 'tis good to be home!"

"Darach!" Cassie smiled. "So good to see you here."

Logan clenched his jaw and started to step forward as she flung her arms around his cousin. Grant's hand clamped down on his shoulder and his sharp words reminded, "'Tis never an easy thing to honor yer clan but ye must my lad. Ye must."

Then Grant said the most damning words. "After all, she's not meant for ye."

Chapter Five

"OH!" CASSIE YELPED when Darach spun her a few times. She hadn't expected such an enthusiastic greeting but probably should have known better. He had been fairly obvious about his attraction to her before.

"'Tis good to see you here, lass." He smiled and finally held her at arm's length. "Are you well? 'Tis no easy thing traveling through time."

"Actually it was pretty painless. If you leave out the part about being thrust into the middle of a battle. *That* was terrifying. But I'm doing a lot better now." She shook her head. "I still can't believe I'm here. I keep feeling like I might wake up from a dream at any moment."

"Nay." He took her hand and led her toward the bonfire. "There will be no waking up from this because you're wide awake already."

Was she *really*? Because everything still seemed so surreal, especially what she felt in Logan's arms on the drawbridge. What *was* that? Her body had responded in unfamiliar ways. Her clothing became too heavy, too constrictive. Every inch of her skin tingled and burned, craving the feel of his flesh against hers. Even now, her heart beat into her throat just looking at him all done up in Highland regalia. So frigging handsome. All she could think about was being back on the bridge and in his arms.

She stepped back when Darach embraced first Grant then Logan.

"'Tis good to see you, son." Grant beamed as he eyed Darach. "Did you go back to the castle and see your Ma first? She willnae forgive you otherwise."

"Nay, not yet." Darach rubbed the back of his neck and shrugged, eyes meeting Cassie's. "But I dinnae think she will fault me for getting detoured."

Grant sighed and shook his head.

"How fares the Colonial in New Hampshire?" Logan interrupted, his expression somewhat stern. "And Uncle Bradon and Aunt Leslie?"

"All is well." Darach received a skin and took a long drag before he continued. "They're caring for more Broun lasses as they arrive."

"Is Nicole okay? Does she know where I am?" Lord, she had been so completely entrenched in being introduced to an ancient society and yes, *Logan*, that she nearly forgot about her friends. "And more Brouns have arrived? Does that mean Erin and Jaqueline are there?"

"Nicole is fine and knows you're here." Darach wrapped an arm around her lower back and pulled her against his side. "Jaqueline has arrived but not Erin."

"How's Jackie? I mean Jaqueline." She worried at the corner of her lower lip, overly aware of how affectionate Darach was being. Better yet, the tightness in Logan's jaw as he watched them. "Has she been filled in on...well..." She looked around. "All that might be heading her way?"

"Aye, your friends will be just fine," Darach assured. "None will arrive here without plenty of knowledge beforehand."

"So all of them are definitely coming?" she said softly, happy and worried for them at the same time.

"Aye," Grant answered for Darach, his eyes shifting between the two young Highlanders. "As they are meant for a MacLomain like the Brouns before them."

"Oh," she murmured, wheels spinning. "What MacLomains *specifically* are they meant for?"

"Those born of the Next Generation," Grant said. "But 'tis not for you to worry over, lass."

"No offense but it sort of *is*." Cassie carefully removed herself from Darach's hold. "Not only because my friends are involved but because I am too."

All she could think about was Rònan and Niall being meant for one of her friends. Darach? Fine. He was a sweetheart. But the other two? She was not so sure. They were damn intense. As to Logan? Well, he was off the table which made her wonder, why the heck was she here? Because—though she might not want to admit it—the only man that slightly...okay, *really*, interested her was Logan.

But she was *so* not a home-wrecker.

And pursuing any man sworn to another woman was close enough.

Yet she had to be sure he wasn't meant for a Broun anyway. Just to ease her peace of mind for his betrothed that is. "Logan isn't born of the Next Generation right?" She kept her eyes trained on Grant because she couldn't believe she was spitting this out with Logan standing right here. "So he doesn't have to worry about this new Broun/MacLomain connection?"

"Nay," Logan answered for Grant, drawing her eyes in his direction. "I was part of the Next Generation but a wee bairn at the time they met their lasses." His expression remained unwavering, but his voice deepened as though he fought emotion. "So I cannae be meant for you or your friends."

Heat flared beneath her skin. Their eyes held and damn if she wasn't back on that drawbridge pressed against him, eager for more. Eager to understand the intense pull between them.

"Good," she whispered but didn't mean it at all. Not even a little bit. And that bothered the heck out of her.

His pupils flared and for a second she swore he was going to close the distance and pull her into his arms. She swore he was thinking the same thoughts as her. Darach cleared his throat and Logan's eyes shot to his cousin.

"When precisely is your intended, Aline MacLauchlin, due to arrive?"

So *that* was her name. *Aline MacLauchlin.* A pretty name, beautiful actually. A name *meant* for him. Cassie took a sip from her skin and looked to the fire. Whatever this was between her and Logan needed to stop *now*.

"In less than a week," Logan said. "But I've decided to go to her on the morrow. 'Tis dangerous and MacLomain warriors alongside her own will help ensure her safe passage."

"You're riding to her?" Darach's brows perked as his lips turned down. "With how many men, cousin?"

Cassie did not like the look on either Darach or Grant's faces.

"Enough," Logan said curtly before he nodded at her. "I wish you a good eve, Cassie. Stay close to either Grant or Darach. They will see you well."

She started to mumble a response, but he strode off. A little stunned and worried, she looked at Grant. "Is everything all right?"

"Aye." Grant nodded at Darach before he left as well. "Stay by her side until she is ready to rest or unless Machara happens along."

"Of course," he murmured, eyes narrowed as he watched his father go after Logan.

"What was that all about?" she asked. "I get the sense that Logan going to Aline is a bad idea."

"'Tis nothing, lass." Darach shook his head and quickly smoothed away his disgruntled expression. He grabbed her hand and pulled her after him. "Let's go dance."

"No." Cassie braced her feet and stopped him. "Tell me what's wrong. Please."

"'Tis nothing for you—"

"Yes it is," she interrupted and tried to voice her concern without sounding like she was overly worried about Logan. Because she was. A lot. "If I'm here then that means I have the right to worry about the MacLomain clan and everything to do with it...including its chieftain."

Hmm, had that sounded vague enough?

Darach eyed her for an awkwardly long moment. Though she thought for sure she had done well with her line of inquisition, he was blunter than she anticipated. "So you're interested in Logan then?"

It was weird hearing a medieval Highlander phrase things like a twenty-first century guy, but then these MacLomains had the bizarre benefit of understanding two eras at once.

"No," she said slowly, cautiously. Darn him for pegging her. "I'm worried about the MacLomains."

A strange look passed over his face. Sadness, concern...determination?

"The MacLomains are strong. Dinnae worry over them." Compassion lit his eyes. "But many thanks for your concern considering what you've been through."

Cassie nodded, trying to be equally compassionate. "What about your clan, the Hamiltons? Are they okay?"

"I am Hamilton in name only, not by blood." A flicker of unease entered his eyes. "But aye, the Hamiltons are fine so dinnae fret over that."

"Okay, sure." But she wasn't one to let things go when she was curious. "So you're not a big fan of the Hamilton clan?"

"Aye, the clan's fine," he muttered under his breath as he again pulled her after him. "Its history, not so much."

She was about to question him further when Rònan approached. Dear God, this guy was overwhelming. If his height, which was a few inches taller than his cousins, and the tattoos wrapped over his muscled chest and arms weren't enough, his confrontational personality was.

"*There* you are, lass," he rumbled.

To make matters worse, Niall was strolling alongside. Not that he had been mean to her in the least, but he was as intimidating as his MacLeod cousin. One thing was for sure, these guys weren't her cup of tea. And clearly tea had *not* been their choice of drink tonight based on their rambunctious attitudes.

At least she had Darach with her. He seemed more like Logan.

Darach embraced the men, a wide smile on his face as they laughed and clapped one another on the back. Maybe she was wrong. Maybe they were alike after all. She clenched her teeth and tried to keep her cool, tried not to be silly and act like she was in over her head. They had all grown up together. They were friends. Nobody meant her any harm.

Still, she wished Logan hadn't vanished.

As if he sensed her distress, Darach returned to her side, his posture protective. "I'm taking Cassie to Machara. 'Tis best she remains with a lass this eve, aye?"

"Is it?" Niall smiled at her. For the first time since they had met he didn't devour her with his eyes. "We willnae hurt ye, lass. This I promise."

"Not so sure I believe that," she said, cursing her loose tongue. But now that it was said she might as well continue. "You guys kinda freak me out...a lot."

Rònan frowned. "Freak?"

Darach shook his head. "You'd ken more if you bothered to visit the twenty-first century."

"It means we frighten her," Niall provided, doing his best to lose his grin. "And that isnae good." Then a genuine frown settled on his face, which oddly enough made him look even more handsome. "'Twas not our intention, lass."

"It *never* is," Machara declared as she joined them. "Ye bunch of bloody arses."

Ronan spoke to Cassie as he wrapped his arm around Machara's shoulders and kissed the top of her head. "I heard you wondered about the Oak out yonder and that I was the lad to tell you more about it."

Scary thought but she was too curious for her own good and after all, she only told Grant so he must trust this guy...she hoped. "That's right."

"Another time, cousin." Machara patted Ronan's stomach as though he didn't possess washboard abs but a pot belly. "Meanwhile, she stays with me. The Laird will have it no other way."

"So Logan asked *you* to keep Cassie by your side?" Niall drawled, clearly not convinced.

"Aye. Can ye believe it?" Machara winked. "His number one enemy."

Truth be told, though eager to escape with Machara she was sorely tempted to follow the devil Ronan to the mighty oak.

"Och, lassie." Machara shook her head. "I'll not see ye tempted by the MacLeod just yet." She pulled Cassie after her. "Enjoy yer eve, lads. Find yerselves another lass's skirt to wander beneath, aye?"

Cassie waved over her shoulder at Darach before Machara pulled her into the crowd and away from the men.

"I'm not sure if I should thank you or not," she muttered as the Scotswoman released her hand and they walked over the drawbridge. "I was super curious about the oak."

"Aye, we all are at one time or another." Machara shook her head. "But Ronan never tells all. At least not beyond what we already know."

"And what exactly is that?" Cassie asked.

"That the oak was born of a dragon. Ronan's Ma, Torra. And that the tree watches over the MacLomain clan to this day."

"Excuse me?" Cassie avoided a bunch of girls scampering over the bridge and did her best to keep her eyes from the wall Logan had her against earlier. "A *dragon*?"

"Aye." Machara looked at her as though she was born yesterday. "Half dragon anyway. Just like Ronan."

Cassie almost questioned whether dragons actually existed but figured that would be pretty redundant considering she *had* traveled back in time and that wizards seemingly existed.

"Listen, if it's okay I'd rather head back to my chamber," Cassie said. "It's been a long day."

"Really?" Machara eyed her. "The celebrations are in full swing."

"Yes, really," she confirmed. "But thanks so much for everything you've done for me." Machara really *had* done a lot for Cassie. She had been very thorough showing her around and made her feel welcome. "I'm sorry. I'm just overtired."

While the tall, thin brunette was not necessarily made of warm moments, she nodded and her face softened. "Fine then, lass. I'll make sure ye get to yer chamber safely."

She nodded, grateful Machara left it at that.

As it turned out, Logan became caught up in clan business and did not leave the next day or even the following one. Though Grant, Machara and Darach kept her entertained, she was always hoping for a glance of the MacLomain Laird. Occasionally he checked in on her, but the moments were fleeting. Niall and Rònan flirted when they got the chance, but Machara was fiercely protective, claiming Cassie deserved time to learn her way around without dealing with their lusting.

On her third night in medieval Scotland, Cassie looked out the window of her chamber, thankful she was *here* and not down *there*. Summer solstice was definitely a big deal around here and the crowd was rowdy. Partying had never been her thing so she was happy enough tucked away with a fire crackling and a tray of assorted foods on the table.

She liked solitude.

Almost as much as history and ancestry.

While not overly hungry, she still sampled the variety of foods. Bannock, a type of bread. Various seafoods including scallops and shrimp. Delicious cheeses. She didn't drink the whisky provided because it seemed foolish to dull her senses in a fairly unfamiliar place.

Eventually, she grew restless and decided to explore the upper level of the castle. Traveling the torch-lit corridor, she walked out onto the first wall walk she came to. It was relatively quiet, the sound of celebrating carried away by the wind. The lilt of bagpipes a faint echo off the castle walls. She liked it. A place less confined by stone but open to the sky.

Hands braced on the battlement, she leaned her head back, closed her eyes and smiled. A temperate breeze blew her hair. The rock beneath her fingertips was rough in some areas and smooth in others. As if generations of hands and perhaps even weapons had rested upon it. The scents here were different. So free of modern day. She inhaled deeply, focusing on each little smell. The torch smoke, salt off the loch, grass, and even wildflowers.

"Ya ves, con todos sus sentidos. You see with all of your senses. *"*

Her heart leapt with excitement at the sound of Logan's quiet voice. She kept her eyes closed and smiled. "So you did learn something from *Handy Manny*."

"Sí, él me enseñó mucho. Entonces hice un punto de aprender español después. Es una lengua hermosa e importante. Yes, he taught me a lot. Then I made a point of learning Spanish afterward. 'Tis a beautiful and important language."

"So is Scottish Gaelic." She opened her eyes to find him leaning against the battlement beside her.

"Not so much anymore," he replied, eyes on the celebrations below. "Or should I say, not so much in the future we both know is coming."

Though tempted to say the particular brand of Scots Gaelic he spoke or even Gaelic in general, would become a world language, they both knew that'd be a lie. So she said, "The minute you stop speaking your native tongue, it dies with you."

That was more intense than she intended, but it was true.

"I know," he murmured, eyes still on his clan. "But to my way of thinking, learning to expand my language will keep my native tongue alive one way or another." His eyes went to hers, shadowed by the torch burning over his shoulder. "How else will I teach future Spanish speaking generations Gaelic?"

Cassie crossed her arms over her chest. "Are you seriously worried about what will happen to the Gaelic language seven hundred years from now?"

His eyes lingered on hers for a few long moments before returning to the crowds below. "Nay, lass, I'm worried about what will become of my clan."

Though she knew a great deal about the Brouns, she knew nothing about the MacLomains. She could not remember them coming up in any of the research she had done.

As if reading her thoughts, Logan said, "Our clan will change over the next couple hundred years. We will become known as the Lamonts. Still, we will be connected with the Brouns." His eyes met hers. "Because of the centuries in which we currently live and those that are behind us."

"*Lamont?* As in the Lamonts slaughtered in the Dunoon Massacre in 1646?"

"Aye." He shook his head. "'Tis a poor piece of history that is."

"*Jesus*," she whispered, sick to her stomach.

"You know your Scottish history well," he murmured.

"Yes," she whispered. "But it's hard to imagine your clan name becomes Lamont."

"Aye," he said. "From *Mac Laomainn*, or Lauman and then Lamont as it becomes known in a few hundred more years. In this era, we were actually called MacLomain. They never did spell it right in the history books, but one thing withstood the ages."

"What's that?"

"The connection." His eyes didn't quite meet hers. "Betwixt your clan and mine. The Brouns and the MacLomains, more easily researched if you look up Lamont. The Brouns and Lamonts have been septs of one another's for ages. Forever tied together. But little of either clan's history was recorded accurately for hundreds upon hundreds of years."

"How can you talk about all of this so loosely?" Her eyes burned as she looked at him. "I can't even imagine what you must be feeling knowing that this..." She looked at the people celebrating below, her mind less on their clans' connection but the massacre on the distant horizon. "That this will all be wiped out..."

"Everything changes. 'Tis part of life." He clenched his jaw and shook his head. "For now, we still thrive and have the ability to help make changes, ones that can see the future of Scotland better than it might have been."

"But we both already know the future of Scotland," she murmured, appalled to say it but unable to stop. "And she's under the rule of England."

"The United Kingdom," he conceded. "Is where we are for now." Then she swore she heard him whisper, "But mayhap not forever," before he said, "And our economy in the future fares well, does it not? So all is not so bad."

"No, not bad," she agreed, baffled that she was having a conversation with a thirteenth century Scotsman about twenty-first century Scottish economics. And, as usual, though she should tread carefully, her big mouth just spit out what she was thinking. "Scotland is rich in natural resources. Tidal, wind and wave energy as well as oil in the North Sea. Fish stocks, agricultural output, and thriving tourism. The list is pretty lengthy. A country that might be better off in charge of its own resources wouldn't you say?"

"You're well-educated about this country in both the present and the future."

"As are you and I'd bet far better than me."

"It would only make sense." His eyes returned to the crowds below. "Because somehow I need to make sure my clan survives its own history."

How though considering the massacre? Then again, hundreds might have died that frightful day but certainly not all. The gene had survived. The MacLomains still lived in the twenty-first century…didn't they? Maybe under the name Lamont but still, that was something…*everything*.

"I understand," she said not sure what else she should say. What she wanted to say was that it would all be okay, everything would work out, Scotland would be its own country. But they both knew that wasn't true.

She almost closed her eyes when his hand rested over hers on the battlement. Yet he was not being romantic. "I know what will happen to my country but I also know what it will take to get her there and it needs to happen."

Her eyes shot to his. "So you're determined to get this country to its current future?"

"Aye." He inhaled as though he smelled something refreshing. "Though you might wish for an independent Scotland in the future, I must focus on what will get her to the point that she even has that as a possible goal."

Cassie shook her head. "I don't get it."

Though it seemed for a minute he was going to stop talking, he exhaled and spoke as if he *needed* to share. "My cousins and I will make sure King Robert the Bruce has his wits about him when he becomes an adult, when challenges are laid before him."

Robert the Bruce? She made to speak, but the words died on her lips. So she tried again. "As in the King of Scotland?" But even that came out as a weak squeak.

"The one and only," he replied, sounding very modern before he once more sounded ancient. "I dinnae know quite how but 'tis part of my destiny…'tis part of my cousins' destinies."

What had she been plunked into? This was *insane*. But so was everything else that was part of her current set of circumstances. "If I remember correctly he was born in the late thirteenth century. What year is it now?"

"'Tis 1281. The Bruce is only seven winters old."

Cassie was overly aware that he had *not* removed his hand from hers. "So when are you and your cousins supposed to help him?"

"Soon." His eyes met hers. "'Tis said that we would assist him when he was a bairn."

"Oh." *Interesting.* And definitely not recorded in any history books. "So how exactly are you supposed to do that?"

"I dinnae know yet." He shrugged. "But there cannae be any doubt that he will need us."

The idea that the future King of Scotland would somehow be protected by wizards and even a dragon-shifter was pretty darn mind-blowing. "Where is he now?"

"Being fostered by a family well north of Ayrshire." He at last pulled his hand away. "'Tis best for him to be raised around those that willnae show him favoritism so that he might grow up strong."

"I see." She frowned. "Sort of sad, though. His mother must miss him."

"She does." Logan leaned back against the battlement, crossed his arms over his chest and eyed her. "You shouldnae be out here alone, lass."

While she would like nothing more than to grill him about the King, she got the sense he needed a break from heavy conversation so she kept it light.

"You're only now chastising me about being out here alone?" she teased.

A small smile curled his lips. "I had to eventually."

"No, you didn't."

"Aye, I did."

"Why?"

"Because I didnae want you left alone." She swore he shifted closer. "Yet here you are."

"I just needed some air." Was he flirting? It almost seemed like it even though she was being reprimanded. "It was so peaceful out here. And free of people."

"I've men stationed on this wall walk," he enlightened. "The only reason you dinnae see them is because I'm here."

"And why are *you* here?" She quirked her lip. "Shouldn't you be mingling with your clan and getting ready for your journey...whenever that is?"

She almost wished she hadn't said it because his body tensed. But it was probably best she reminded them both that he had somewhere else to be. More so, someone else to be *with*. Because there was some serious heat fluctuating between them and she knew it wasn't just her imagination.

"I enjoy time spent alone when given the opportunity, which is rarer and rarer lately," he said. "It gives me time to think and plan."

"I get that." She nodded. While she should probably leave it alone, she had been curious for days and was now given an opportunity. "So why did Grant and Darach seem so concerned about you going to get your betrothed?"

"They worry overmuch." A flicker of discomfort crossed his face before his expression smoothed. "The times are perilous."

"Without a doubt." She narrowed her eyes. "But there's more to it, isn't there?"

He considered her for a long moment before he sighed. "There are some who would not see Aline and I married. That dinnae want the connection betwixt our clans strengthened."

"I understand...I think," she said. "So both of you traveling together are double the target?"

"Something like that. However 'tis for the best that I escort her here and sooner rather than later." He clenched his jaw. "Things are only becoming more dangerous."

There was a strange edge to the way he said those last few words, the way his eyes suddenly locked with hers. She knew in that riveting moment that the danger he referred to did not entirely have to do with the current state of his homeland. While Cassie thought he had barely noticed her over the past few days, she could see in his eyes that she had been dead wrong.

"Then you should go," she said softly, trying to unravel from the overflow of emotions wrapping around her. "But stay safe."

"I will," he murmured, so close now that their arms nearly touched. Then, almost as if he didn't mean to but could not help it, he said, "Tell me about yourself, Cassie."

She could smell the light spice of his skin and all but feel the burning heat in his eyes.

"I don't think that's a very good idea," she whispered.

"You're my guest." His voice was gentle yet inquisitive. "So know that I only ask as a curious chieftain…and hopefully someday a friend."

He knew as well as she did that they were playing with fire. Friendship was not on either of their minds. Or maybe this was one sided. Maybe she really *was* imagining the strong attraction between them. But she didn't think so. She had *never* felt anything like this. On the other hand, she didn't have a lot of experience to go off of.

So though she knew she should leave it alone, she figured sharing a little wouldn't hurt. "I was born in upstate Maine but more recently moved to the coast." She shrugged. "I did the whole college thing but never really settled on a major I enjoyed so it was sort of a waste of time and money. Though I love history, I never went for a degree in it but instead ended up fascinated by ancestry. That's when I decided to create an ancestry website. It's no ancestry.com, but I've done okay with it and really enjoy running it."

"So you have some experience with software engineering then?"

Again, weird that he even knew to ask that question. "Enough." She shrugged a shoulder and eyed the bonfires. "One of those majors I never saw through. I ended up hiring a small team to help me launch and maintain the site."

"What made you so interested in ancestry?" he asked. "Enough to devote so much work to it?"

"I just think it's fascinating." Definitely not the reason she pursued it. "Everyone should try to reconnect with their family history. You can learn so much." Now *that* edged a little closer to her reasons for launching the site.

"You forget I'm a wizard," he murmured.

Her eyes went to his, confused.

"You give me little truth." He took her hand and ran his forefinger lightly over the vein on the underside of her wrist. Her knees almost buckled as shivers ran through her and gooseflesh spread over her skin. "I dinnae need to touch this to feel your unsteady heartbeat. A telltale sign of nervousness caused by possible deceit."

Before she could respond, he continued. "I dinnae want you to feel as if you need to give me all your truths but know I'm always here if you want to share them, aye?"

He meant it. She knew he did. Still, it made her chest burn and throat tighten so she offered no response. God, would it be nice to share, to release all her pent up feelings about what life had dealt her. How scared and lonely she really was.

Could they become friends? Hands down, yes. But would his wife be all right with that? Better yet, would Cassie knowing full well that she was so attracted to him?

"No," she murmured, not entirely sure what she was saying no to. Her eyes drifted down to his hand still locked around her wrist and she shook her head, trembling. "I'm sorry."

"Nay, ye dinnae ken," he whispered, brogue thickening. "Or mayhap I dinnae."

Her eyes again shot to his and held. The bagpipes playing in the distance faded and even the wind seemed to quell as his brows lowered, breath hitched and his grip tightened.

Pull your hand away. Walk away. Run! She screamed inwardly.

But no.

She did the *very* last thing she should do.

Chapter Six

LOGAN FROZE WHEN Cassie flung her arms around his waist, pressed close and rested her cheek against his chest. He kept his arms akimbo knowing bloody well if he embraced her he might never let go.

And he *had* to let go.

Of her. This. Them. Everything he suddenly realized he wanted. No, that wasn't true. Every second of every minute of every hour since she arrived he had wanted her. But he had done as asked, done what was right, and kept his distance.

Until he saw her come out on this wall walk.

Then he had only meant to check on her.

But he should have known better.

Now the feel of her soft curves pressed against him and the flowery scent of her hair was breaking down his defenses. When he heard her breath catch and knew that a tear rolled down her cheek he was done for.

Completely, thoroughly, *undeniably* done for.

Wrapping one arm around her lower back, he cupped the back of her head and held her close, made her feel safe. Because if he was not mistaken, she was terrified of something and made a habit of showing the world a brave face. But what had her so scared? He could search her mind. He had that power. Yet he wouldn't. It would be an invasion of privacy. Still, he was sorely tempted...anything to search out and help assuage her pain.

Trying like hell not to get aroused by her closeness, he did his best to remain focused on the friendship he hoped to develop with her. *Friendship.* How would he manage that? Maybe it was better to focus on his journey on the morrow while still comforting her. A journey he had been putting off whether or not he wanted to admit it. That might work. But when she nuzzled even closer he knew it was a lost cause.

He had never wanted to possess a lass so much.

Kiss her.

Feel her.

Take her to his bed.

But more than that, he wanted to know absolutely everything about her. What demons did she fight? What made her happy? Sad? Serious? Did she want bairns? Did she want to wed if she found the right lad?

That last thought soured his stomach.

Because that lad could *never* be him.

He closed his eyes and lowered his head. Though he didn't inhale, he gently lifted a few strands of her hair to his cheek and felt its softness. So, so, soft. Like cool silky grass on a hot summer day.

"Logan. Trouble."

Grant's words slammed into his mind moments before the Hamilton Laird and Darach appeared on the wall walk. Cassie pulled away as though she had been caught doing something wrong.

"'Tis okay, lass," he started to assure her, but Grant cut him off.

"There is grave trouble, lad. I tried to tell you before I got up here, but your mind was closed."

Closed? Shocked, Logan frowned. Not once had he closed his mind to anyone. It wasn't a luxury he could afford when leading a clan. That he did so now said much. That he had done it without realizing said even more.

"Tell me," he bit out.

"There's been an attack," Grant said. "On the MacLauchlin clan."

His muscles locked and his gaze swung out over the distant forest as though he might be able to see the harm done in the distance. While tempted to flee immediately and help save them, he realized how irrational his thoughts were.

His eyes went to Cassie and he squeezed her hand in reassurance. "All will be well." Then he glanced at Darach. "See her to her chamber. Make sure there are guards outside her door then meet me in the courtyard."

"Aye." Darach took her elbow and led her away.

Logan joined Grant as they strode toward the great hall. "What happened?"

"Nothing good," Grant said under his breath. "'Twas bloody ugly."

The clan celebrations had simmered down considerably as rumor spread about what had happened. When he saw Grant's daughter, Lair, making her way through the crowd with a heavy frown on her face, he knew it was as bad as it could get. She had been visiting outlying homes caring for those with ailments and he had not seen her for days.

When she reached him, she whispered in his ear, "Ye must travel swiftly, cousin. She is in great pain."

Logan nodded, kissed her on the cheek and headed down to the courtyard. If Lair said things were dire, then any hope of a good outcome was dwindling. He swung onto his horse, received weapons from one of his men and shot Grant a look when he joined him astride his own horse. "Ye are too important to this clan, m'laird. Dinnae come."

"Just as important as ye are," Grant shot back and nodded to Logan's cousins as their horses came alongside. "And as important as they are."

Rònan nodded at Logan. "Where ye go I go."

"As do I," Niall said.

Darach nodded. "Me too, cousin."

Before Logan could ask about Cassie, Darach said, "She's safe. Four guards watch over her."

Logan nodded and eyed them all with thanks.

"Dinnae forget about me," Machara declared as she joined them. "If yer fighting, so am I."

Logan nodded again and spurred his horse, his kin and dozens of warriors in tow. The MacLauchlin clan wasn't all that far north of their border but because of magic, they were able to shorten what would have been a few days ride into several hours. What they found as the sun crested the horizon was a village that had once been thriving now in complete devastation.

There would be no battling here.

There would be no saving of lives.

As far as he could tell there was little left except stray dogs feeding on scraps and the pressing circle of vultures overhead. Logan swung down from his horse and staggered through the dead bodies. Numb, without direction, he scanned his surroundings. His cousins were by his side, eying the destruction with part sadness and part fury.

Niall was crouching as he moved forward, turning over body after body, angry and desperate to find life. Darach had never looked sadder as he pulled a whimpering but dying lass into his arms.

Rònan was downright furious as he strode through the bodies, eager for a target, eager to destroy whoever had killed so many.

"We must find her," Grant said softly. "We must find Aline."

Logan nodded and kept scanning everything. The village had been massacred. Its people treated mercilessly. While such tragedies happened often enough, this was worse than usual and done on a larger scale. Women had not just been killed but beaten and raped first. Men had been ripped apart, some of them disemboweled. Even the elderly and young weren't spared.

"I should have been here days ago," he whispered. "I could have stopped this."

"*Ye* could have stopped *nothing*. Dinnae for a moment blame yerself for this lad. If ye'd been here 'twould verra likely have meant the death of ye and yers as well," Grant said sharply. "Focus on what is important. Find Aline. Yer cousins will round up anyone who might have survived then we leave immediately. The air smells of the enemy."

Logan nodded and pushed past the haze of complete loss, pain, and devastation he felt. "Aye."

Gesturing to his men to span out, he hollered, "Aline, are ye here? Aline MacLauchlin, 'tis I, your betrothed, Logan MacLomain. Call out, lass. Ye are safe. I am here."

Again and again he called out those words.

Fear filled him. Please don't let her be part of this slaughter. *God forgive me for desiring another lass while she was going through such pain. What kind of monster am I? I should have left earlier. I should have been here. I could have saved these people.* Self-loathing filled him as he searched.

Logan had just reached the edge of the carnage when he heard a faint murmur. Like the sound of a small squeaking bird struggling, caught in a distant cave. Then it changed and became weak words. "Here. I am here."

Logan tore through the rubble, desperate. *Frantic.* He tossed aside straw, loose wood, but the heavier beams were harder to move.

"Easy, cousin. I'm here to help." Niall started to push and pull but remained careful as he helped Logan try to uncover Aline. Though it seemed to take two full turns of the moon, they finally removed enough.

Dirty faces stared up.

None moved.

All were lifeless.

"Nay," Niall muttered and kept going.

Logan threw a scrap of wood over his shoulder then froze when a hand snaked up and grabbed his wrist. "Here. I am here."

He and Niall started digging. Within moments, they pulled her free. Covered in soot, she tried to gasp but it was clear her lungs were full. Yet she kept trying to say something. He brushed his hand over her lips and summoned magic. As it had been the day he helped Robert the Bruce into this world, he used the power of Mother Earth. Though by no means the gift of healing, it seemed to help based on her coughing.

Grant joined them. He had retrieved a bucket of water and a washcloth. "Here. The water will help her."

Logan gently washed off her face while she at last inhaled deeply several times. As he wiped away the soot, he finally looked at his betrothed for the first time. While not a stunning beauty, she was lovely in a gentle sort of way. With rounded cheeks and a creamy, smooth complexion, she was anything but long in the tooth.

"Ye must get me back to yer castle," she breathed. "Then ye must go after him."

What did she mean by that? Better yet, what was he sensing? Some type of magic fluctuated around her. Based on Grant's quizzical expression, he sensed it as well.

"Now!" she pleaded, snapping him out of his curiosity.

"Aye, lass." He lifted her and strode for his horse. Meanwhile, the few who had survived were already being taken back to the castle.

He spoke to Grant within the mind so as to not upset Aline. *"Either the MacLauchlin Laird doesnae know what has happened here or his castle is under attack."*

"Dinnae send anyone yet," Grant warned. *"There are bad things afoot in this area. Evil. 'Tis best to get back to yer castle and defend the MacLomains until we know more."*

Though sorely tempted to go lend aid to the remaining MacLauchlin's, he knew Grant was right. Despite his concern, his clan must come first.

"I willnae stay on long," Grant said, distress in the essence of his voice. *"Nor do I suspect will Darach or Rònan."*

Logan understood. If a new threat was loose in Scotland, the men would want to protect their clans, the Hamiltons, and MacLeods.

They had not gone far when a cry rang through the woodland. Logan's men surrounded him, weapons drawn, ready to protect their laird as a man staggered through the trees.

"He's a MacLauchlin," someone said.

Still, his men kept their weapons at the ready.

"Help. *Please* help." Bedraggled, face ravaged by grief, he held a lass. His bleary eyes scanned the warriors. "I've the MacLauchlin Laird's daughter, Aline. She's been hurt."

Confused, Logan's eyes went to the lass in his arms but she was passed out cold. His eyes snapped back to the other woman. "'Tis the same lass."

"Aye, so it appears." Grant's eyes narrowed. "Yet Aline doesnae have a twin that I know of."

If things weren't strange enough, the man's voice grew more desperate. "Please help. I dinnae want my wif to die."

"By the bloody rood," Niall said as he joined them. "But Aline MacLauchlin is betrothed to Laird MacLomain."

What the hell was going on? He intended to find out as soon as the lass in his arms awoke. Logan nodded at one of his men. "Take the lass to the castle." Then he nodded at another. "The lad can ride with ye."

Little was said as they raced back. The bonfires had been doused by the time they returned. As expected, all villagers who lived close had taken sanction within the castle walls and the portcullises were closed after Logan and his men entered. Though most warriors stayed to protect the castle, many bands patrolled the clan's land lending protection to those who lived further out.

It was fortunate that Lair was visiting as she had the gift of healing. He suspected Grant would want her to stay here rather than attempt to travel. She was already directing several lasses to help the wounded when Logan swung down from his horse. He didn't have to say a word as her eyes went from the lass in his arms to the lass his warrior held. "Ye'll want them in the chambers close to yers."

"Aye," he said, striding after her.

When the man claiming to be the husband of the other lass tried to follow, he was held back.

"I need to be with her," he cried, struggling. "Please. She shouldnae wake without me there."

Assuming she would awaken. Logan glanced at the man and shook his head.

"Please, m'laird, dinnae keep me from her," the man pleaded.

Though frustrated that this man called Logan's betrothed his wife, he was not without compassion. So he gestured at the warrior retaining him. "Bring him then stand guard. He doesnae go near her."

"Aye, m'laird."

"Thank ye," the man said repeatedly. Logan ignored him and strode into the great hall. The celebrations were over and those that remained were somber. Obviously, Lair had hoped for the best because one chamber was already prepared. "Give the other lass this one." He nodded at the woman in his arms. "I'll take her to mine."

"Aye, of course." Lair must have sensed the strange magic surrounding the lass. "Ye shouldnae be alone with her, Logan. Keep my Da with ye until I've seen to the other, ye ken?"

"Aye." But there was no need for the request. Grant was already following.

Logan kept his eyes averted as a servant attended to Aline as best she could then tucked her into his bed. Despite the time of year, the air had chilled enough that a small fire was lit on the hearth. Grant sat while he paced, eyes occasionally flickering to the bed. "I dinnae ken this."

"Nor do I," Grant murmured. "But fear naught. We will soon enough get answers." He cocked his head slightly as if he sensed something. "Your Da is nearly here. I will leave once he arrives."

"Aye." Logan frowned. "Take some of my warriors with ye for protection."

"Och, ye forget that I've my magic." His brows perked. "And though I'm older, I'm still one of the best warriors ye know."

"Still," Logan said. "I'll not see harm come to ye. Take a few of my men."

"Nay." Grant shook his head. "Ye'll need every lad ye have."

Logan knew how Grant could be on occasion, especially when it came to protecting his people, so he nodded his consent. There would be warriors sent regardless. He was about to turn the subject back to Aline when a soft murmur came from the bed.

"Shh." Logan sat and took her hand. "All is well. Ye are safe, lass."

Her eyes fluttered but remained closed as Lair joined them.

"How fares the other lass?" he asked.

Lair placed her hand on the woman's head and chanted softly before her eyes met Logan's. "Worse off than this lass I'm afraid."

His cousin resumed chanting then suddenly stopped. "There is an enchantment on this lass. It soon wears off."

"What sort of enchantment. I dinnae recognize it."

"'Tis a type of glamour, aye?" Grant said as he joined them.

"Aye," Lair said. She looked a lot like her mother with her rich brown hair, auburn highlights, and soft blue eyes. Even her lovely features resembled Aunt Sheila's. Yet right now those features were set in a hard line. "'Tis indeed a type of glamour but of a magi in which I'm unfamiliar."

While Lair might look like her mother, her personality was more like Grant's. Her nature leaned less toward bubbly and more toward a quiet wisdom. Though her magic wasn't as strong as her father's, it was stronger than most of the children born of the Next Generation.

"Logan," Aline whispered and squeezed his hand.

It was unusual for anyone save family to leave off his title, especially she who was not yet his wife. "I am here, lass. All is well."

She shook her head and croaked, "Nay, 'tis not."

Though she could barely open her eyes, Logan brought a mug of water to her lips. "Drink. 'Twill help."

Aline managed a small swallow then turned her head away, her voice a wee less raspy when she spoke. "Ye *must* listen to me. Trouble has alas come and he must be saved."

A strange sensation rippled over him and he narrowed his eyes. "Who?"

"My son," she managed as she grabbed his wrist. "Has been taken."

Logan was about to respond when the air seemed to compress around him. It was clear Grant was about to weave a protection spell around Logan and his daughter when Aline's visage wavered. Yet soon enough, it became obvious it was not needed.

When the enchantment spell wore off, Aline was gone.

Instead, Marjorie, the Countess of Carrick, lay there.

The future King of Scotland's mother.

Chapter Seven

AFTER WATCHING THE commotion in the courtyard for a long time, Cassie tossed and turned in bed all night as images of slaughter and death plagued her. Faces flickered in and out of a dark forest. Sometimes they mocked her. Other times they called to her. Eventually, she decided trying to sleep wasn't such a great idea so she woke early and watched the sunrise the best she could from this vantage.

Her chamber was nice with several nautical tapestries and a comfortable bed. There were two windows, both flat on the bottom and rounded on top. Though a bath, clothes, food and drink had been provided, the guards outside her door would not allow her to leave and it was getting pretty old. It almost felt like she was being held prisoner.

Cassie knew nothing of the events last night except what she could surmise. Logan had a woman in his arms when he returned so she assumed that was Aline. It appeared the castle was in some sort of lock-down because save Grant, Rònan and Darach leaving a while ago, nobody had come or gone. She was sad to see Grant and Darach go but figured they were eager to get back to the Hamilton castle.

Though she had been trying all morning, she leaned against her door again and eyed the youngest guard. He seemed to have softened the most to her relentlessness. "I really need some air. Maybe just a few moments on the closest wall walk?"

"Och, nay, lass." His grin dropped under the scowls of his fellow guards. "The Laird would have my hide, he would."

Cassie was about to attempt flirting, something she had no practice at, when a strange sensation overwhelmed her. Seconds later, her vision started to blur and she grew dizzy. Uh oh. Not again. She stumbled and tried to grab the door but panic was taking over.

"Lass, are ye well?" she heard the young guard say from somewhere far away. Then, "Go get Lair!"

The room grew very dim and blurry as a small voice reached her ears. "Can ye save me then?"

Cassie spun the best she could, fighting dizziness. Though everything else blurred, she could see a young boy huddled in the corner of the room. Yet it wasn't really the room but somewhere else. A cave maybe? It was hard to tell.

Concerned, she crouched, glad she didn't fall over. His features were hard to make out so she squinted. "Are you okay, sweetie?"

"Where are ye?" he whispered. "I can barely see ye."

"I'm right here," she said softly. When she moved closer, he only seemed to get further away. "You're not alone."

"Please come." She got the sense he tried not to cry. "I dinnae want to be alone."

"I will." Cassie reached out. "Take my hand so you know you're not alone."

But it was too late. Her vision dimmed more and the boy vanished.

"No, come back," she cried.

"All's well, lass," came a deep voice. Only when a hand cupped her chin, did she realize she was in bed. "Can you see me then?"

"You're all right," came a woman's voice. A cool hand touched her forehead. "Just try to focus."

Though a little freaked out by hearing two unfamiliar voices, she was more frightened by her lack of vision. Slowly but surely, things started to brighten and grow less fuzzy.

"There you are, lassie," the woman murmured.

Cassie blinked, eyes going first to the man. There could be no doubt who he was. Though older with a starburst of lines on either side of his eyes and silver peppered through his black hair, this was the guy in the photo. Ferchar MacLomain. Logan's father. Save the age difference, the two looked so similar it was uncanny.

"Ferchar," she murmured.

"Aye, you've the right o' it, lass." He nodded at the woman. "This is Lair, Chieftain Grant's daughter."

Cassie nodded at the pretty woman, embarrassed by her situation. "Sorry about this."

"No need to be sorry." Lair sat on the edge of the bed and took her hand. "How often does this happen to you?"

"Never." She glanced at the corner of the room. "Where'd he go?"

Ferchar frowned. "Who?"

"The boy. He was Scottish." She tried to sit up, but Lair gently pushed her back down. "He was scared and wanted me to save him." Cassie tried to sit up again. "I have to save him."

"There is no one here," Ferchar said softly. "You had some sort of problem with your eyes and balance. I lifted you off of the floor."

"There *was* someone here," she said, desperation in her voice. "And he needs help."

Ferchar and Lair glanced at one another before Grant's daughter nodded and squeezed Cassie's hand. "All right then, lass. We believe you."

There was no way that little boy had been a figment of her imagination. She was about to ask more when Logan appeared at the door with a deep frown on his face. His eyes locked on hers, concerned. "Are you okay, Cassie?"

"I'm fine," she said, more and more embarrassed by the moment.

"'Tis inappropriate for you to be here, son," Ferchar murmured as Logan entered. "You're set to be wed."

"My betrothed is married to another man," Logan muttered, sitting on the bed when Lair stood. "*That* makes this a tad less inappropriate, aye?"

Her heart leapt in her chest. His betrothed was *what*?

Ferchar nodded at her. "'Twas good to meet you, Cassie." His eyes went to Logan. "Dinnae overly linger. You are Laird and should behave as such."

"Tell the guards they are no longer needed." Logan looked at Lair. "What happened to her?"

Cassie got the overwhelming feeling that Lair knew precisely what was going on with her eyes and her breath caught in her throat. She didn't want him to know. Not yet. Hopefully not at all.

Lair eyed her for a long moment before she spoke. "It seems she may have a wee gift that allows her to see things we cannae."

Logan's eyes roamed Cassie's face with both interest and renewed concern. "Is this true?"

"I have no idea," she fibbed. "This is the first time this has happened."

Lair told him what Cassie had seen then met her eyes. "But I dinnae think this is the first time such a thing has happened to you."

"Nor do I," Logan added, voice gentle as he took her hand. "'Tis nothing to be ashamed of, lass."

"I'm not ashamed," she said a little too quickly and though she meant to pull her hand away, she couldn't seem to do it. "It's nothing. Probably just my imagination."

"Yet you were so passionate moments ago about the lad being real," Lair reminded.

"He was," she said. "Just not the other stuff...before...well, not for the most part."

Logan's brows lowered. "What happened before?"

Cassie sighed. "Darach didn't tell you?"

She *really* did not want to have this conversation with him. But it looked like she didn't have much choice. So she reluctantly told Logan about seeing him on the horse, Athdara in New Hampshire and seeing his eyes glow in the picture on the mantle.

His gaze narrowed as she spoke. When she finished, he said, "And Darach knows of this?"

"Yeah." She shook her head. "I had no choice but to share with him, Leslie and Bradon because they were there when I had one of my episodes."

Logan muttered something under his breath, his eyes going to Lair. "Give us a moment alone."

"Nay," she murmured. "'Tis not a good idea."

His voice grew stiff. "'Tis a fine idea."

"Och, nay." Lair stood her ground, accent thickening. "There's naught but ye, this lass, and a bed in this chamber and ye've another lass just down the hall that's meant for ye even if she is with another lad."

Cassie shook her head and swung her legs over the side of the bed. "Excuse me but I have no intention of doing anything that involves Logan and this bed."

Lair made a soft sound and shook her head. "Ye might not intend it, but yer body doesnae agree."

"My body," Cassie choked out. "Sorry, but I'm not sure what you're getting at." She certainly did but was horrified it had been said with him *right here*.

Logan scowled fiercely at Lair as he came around and sat next to Cassie. "Forgive my cousin. 'Tis typically Machara's way to be rude on occasion, *not* Lair's."

Her heartbeat kicked up a few notches. He was sitting *way* too close. Fire flared under her skin and Cassie knew her eyes looked guilty when they met Lair's. Though it sounded self-condemning, she understood Lair only had Logan's best interests at heart. And there *was* the fact that it didn't appear the Scotswoman was going to share any more details about her vision issues. "It's fine. She's just looking out for your good name."

Logan caught her off guard when the corner of his lip shot up. "You say that as though 'tis in jeopardy."

Lair snorted, but a small grin came to her lips. "Ye need to stop flirting with the poor lass, cousin."

Cassie bit back a groan and carefully stood. This conversation needed to end. Now.

Logan stood as well and took her elbow. "Take your time, Cassie. 'Twould be better if you rested more."

"I'm tired of resting," she complained, too aware of his close proximity, of his touch. "I'm okay. You can let go."

"Nay," he said, voice a little guttural. "Not until I know you're well enough."

"I am," she assured, winded by the way his hand touched her lower back and his large body came even closer.

"Well, I suppose you cannae be too upset with Aline marrying another, Logan." Lair's eyes flickered between them and she shook her head. "Not if ye keep this up."

"He's not keeping anything up," Cassie said, then coughed when she realized what she said...what it might imply. To make matters worse, her traitorous eyes lowered to his plaid. What, to confirm nothing was *up*?

"Oh man," she mumbled and stepped away from him before he could stop her. What was *wrong* with her?

Logan chuckled.

Lair's brows edged up and her eyes widened. "Och, lass."

I'm s-sorry," she stuttered and wished she had a cell phone to fiddle with, anything to keep her from having to meet their eyes. "I didn't mean that how it sounded."

"You dinnae need to apologize." Logan grinned. "It didnae sound offensive in the least."

Her eyes shot to his. He was definitely flirting now. It threw her off to think a guy like this was attracted to her. But then she was still getting used to life without thick glasses. Regardless, Lair was right. Somewhere in the castle there was a woman meant for him, even if she was married to another. How was that going to work out anyways? And was that why he seemed more open about flirting with her now? Obviously. He had been screwed over by his fiancé and he was probably rattled by it. Who wouldn't want some sort of revenge? But she was not going to be his means to get it.

So she focused on Lair, *not* Logan. "Thanks for being here for me when I passed out."

Lair seemed to sense that Cassie at last had her wits about her because she wrapped elbows and led her from the room. "Ye dinnae need to thank me. I will be keeping a close eye on ye now and hopefully be there if it happens again."

"As will I," Logan said as he joined them. "I think 'tis best you try to sit if you feel it come upon you again."

If she could push past the panic, she might just do that. "You're right. I'll give it my best shot." Her eyes went to Logan. "What about the little boy? Who do you think he is?"

Cassie was surprised when Ferchar met them halfway down the hall and nodded at another set of stairs winding into a tower. "Son. Cassie. Please join me."

She was mildly alarmed by the look on Ferchar's face but followed when Logan took her hand and led her up the stairs.

"'Tis nothing to worry over," he murmured and squeezed her hand. "He but wants you to meet someone important."

When they arrived at the top, Ferchar knocked softly and called out, "'Tis I, Ferchar, Logan and a lass you should meet."

"Come in," said a soft voice.

They stepped into a room with an exquisite view of the loch beyond its three windows. A warm breeze blew in as a woman with long dark hair turned to them. Cassie had never met anyone who held themselves so nobly. Shoulders back, she had a way of tilting up her chin without giving the impression she was looking down her nose at you.

Logan gestured toward a chair. "You should sit, Cassie."

The woman's brow arched slightly, but she nodded her agreement.

"I'm all right," Cassie murmured.

Ferchar made introductions and Cassie soon learned why Logan was worried about her hitting the floor once more.

"Cassie, this is Marjorie, Countess of Carrick," Ferchar said. "Wife of Robert de Brus, 6th Lord of Annandale and mother to Robert de Brus, Earl of Carrick and the future King of Scotland."

Cassie was never more grateful for the supportive arm Logan wrapped around her lower back. Incredibly humbled, she lowered her head and made her best attempt at a curtsy. "Nice to meet you, Countess."

Seriously overwhelmed and impressed, she really wasn't sure what else to say or if she had even greeted the woman properly.

The Countess nodded. "Nice to meet ye as well, Cassie. 'Tis an unusual accent ye have."

Before she could respond, Marjorie continued. "But I would expect nothing less of a Broun from the future."

Startled, she met her eyes and stated the obvious. "You know where I'm from?"

Brilliant, Cassie. Keep sounding like a genius.

"Aye, I know of the Brouns." The Countess lowered into a chair and gestured to another. "Please. Sit."

She didn't hesitate but sat. This was a woman who was used to being obeyed.

Ferchar shocked Cassie when he began filling the Countess in on her vision of the little boy. Marjorie's face went from semi-serene to upset in a heartbeat. "Was it my lad then?"

Her lad?

"Aye, I believe 'twas." Ferchar crouched in front of the Countess. "'Tis good, this."

Marjorie's eyes grew moist as they met Cassie's. "How is he? Is he well?"

"Who exactly are we talking about again?" she said slowly even though she had a feeling she knew.

"'Twas her son, Robert," Logan said.

"The future King of Scotland." Cassie blinked a few times. "Are you trying to tell me that Robert the Bruce was the little boy I just saw?"

"Aye." Ferchar nodded. "It can be none other."

"And how would you know that?" she whispered.

"Because long ago 'twas said that he would be taken," Logan explained. "And that 'twould be a connection of true love that brought him back to safety."

Ferchar's gaze went to her ring and if she wasn't mistaken pain flashed in his eyes. "Och, I didnae see so clearly when first we met." Cassie's eyes widened when he crouched in front of her and fingered the ring, disturbed, heart in his eyes. "'Tis her ring. How can this be?'"

"Whose ring?" Logan said, alarmed.

"I must go." Ferchar went to Logan, clasped his shoulders firmly and ground out, "Ye follow yer path son and see the King safely returned. That is yer sole focus and purpose now. Nothing else, aye?"

Logan nodded, frowning. "What's going on, Da?"

"Nothing that need concern ye." He squeezed his shoulders tighter. "Ye see to protecting yer clan and the future of Scotland. Swear to me ye will see this quest through."

"I swear," Logan promised. "Ye have my word. 'Tis a quest that will end well."

Ferchar ground his jaw, eyed his son then nodded once before turning back to the Countess. "I must go. My son will save yers. Ye have my word."

"Aye, I dinnae doubt it." She stood, equally concerned about him. "Please travel safe, my friend."

Ferchar nodded then strode from the room. Cassie twirled the ring on her finger, thoroughly confused. Why had her ring upset Ferchar so much? And what was this about a quest to save Robert the Bruce?

One thing was for sure, she wanted to help. *Needed to help.* She could not explain why. All she knew was that she was being persuaded by a power she couldn't explain, and knew nothing about.

"I want to go too," Cassie blurted and meant it. Her eyes went to Marjorie's. "If I really saw him then he might come to me again which means I'm the best chance you've got to find him."

"Nay." Logan shook his head. "'Tis far too dangerous."

The Countess considered Cassie. Though she tried to remain calm, her fear and worry was palpable. "Would ye do such a thing for a perfect stranger? Logan is right, 'tis verra dangerous."

Cassie remembered the fear in Robert's voice, the terror he tried to keep hidden. Though who he would become in the future was certainly impressive, she was far more concerned about the little boy he was *now*. "I absolutely would."

"Och," Logan muttered. "'Tis a verra bad idea, Countess. She knows nothing of how to defend herself and we both know what will become of her if she's taken from me."

"Then dinnae let her be taken, lad." Marjorie's eyes never left Cassie as she leaned over and took her hands. "Are ye sure about this, lass? 'Tis a lot to ask."

"Yes." Cassie nodded. "I'm sure."

"Ye are verra brave." The Countess squeezed her hands. "Thank ye. I willnae forget what ye are willing to do for my bairn."

Logan was clearly struggling through several emotions between his father's hasty departure and Cassie's commitment, but he soon pulled it together and nodded at the Countess. "We leave soon. 'Tis best that ye stay here under my clan's protection until we return with Robert."

"Aye, of course," she murmured, still holding Cassie's hand. "Ye will bring yer cousins with ye, aye? I know the four of ye alone could take the whole of Scotland if put to the test."

"Niall at least," he conceded. "The others returned to their clans this morn, but I will send word to them that ye wish them on this quest."

"Only if their clans are well protected without them," she said.

"Their clans will always be best protected if yer son is well protected," he returned. "We would do anything for yer bairn, Countess."

She nodded and again squeezed Cassie's hands. "Then I thank ye both so verra much."

"Ye need not thank us." Logan sank to a knee in front of Marjorie and took one of her hands. He lowered his head. "I am sworn to ye, yer wee bairn and to the future of Scotland. I willnae let ye down."

The Countess pulled her hand from Cassie's and tilted up his chin until their eyes met. "Ye havnae let me down thus far lad. I have complete faith in ye, ye ken?"

"Aye," he murmured. "I ken."

He kissed the back of her hand and stood. "Will ye be staying here or coming below stairs?"

"Here," she said. "'Tis best that none know I am here for now."

"Aye," he said. "Then only Lair will see to yer needs. Always know, however, that ye may roam the castle and courtyard if ye change yer mind. The MacLomain clan will never betray yer presence here but be proud to house ye."

"Aye." The Countess walked to the window, a motion that even Cassie recognized as a need to be alone. "Travel safe, my friends."

Logan took Cassie's hand and pulled her after him, closing the door behind them. He said nothing as they traveled down the winding stairs, but she knew he was tense. Instead of going back down the hallway when they reached the bottom, he pulled her to the right, down another narrow hallway and into an alcove with nothing but an arrow slit window.

Cassie backed up against the stone wall when he raked his hand through his hair and eyed her with fury. "What are you *doing*, lass?"

He might be formidable and blocking her only way out but his anger frustrated her so instead of cowering, she stood up straighter and jut out her chin. "I think it's pretty obvious. Helping a little boy."

Logan made a sharp gesture with his hand as if encompassing Scotland. "You know nothing of these times, nothing of how truly dangerous it is." His brogue grew thicker with his passion. "What if I cannae protect ye out there, lass. What if ye fall into the hands of the enemy? Do ye ken what they'll do to ye, a pretty lass such as ye are?"

"Yeah, I have a damn good idea," Cassie spat. "But what sort of person would I be sitting here when I have the ability to *see* Robert, to communicate with him? I'm not a coward, Logan. I'm not afraid to face this."

"Ye should be ye bloody fool," he growled, stalking closer. "The Scotland ye've been thrust into is not one that will go away with the turn of a history book page. 'Tis real and deadly and without mercy. They might start with rape but trust me, there are far worse things they'll do to ye afterward. Then when they're done with that, they'll return to the raping."

"I know." But she didn't. Not at all. Still. She tried to keep her voice level. "I couldn't live with myself if I didn't go."

He braced a hand against the wall beside her head, his eyes such a lethal pale blue it was hard to hold his gaze. "Ye might not be able to live with yerself after what could happen, lass. Do ye not ken that?" His body trembled he was so upset. "And now ye've committed to it, committed to something ye know nothing about."

"I'm used to committing to things I know nothing about, used to committing to fear." She tried not to shake, tried not to let his words feed into her fear. "Running away from things that frighten me won't do me any good. It's best to face them head on." Cassie jabbed a finger at his chest. "And I won't run from this when I can save that boy. Do you have any idea how scared he is right now? Any idea at all?"

"Nay, I dinnae." Logan grabbed her hand and held it against his chest, anger warring with something else, voice lowering a fraction. "But do ye really, lass? Was he so frightened?"

"Yes." Cassie blinked away angry tears. "But he's afraid to show it."

The set of Logan's jaw unclenched a scant fraction and his brogue lessened. "Are you sure he knew you were there, that you two made contact?"

"I'd bet my life on it," she said softly, no longer struggling to pull her gaze from his but drowning in it instead.

"'Tis so bloody dangerous," he whispered. His free hand came to the side of her waist, almost as if he was trying to ground himself while his eyes wandered her face. "Too much for a lass used to the twenty-first century and all its luxuries, all its safety."

"I can do this." She meant it. "I'll pay attention and learn how to protect myself as we travel. I won't be a burden, I promise."

"You're no burden, Cassie." His hand tightened on her waist and his eyes held hers. "But you are vulnerable and I fear for you."

She shook her head. "Don't."

"But I do." The hand on the wall lowered as he moved closer. What was moments before heated anger became a different sort of heat altogether. "You spoke of things you have to commit to that you know nothing about, that you were committed to facing fear. What did you mean?"

Though she meant to shake her head, it only jerked a little as her eyes dropped and she focused on anything but his steady gaze. "Nothing. Just stuff."

"Stuff?" he murmured, so close now that there was barely half a foot between them. "What kind of stuff?"

"It doesn't matter." Pressing her lips together, she put a defensive hand against his strong chest and kept her eyes averted. "We need to focus on what's ahead, saving the future King of Scotland."

"We are." He tilted up her chin until she was forced to meet his eyes. "And to do so, you need to be honest with me. You just became part of my band of warriors set to save the future King. So tell me, what is it in your past or mayhap even in your future that makes you so brave now?"

"Can't bravery just be part of who I am," she murmured, her lips suddenly throbbing. She licked then pressed them together, unsure of her body's strong reaction.

"Why won't you just tell me," he said softly. "About this fear within you that has made you so bloody strong."

She wanted to say, "Is that what you see? Strength?" but it would work against her case so she said, "Life. Simple as that. Being a single girl in the twenty-first century isn't all that easy."

Logan's eyes narrowed. "Again you fib." He leaned closer, so close that mere inches remained between them. Their height difference was substantial, but he had lowered enough that his mouth was only a few inches above hers. "I need honesty from my warriors." Then he whispered, "From ye, my lass."

His lass? "I'm being honest." Sort of. Not really.

It became hard to breathe as her eyes focused on his lips, on the way they parted slightly as if ready to close over hers. She stopped breathing altogether when his hand wrapped around the back of her neck and he leaned his forehead against hers.

She barely heard his words they were so soft. "Bloody hell, lass, this is torture."

A deep throb shot through her and she squeezed her thighs together. Moisture seemed to break out over every inch of her skin. Her mouth went dry then grew wet all at once. Her lower lip started to tremble and she worked to drag in a shallow breath. *Torture?* Was that the word he used? Whatever she was feeling now felt far worse…or better. It was impossible to know.

Logan's lips didn't meet hers but instead brushed her cheek then fell by her ear. His breathing was harsh, irregular, his body pressing against hers. It was then that she felt the hardness against her stomach. His arousal. *Damn, then double damn.* A sharp shiver went through her and she pressed her hands against the rock wall. Because if she didn't she was going to wrap her arms around him and never, ever let go.

At first she thought the loud cry she heard was the increased buzzing of blood rushing through her. Desire. Yet when he stepped away, she knew it was not. Torn from someplace she didn't recognize, Cassie realized a man was wailing.

"Come." Logan pulled her after him. He released her hand when they returned to the main hallway and ordered her to stay put. Worried, drawn by the mournful cries, she inched along the wall as women came and went from a chamber. Peeking around the corner, she put a hand over her mouth as a woman arched and flailed in bed. Soaked in sweat, her brown hair was plastered to her head, skin pale and eyes vacant.

A man tried to hold her down, tears in his eyes as Lair chanted over her. Logan rushed in and helped restrain her. She released an ungodly scream as she clawed at everyone. Though it was impossible to be sure having seen her from a distance, Cassie was fairly positive that this was Aline MacLauchlin.

"Shh, lass, all is well," Logan murmured, stroking her cheek. "Ye are safe. Always safe with the MacLomains."

"They killed everyone," she cried, eyes unseeing. "They killed my wee bairn. I tried to stop them, but they...they..."

"Shh." Logan pressed his face close. "'Tis all right, lass. 'Tis all right."

Horrified tears rolled down Cassie's face as she watched. What hell had this woman witnessed?

"Please, lass, stay with me," the man on her other side whimpered, coming as close as Logan. "Dinnae cross over, aye?"

Lair chanted louder until the woman at last calmed, her body jerking slightly as she fell back.

"Everyone out save my women," Lair said.

Logan eyed her. "Are ye sure?"

"Out," she repeated.

"Aye." Logan grabbed the other man when he shook his head. "Yer coming with me, lad."

Held by the scruff of his tunic, Logan led him past Cassie then down the stairs to the great hall. Everyone left as Logan didn't quite shove him into a chair but wasn't necessarily gentle either. Not sure what she should do, Cassie trailed down the stairs, grateful when a servant handed her a mug of ale.

"Come." Logan gestured to her. "Sit with us."

Cassie was surprised when Niall came alongside and murmured, "Sit by me, lass, as the Laird is in a bad mood indeed."

She never thought she would be so glad to see his intimidating cousin. "Sounds good."

The foreign man was sweating profusely, his worried gaze torn between the landing above and the MacLomain Laird standing in front of the fire with his arms crossed over his chest. Cassie sat in a chair beside Niall and took a good long swallow of ale. It was rough going down, but it warmed her belly.

"I've not had the pleasure of making yer acquaintance," Logan said to the stranger, his brogue thick and his r's rolling. "Who might ye be?"

The man sat up a little straighter, hands shaking as he wrapped them in his lap. "Ye already know who I am, Laird MacLomain. Husband to Aline MacLauchlin."

"So that is yer name then?" Logan said. "Husband to Aline MacLauchlin?"

The man stilled and though he might be afraid there was something else altogether in his eyes when they met Logan's. "I am Baird." His voice lowered. "Baird of the Stewart Clan."

Logan's eyes flickered with surprise. "Nay, I dinnae believe it. The Stewarts wouldnae betray the MacLomains."

Baird's eyes held Logan's and Cassie had to give him credit for not throwing his clan under the bus. "The Stewarts dinnae know of our marriage. 'Twas done in secret."

"Did ye know she was promised to marry me?"

Baird's eyes again flickered to the landing above before lazily, almost arrogantly dropping to Logan's. "Aye, I knew it."

A fury unlike what she saw earlier lit Logan's eyes as he grabbed a sword off the wall. "Ye bloody bastard."

"Och, I thought we'd get in a wee bit more talking before fighting, but something beyond the obvious has m'laird's blood stirred up." Niall chuckled, grabbed a blade off the wall and tossed it to Baird before he winked at Cassie. "Best to give the fool half a chance, aye?"

Cassie gasped when Niall shoved the table aside with his foot then yanked their chairs back before plunking down beside her and taking a swig of ale. "Now 'tis time to enjoy a good fight." He shrugged, grinning. "Mayhap."

"What the hell?" she started but snapped her mouth shut when Logan drove his blade against Baird's. The Stewart might be distressed, but he met Logan's sword with force and skill even as he was driven across the hall.

Niall kept chuckling until he realized she was watching him. "Why are you looking at me like that, lass?"

"Because you're enabling this!" she cried. When she made to stand, he grabbed her wrist and pulled her back down.

"The Laird needs to defend his honor." Niall shook his head and nodded at her mug. "Drink and let things happen as they will. This isnae a battle you need to interfere with."

Frowning, she tensed as swords clashed. Logan was vicious and as far as she could tell the better fighter as he slashed his blade against Baird's. His arm muscles bulged, seen much easier thanks to his sleeveless tunic. "This is..is..is..."

"Is what?" Niall said.

Eyes glued to Logan she murmured, "Crazy." When Baird spun away and slashed back, Logan dodged and the slight lull she had been under vanished. Her eyes shot to Niall. "You need to stop this."

"Och, nay, I'll do no such thing." He offered a crooked grin. "Logan has every right to fight this man."

"Why? Because he married the woman he was meant for." She shook her head. "Hey, Logan's no saint. What about..."

She trailed off, surprised by what she nearly said.

Niall arched his brow. "What about what?" He kept on grinning. "His desire for you?"

Way to be blunt. "No, that's not what I was getting at."

His eyes darted between the warring men who had already managed to knock over half a dozen chairs. "'Tis exactly what you were getting at." When the men came close, Niall kicked a chair and Baird tripped backwards. He fell on his ass, squirming as he kept meeting Logan's blade from the floor. "The difference is Baird was part of breaking a vow when 'twas still in the making. You are part of breaking a vow after 'twas already broken.''

Logan slashed his sword and knicked Baird's shoulder. Fueled by pain, Baird scrambled after Logan. Niall, casual as could be, again pulled their chairs back further and out of the men's way as he continued talking. "Do you ken, lass?"

"I don't ken a damn thing," she said as Baird slammed Logan to the floor.

"Well, you need to." Niall took another long swig and laughed as Logan flipped Baird. Over and over they went until they were once more on their feet and clashing swords.

"Aren't you worried about your cousin?" she seethed.

Niall cocked his head one way then the other as he studied their fighting. "Nay, not really, but 'tis well matched this fight."

"And that's *bad*." She frowned, took a deep sip of ale then muttered, "Really bad."

"Nay." Niall shrugged. "Not so bad at all."

Clang. Clang. Clang.

Metal rang against metal as they fought on chairs, then tables then up and down the stairs. "This is beyond ridiculous."

"This is how Scotsmen settle things," Niall murmured.

She was about to say yet again exactly what she thought of that when the battling men once more headed in their direction.

"Oh God," she cried when Logan drove Baird toward them so fast that he landed on his back at her feet.

Logan braced his legs on either side of Baird and held the tip of his sword against the man's lower sternum.

"Ye married another lad's lass," Logan roared.

Before Baird could respond, Niall crouched and put a dagger to his neck, words soft. "What have ye to say to that, Stewart? It had best be something worth hearing."

Baird swallowed and though his eyes remained rebellious his words were not. "We fell in love when *bairns*. Who are ye to take my lass from me?"

Niall tightened the blade. "Ye address my laird the proper way when in his castle."

"Nay," Logan said, words soft but still hard, his blade unwavering as his eyes held Baird's. "Did ye truly love her since ye were bairns?"

"I have loved Aline MacLauchlin since first I laid eyes on her," Baird ground out, even as a tear trickled down his cheek. "How could I not?"

"Yet ye knew she was betrothed to me. Promised to another, a MacLomain no less, your ally." Logan shook his head. "How did ye right that with yer conscience, lad?"

Baird relaxed beneath the blades meant to kill him, closed his eyes and murmured, "There is no controlling the conscience when it comes to true love. It just is what it is."

Logan's brows shot together and he inhaled sharply, jaw grinding as he pressed his blade tighter against Baird's chest. Yet he made no further move, just stared at the man.

Niall's eyes went to Logan's face, but he made no move.

He was waiting for his Laird's orders.

When Logan spoke, he said the last thing she expected. "Ye fight well, Stewart and I will offer ye a way to redeem yerself. A way that our clans might not see ye as the traitor ye are."

Baird's eyes narrowed. "And what do ye propose."

"*M'laird*," Niall ground out, pressing his dagger tighter. "What do ye propose, m'laird."

"M'laird," Baird croaked, the defiance never leaving his eyes.

Logan tossed aside his blade and crouched, secure enough in Niall's dagger as he leaned close. "I need something of you." Cassie blinked once and Niall's dagger was in Logan's hand, wedged tight against Baird's neck as the MacLomain came almost nose to nose with the man. "I need a good warrior by my side on my upcoming quest." He pressed the blade tighter. "Will ye travel and fight for me?" Then he offered a grin that by no means met his eyes. "Some might say ye owe it to me, aye?"

All the while, Cassie drank, baffled by what she watched. No history book could have ever prepared her for this. These men were notably insane.

Every. Last. One. Of. Them.

"M'laird."

Logan's eyes went to Lair on the landing. Their gazes held for a long moment and she knew the news wasn't good. His eyes fell to Baird's. "Yer wife struggles for her life. Will ye make right by her and fight for me?"

Cassie shook her head. Baird should be by his wife's side if she was dying. "This is wrong."

But she might as well have said nothing because she was completely ignored as Logan and Baird stared at one another. Long, silent, seeking, their eyes held before the Stewart whispered, "Only if ye'll see her well, m'laird."

Again their eyes held, searching out one another's, before Logan at last spoke. "I will."

The second he said it, Niall pulled away and sat beside Cassie. This time there was no grin on his lips or even a chuckle.

When Baird stumbled to his feet, eager to return to Aline's side, Logan grabbed his wrist. "Might I be by yer side now warrior?"

Baird swallowed, not sure at first. A long minute passed, the men eyeing one another before he nodded and they left.

"They want to kill each other one second now they're best buds," Cassie muttered as she stood to follow, but Niall pulled her after him before she could get too far.

"The lass has a truly hard time ahead of her. As do you. Let us go to the stables."

Cassie staggered after him, determined to go in the opposite direction, but Niall was having none of it.

"You need to spend time with your horse, Athdara now, lass," Niall said. "After all, she is your best hope of surviving the journey ahead."

Chapter Eight

LOGAN SIGHED AND hung his head as Aline MacLauchlin struggled for her life. Nothing seemed to work. Lair had tried her best with healing magic, but the poor lass would likely lose an arm. Baird sat on the bed with his wife's head in his lap, stroking her hair as she suffered through a fever.

"Ye will stay with her until her fever breaks and ye know she is well enough," Logan said softly. "Then ye can pursue me and my warriors."

Baird nodded, eyes never leaving her face.

"'Tis my fondest hope that she makes a speedy recovery," Logan said.

"Aye," Baird whispered. His pained eyes skirted over her arm.

Was Logan still upset? No. In truth, he had not been all that upset about Aline's betrayal but by how injured she was. The devastation of her people...the loss of her son. "And I'm so verra sorry about yer wee bairn. Know that when ye ride with me and my men 'twill be part of a quest that will avenge the harm done."

Baird swallowed and again nodded, his jaw tight. "Aye, 'tis good that, m'laird." His eyes went to Logan. "And ye have my endless thanks for yer help." He inhaled deeply and shook his head, voice soft. "And may ye forgive my transgressions. May ye forgive me for marrying yer lass."

Logan considered him for a long moment. "Ye have my forgiveness, lad. What we did below stairs had to be done but 'twill be known by the MacLauchlins and Stewarts that yer paying yer debt by fighting for me."

He stood, murmured a brief prayer for Aline's recovery then paused at the door. "The MacLauchlins will also know that the arranged betrothal betwixt Aline and I is no more. That with my blessing, she has taken another."

Baird's eyes went to his, churning with deep emotion. His words were hoarse. "Thank ye, Laird MacLomain. That is most generous of ye, indeed."

Logan said nothing but left, his mood dark as he headed down to the great hall. While he was certainly irritated by the betrayal of his betrothed, he was also relieved. It had never been a particularly easy thing being promised to someone he'd never met. But though he tried to keep telling himself that was the only reason, he knew better.

His desire and need for Cassie was remarkable. Increasing. Unavoidable.

Cassie.

A lass who was clearly going to be the death of him.

Logan tied back his hair with a swath of plaid and pulled his favorite broadsword off the wall before he strode out the door toward the stables. He still couldn't believe that she had managed to commit herself to this quest. Though he understood her reasons and admired her for them, it continued to infuriate him. That was the real reason he had battled with Baird so viciously. He needed to get out his aggression. Not to say the battling itself didn't need to be done. It did. For the sake of not only his honor but his clan.

The MacLomains would have every right to cease their ties with the MacLauchlins based on Aline's actions. Not to mention the Stewart clan. And that tie was deep and long and far too important to forfeit. So it was best Logan made a show of it with Baird then grant forgiveness afterward.

All was well that ended well.

But then things, in general, were not all that well at all.

Robert the Bruce had been kidnapped and Logan had no idea by whom. Grant's warning about evil being afoot was alarming. Scotland hadn't dealt with anything quite like that since the Next Generation of MacLomains had battled Keir Hamilton almost thirty winters prior.

If all of that wasn't enough, his mind kept returning to his Da. Something had distressed him greatly when he looked at Cassie's ring. But what? Logan knew his Ma wore a ring like that, but he was trying his damndest to put that from his mind. Because if something was wrong with his mother, focusing on what lay ahead would be nearly impossible. And right now he needed to be incredibly focused. He had promised his Da and the Countess. More than that he had promised the wee Bruce before he was even born.

As he knew she would be, Cassie was with Athdara. Strapping the sword to his back, he watched her for a few minutes. He couldn't help but contemplate what she had shared about her time in New Hampshire. How she saw him on her horse in a vision. Her connection to him as a bairn in the picture. What was that all about? As a wizard, he should have felt something when they first met. Not to say he hadn't felt anything. He had.

Attraction.

Lust.

But a connection like those found in the past between MacLomains and Brouns? True love? He just didn't know. Yet his need for Cassie grew as he watched her. God, she was beautiful. Hair tied back in a high ponytail, she was murmuring in Athdara's ear.

The horse's voice entered his mind. *"She still cannae hear me. 'Tis frustrating."*

"Soon enough, my friend," he responded. *"'Twill happen when the time is right."*

He still wondered where the horses came from to begin with. He wouldn't be surprised if Grant had something to do with them. Or mayhap even Adlin from beyond the grave. Who knew with that old wizard. He had been capable of most anything in life so Logan suspected he was just as busy meddling in the affairs of his clan from the afterlife.

Unable to stay away any longer, Logan headed toward Cassie. Both pleasure and irritation flashed in her eyes when they met his. He knew she had not been crazy about the fighting between him and Baird. "We leave soon, lass. If you prefer trousers for traveling, there are some in your chamber."

"That's probably a good idea," she murmured. "Considering the horseback riding and all."

"Either way, 'twill not be easy for someone not used to riding." His eyes narrowed a fraction. "Or for someone who knows nothing about riding at all."

Add that to the dozens of reasons she should *not* be going on this journey.

"Like I said, I learn quickly." Her eyes narrowed as well. "Are you gonna be like this the whole time?"

"Like what?"

"With that scowl on your face." She sighed. "Doubting that I can handle myself and that I'll be a hindrance."

"Aye, lass, 'tis likely. But 'tis with good reason." Logan regretted that he made her feel that way but was in no mood to appease her. She *needed* to understand what she had gotten herself into. "You're going into this with almost no means to protect yourself. Not only physically but mentally. Little can be learned in a few short days to prepare you for the reality of this country."

"Yeah, I got that." Now her eyes avoided his though he stood next to her. "All I can tell you is that I'll try to stay out of the way, okay? I've got to go meet Niall in the armory. He was gonna show me a few tricks."

Logan had positioned himself between the horse and the stall door, making it impossible for her to pass. He was beyond frustrated with her because of her foolishness. Yet he knew starting the journey with tension between them was not good for her spirits. And a somewhat optimistic spirit was all she had going for her right now.

"Niall can oversee preparations." He took her hand. "*I* will spend a few moments with you in the armory. I know all the same tricks if not more than my cousin."

When her brows rose and her eyes shot to his, he realized that hadn't sounded rallying in the least but downright flirtatious. Despite his frustration, he cocked the corner of his lip. "I didnae mean that how it sounded."

"I guess we're both not too good at saying what we mean." Clearly aware that he had shifted closer, her cheekbones reddened.

"No. Don't look at me like that." She shook her head and tried to squeeze by. "The woman you're meant to *marry* is in the castle. Heck, you just put on one hell of a show to prove that point."

"'Twas a necessary show, done for the honor of my clan. You may not have liked what you saw, but I'm not the bad guy in this situation." Logan put a hand against the stall door and angled his body so that she was unable to pass. "And the lass I'm meant to marry isnae in the castle." His voice grew intentionally soft. "In all truth, I dinnae know where she is."

Cassie backed up a step and frowned. "Oh no." Her eyes widened and she whispered, "Did Aline die?"

"Nay, but she fights for her life." He took a few steps forward when she took a few backward. Logan knew he should focus on preparations yet he wanted her close again. He wanted to return to their moment in the chamber above stairs. "But she is no longer my betrothed. I've released her from her commitment to the MacLomains. She is the wife of Baird Stewart and will remain such."

"Oh," she whispered, back against the wall and eyes wide.

"Kissing the lass now willnae help her much in focusing on the dangers ahead," Athdara said.

Logan ignored the horse and rested the underside of his forearm on the wall above Cassie's head. Unable to stop himself, he trailed a finger lightly up her arm, fascinated by the way a shiver rippled over her. He ran the same finger over her collarbone then up the side of her neck until he traced the velvety curve of her jawline, words a murmur. "Are you still set to see this quest through knowing that I am no longer committed to another?" He traced the soft curve of her lips, mesmerized, desperate to taste them. "And that I desire you."

Cassie blinked several times and swallowed hard, her eyes rising to his. It seemed to take her a moment before she could speak. "Yes, I'm still set to see it through."

If he wasn't mistaken, her words had a double meaning. One she intended. Or so he thought. Her next statement threw him off as did the fire that flashed in her eyes. "That's why this attraction needs to stop now." She stepped around him. "Consider that my first contribution to *not* being a hindrance."

Logan released a low chuckle, took Athdara's lead line and followed Cassie out of the stables.

"'Tis a smart lass she is," the horse murmured, a smile in her voice.

"I'm running up to change then I'll meet Niall in the armory," Cassie said over her shoulder, not bothering to look at him.

"Aye, lass," Logan said. "You need not worry over a change of clothes for the journey. A satchel's been made ready for you."

Cassie nodded and made her way up the stairs to the castle. Logan left Athdara with the other horses being prepared for the jouney then spent some time with his warriors before heading toward the armory. Niall fell in beside him, a wry grin on his face. "So ye ended it with the MacLauchlin lass, aye?"

"There was nothing to end," Logan grunted. "She's taken."

"Which conveniently freed ye up for the other lass."

"Lasses are the last thing on my mind right now, cousin."

"Och, ye lying bastard." Niall shook his head as they entered the armory. "But I cannae blame ye. My mind's been on her too."

"Who?" Logan frowned as he studied the daggers. "Cassie?"

"Aye, who else?" Niall grinned as he strapped a sword to his back. "She's a bonnie lass if ever I did see one." His cousin continued to watch Logan a little too closely. "If only she had eyes for me as well."

Logan said nothing as he pulled a few daggers down and started strapping them to his body.

Niall leaned against the wall and crossed his arms over his chest. "Why dinnae ye just say ye want her and be done with it."

"'Tis best that we both leave her be." Logan met his eyes. "How are we supposed to protect her if we're lusting after her? Ye know as well as I 'tis no good thing that she travels with us. We must have our wits about us, cousin."

"Aye." Niall was no fool. He knew Logan wanted her. "But then 'tis a thing to deny lust. Some might say 'tis best to give into the lusting to keep the mind clear. 'Tis no good to have the extra tension when there will be battling afoot."

Logan headed for the bows and arrows. "There'll be no giving into lusting with Cassie." His eyes narrowed on Niall. "For either of us."

"Aye, m'laird." Niall followed. "'Tis good though that ye are free."

"A tie betwixt clans has been forfeited." Logan studied the bows then opted for his favorite. Heavier than most, it was made of a rich, stained wood. "How is such a thing good?"

"Because ye have done nothing but devote yerself to this clan and deserve to be happy," Niall said softly.

"I would have found happiness." But Logan had never been so sure he would. Yet he had been willing to sacrifice himself if it made the MacLomains stronger.

"I wasnae sure before," Niall said. "But now I think mayhap the gods are showing ye favor after all."

Logan arched a brow at him as he attached his bow to his back and slid arrows into a pouch. "How so?"

"Deny it all ye like but I see the way ye and Cassie look at each other." Niall shook his head. "'Tis only a matter of time before ye act on it and it should be sooner rather than later. If we're riding into war and facing evil, ye should do it having found the happiness ye deserve."

Logan was caught off guard. Niall wasn't typically known for being sentimental. That was more Darach's thing. Before he could respond, his cousin spoke, returning to his normal self.

"'Tis good I convinced ye to lay with a lass or two, aye? Got in some practice." A wide grin split Niall's face. "'Twould have been a sad thing at thirty-one winters not to know what to do with yer cock when the opportunity presented itself."

Considering his current circumstances, his cousin made a valid point. But then again, Logan had traveled to the twenty-first century more than Niall, which meant he had access to the internet and TV. And there was plenty of sex to be found on both.

When Cassie cleared her throat at the entrance, Logan scowled at his cousin. He wanted to throttle him for broaching the conversation to begin with. How much had she heard?

Niall being Niall shrugged and grinned at Cassie. "My apologies if ye heard anything overly offensive. 'Twas not my intention."

"Uh huh." Her eyes scanned the walls in amazement as she entered. "Look at all the weapons."

"Aye, lass." Niall grabbed a few more daggers then headed for the entrance. "Logan will help ye choose a few that suit ye."

Cassie nodded, eyes still roaming over the weaponry as she went from room to room. This was the first time he had seen her in pants not covered by a long shirt. They showed off her arse considerably well. His gaze roamed down her backside with avid appreciation. When he saw Niall paused at the entrance doing the same thing, he narrowed his eyes and spoke within the mind. *"Get your eyes off her arse."*

"Can't blame a lad for looking." Niall winked before he left.

Logan was about to follow her when he heard a commotion outside and looked through one of the windows. Though the outer portcullis would not be raised without permission, he knew someone important was coming. Grabbing a few daggers suitable to Cassie's weight and size, he took her hand. "Come, lass. Dinnae wander far from me unless I say so. Do you ken?"

She nodded. "Absolutely."

Logan released her hand before they left the armory and strode through the courtyard, eyes to the battlement above. A warrior yelled down. "'Tis a MacLauchlin warrior, m'laird."

Niall joined him. "Should I go get Baird to confirm the lad is who he says he is?"

"Nay." Logan shook his head. "He stays by Aline's side. I've magic enough to know if the MacLauchlin is being truthful."

Niall scowled. "I'm staying with you."

"Raise the first portcullis," Logan said to a warrior then turned to Niall. "Remain here and watch over Cassie until I've spoken with this lad." He narrowed his eyes. "Do ye ken, cousin? Because 'twill be verra bad for ye if ye dinnae listen."

Niall locked his jaw, his scowl growing fiercer. "Aye, I've the right o' it. But I dinnae like this."

"Nay, but you'll listen to your Laird," Logan growled then strode onto the drawbridge when the first portcullis was raised.

The MacLauchlin warrior swung off his horse. He threw down his weapons and raised his hands in the air as he stood beyond the second portcullis. "I come in peace."

When he clasped the metal bars, Logan unsheathed his sword. "Who are ye?"

"I am Deargh MacLauchlin," the man said, desperate as his wild eyes met Logan's. "I come on behalf of my Laird, Clyde MacLauchlin. The castle has been taken, many killed, but m'laird still lives and needs Laird MacLomain's help."

Logan stemmed out his magic. It seemed the man told the truth. But what if this was of the evil Grant warned him about?

"Deargh, is that ye, brother?" Baird said, trotting to the gate.

"Aye, 'tis me!" Deargh shook his head. "'Tis good to see ye alive and well." Then he frowned. "Where is my sister? Where is Aline?"

"Resting." Baird and Deargh clasped arms through the portcullis. "Her fever just broke. There great hope now of a recovery."

Deargh's eyes were wet as he worked at a smile. "And yer wee one?"

Baird shook his head and said nothing.

"Och, nay," Deargh whispered, pained.

116

Logan lowered his blade and motioned for a warrior to raise the portcullis. Once it was lifted, the men embraced before Baird made introductions. It seemed Deargh was the only MacLauchlin who knew about his sister's clandestine marriage to Baird as well as their bairn.

"M'laird hides in a cave not far from his castle," Deargh said to Logan. "He's requested that ye come, that he has dire news indeed."

"Why did he not travel here himself?"

"Many of our people are being held prisoner." Deargh shook his head. "My Da willnae leave them. He intends to take back his castle."

Logan well understood that but had little trust in the situation. Nonetheless, he was given no other direction to go in thus far so it seemed he would be heading back toward MacLauchlin land. "Baird, stay with Aline until she awakes. She willnae want to be alone in those first few moments." His eyes went to Deargh. "Ye will travel with me."

By the time he made it back to the courtyard, Niall was already rallying the warriors who would be traveling with them. Logan swung onto his horse and came alongside Cassie, who stood by Athdara. He held out his hand. "You'll travel with me until you learn how to ride a horse properly, lass."

"What about Athdara?"

"Dinnae worry. She'll keep up."

Cassie patted the horse and murmured in her ear, "No worries, we won't leave you behind."

When Cassie's hand slid into his, Logan pulled her up in front of him. He still couldn't believe she was coming but oddly enough as they crossed the drawbridge, fifty MacLomain warriors in front of him and fifty behind, he was glad. The idea of having her anywhere that he couldn't keep a close eye on her left a sour taste in his mouth. Yes, his castle was well-protected but even so—and some might call it arrogant—there was no safer place to be than with him and his cousins. They had been training for what lay ahead for a long time and few if any were fiercer or more skilled.

Dark clouds rolled overhead as they left the drawbridge behind, passed beneath the mighty oak then headed across the wide field. As Niall was his first-in-command, his second-in-command, Conall would oversee the castle in his absence. He spoke to him earlier and had every faith in his ability to defend the MacLomain's well.

So when the first swollen raindrop fell from the sky and they entered the forest, Logan at last felt a sense of purpose.

Of destiny.

Of fate.

At long last, everything he had prepared for was happening. He *would* save Robert the Bruce. Scotland *would* have her king. And his clan stood a fighting chance. But even beyond that what pleased him most despite the circumstances was the lass in front of him.

Though he worried for her, downright feared for her, there was a rightness in it.

Cassie was *meant* to be a part of this.

A part he would not trade for anything.

Chapter Nine

THREE DAYS LATER, they were nearing their destination. Apparently because of the number of warriors with them and the inclement weather, they were unable to travel via magic and arrive sooner. Regardless, the journey so far had been an experience. As it turned out, learning to ride Athdara was more challenging than expected. Even so, Cassie was slowly but surely getting the hang of it. Sort of. And while the weather remained fairly dismal, she wasn't all that bothered by it.

Not with Logan around.

She had enjoyed getting to know him better and though their current situation was far from romantic, there had been more than a few heated moments between them. He hadn't tried to kiss her, but a few times it almost seemed like he wanted to. She was definitely flattered considering she was no sexy thing, especially with the weather and traveling. Thankfully, not only did they have the opportunity to bathe that morning but the rain had finally let up.

At his insistence, Cassie continued riding with Logan and had long since settled back against him. The air was warm enough and even though she was nervous about what lay ahead, the beauty of Scotland kept her mind occupied. It reminded her of both New Hampshire and Maine, but more hilly. Yet somehow, though the vegetation looked similar, there was a certain mystical beauty that set Scotland's forest apart.

Then there was the guy she was leaning against.

As he had often done over the past few days, he chatted on and off with her. With an obvious love for his homeland, he was thorough in his explanation of a variety of trees, bushes, flowers and even wildlife.

Voice soft because of possible trouble in the area, Cassie said, "I've always been more of a fan of oaks than pines."

"Why?" he asked. "Pine trees weather the seasons better. They create a more solid canopy."

"And their sap is damn hard to get off my car," she mumbled.

"And what of the oak's acorns?" There was a smile in his voice. "I remember Ma complaining about them dinging her car."

"Oh, I don't care about acorns." She smiled too. "You just have to learn how to dodge them when you're outside. Those little suckers can hurt."

Logan chuckled. "Aye." He hesitated. "Tell me about your car. Do you love it like Aunt Leslie loves hers?"

It was strange hearing him refer to a woman who had to be around the same age as him as his aunt. "Actually, yeah, I do." Cassie shrugged. "It's no Lexus." She kept smiling. "But *way* better."

So she told him about her Chevette.

"'Tis a classic then, aye?"

"She turned twenty-eight this year so yup, as far as cars go, she's a classic for sure."

"'Tis good you love your car but you live in Maine," he said. "Hard winters. Is it so safe?"

"Safe enough," she defended. "And it's got a stick shift. You're better off in one of those on icy roads."

Cassie could almost hear his mental wheels spinning. She knew Logan wasn't quite buying her being safe in an 87' Chevette. "Have you not considered buying something newer? I've heard at length what Aunt Leslie's car can do and it includes traction control. That sounds just as good if not better than a stick shift."

Oh, but the conversations you never knew you would have with a medieval Highlander.

What she did *not* want him to know was the real reason there was no point in buying a new car. "I mostly work from home so it doesn't make sense right now."

"Ah." He tucked her cloak more securely around her as random drops fell off of the trees. "Well, I hope to see your Chevette someday, Cassie."

She pursed her lips, suddenly a little emotional at the thought of him seeing her car, of him being in the twenty-first century at all. Though she knew he was born there, it seemed so opposite of who he was supposed to be. Logan might have been born in New Hampshire, but he was so entirely *Scotland*.

But she wouldn't be rude. "Yeah, I'd like that too."

Yet she wondered if her emotions had more to do with the idea that there was a very good chance he might never see the twenty-first century again. That they were riding into something that might take his life. Cassie didn't care in the least that she might never see home again because it was an upcoming reality and in a very literal sense. But Logan? He wasn't going blind. He was just determined to put himself in harm's way.

Cassie nibbled on her lower lip, mind suddenly on what he had said in the stable. How he desired her and was she willing to go on this journey knowing that. Though she came because she wanted to help find little Robert the Bruce, she could admit that she also came because she was worried about Logan. Did it piss her off that he said she would perhaps be a hindrance?

Hell yes.

But she understood it. This was serious and she was one more person he felt he needed to protect. From what she gathered, Logan had devoted his life to protecting people, to putting his clan first. But he needed to understand she would never forgive herself if she did not try to help.

So he had his reasons and she had hers.

But she was here and his attitude had improved so they were on the right track. *She hoped.*

And what a track it was. She could barely believe that his betrothal had fallen through. That though Aline was already married, he had so graciously given her over to Baird. She knew her history. Based on the promise between the clans, Logan could have made things truly miserable if he were another sort of man. But it seemed he wasn't. And thank *God* for that. Even if Aline had betrayed him, Cassie couldn't imagine a guy who would cause problems after knowing a woman had lost her child.

"M'laird." Deargh came alongside. "We will need to head Northwest soon. Then 'tis best yer men fan out. 'Twill not be good to have too many approach the cave."

"Aye," Logan said. "Verra well."

Cassie shivered at the mention of a cave since she speculated Robert was in one. Then again, she imagined there were thousands of caves in Scotland.

When Deargh lingered by their side, Logan said, "Out with whatever ye wish to say, lad."

Deargh paused for a long moment, clearly uncomfortable before he spoke. "'Tis just that...well, as I mentioned afor..." He cleared his throat. "My sister went against the promise made betwixt our clans and mayhap whilst my Da is going through trying times ye'll not share something that will overly distress him."

"Och." Logan's voice was a deep rumble against her back. "I'll deal with things as I see fit. Now off with ye. Lead Niall in the direction ye want me. My men will follow along from there."

"Aye, of course, m'laird." Deargh nodded and trotted ahead.

"I sensed that Robert the Bruce was in some sort of cave," Cassie warned softly.

"Aye, dinnae worry, lass," Logan said. "My eyes are wide open." His arm came around her and he squeezed her hand. "But I'm grateful for your concern."

Though her skin heated at the intimate gesture, Cassie squeezed back. She liked the friendship developing between them and remained determined to keep it at that. "No problem."

Niall trotted alongside and nodded before he pulled ahead.

Though the skies had brightened through the canopy of leaves overhead, she felt the shift in the atmosphere. The tension and wariness. MacLomain warriors started to spread out, but several stayed both in front and behind her and Logan.

"'Tis a thing to be chieftain," he murmured. "I'm never given much privacy."

"You're important." Without thinking, she entwined her fingers with his, marveling at their weapon-roughened texture. "When they watch over you like this it's a good reminder that they have a lot of faith in you to protect their clan, their families. What better compliment is there than that?"

"Aye, I know lass," he whispered. "I know."

Cassie knew he did, but it didn't hurt to remind him. She wondered how often people took the time to do that. To be thankful that he cared so much. That he was willing to give up everything for them, including his own life.

Of all people, Machara trotted up alongside, a frown on her face as she eyed Logan. "Ye thought to leave me behind, cousin? It took nigh on two days to convince that bloody bastard Conall to allow me to follow!"

Logan sighed. "Aye, few can look over our clan as ye can."

122

Machara humphed as she scanned the forest. "I serve my clan best by protecting its Laird." Scowl fierce, words disgusted, she muttered, "Such as he is."

Then she spurred her horse and vanished ahead.

Cassie shook her head. "It doesn't take much to piss her off, eh?"

"Nay, it never has."

"What you should have done was leave her in charge while you were away," Cassie said. "That's called killing two birds with one stone."

Logan chuckled and spurred his horse forward. "You might just be right about that, lass."

Nothing more was said as they stayed behind Niall and Machara with Athdara trotting alongside. The further they traveled the edgier Cassie felt. Though she by no means enjoyed the bizarre episode she experienced when Robert first appeared to her, she was eager to have another vision. Was he okay? Was he still frightened? Seven years old was so young. She still wondered why Robert and his mother had been in the MacLauchlin village to begin with, but Logan had remained vague.

The reprieve from inclement weather seemed to be shifting because the forest grew darker. Or maybe it was just the thickening trees. Large clumps of bushes became more frequent until they were trotting alongside what looked to be one long bush. Then it was a mountainside caked with moss.

Niall and Machara slowed as Deargh joined them, making soft whistling sounds. Though it might have been the wind, Cassie swore she heard whistles returned. Logan swung off of the horse then helped her down. Like they had been the past few days, her legs and backside were sore from riding. Supportive hands on her waist, Logan backed her against the mossy rock and murmured, "Stay here, lass. Sit if you need to. I'm not going far."

Cassie nodded, surprised when Athdara trotted up and stood in front of her. Was the horse protecting her? She peered around and watched as Logan and his cousins drew their weapons, scanning the woodline. Niall and Logan vanished for a few moments before returning.

Logan took Cassie's hand and pulled her after him. She lowered her hood as they entered a small opening in the rock she had no idea was even there. Then they traveled down a long hallway before entering a small, dimly lit cavern.

Several warriors wearing the same color tartan as Deargh stood in a semi-circle around a monster of a man. Overly tall, muscular, sporting a big belly and a harshly receding hairline, his sharp eyes took her in then went to Logan. Though she suspected he typically had a booming voice, right now he was soft-spoken. He opened his arms and said, "Ye came, my lad. Ye really came."

Logan embraced the man. "Of course I did, m'laird. As soon as I heard ye were alive."

The MacLauchlin chieftain didn't seem inclined to let go so Logan murmured, "All will be well, my friend. Ye lost a lot but not yer daughter. Aline still lives."

The MacLauchlin Laird pulled back and held Logan's shoulders. "Aye, she lives? Truly? I told her not to go to the village. To stay close."

"Aye," Logan assured. "She is safe and well-protected at my castle."

"'Tis good news this," the MacLauchlin grunted and looked Logan over. "And how fare ye, my good friend? 'Twas a bloody slaughter. Were any of yer people injured? Are all well?"

Cassie didn't think anyone could make Logan and Niall look small, but this guy did as he wrapped an arm around Logan's shoulders and led him further into the cave. "Tell me everything. I have done nothing but sit here and fret."

"Come, lass," Machara murmured, leading her after them. "And say nothing lest spoken to, aye?"

"Okay."

Though there were several MacLauchlin men here, the majority that followed and surrounded them as they entered a wider cave were MacLomain warriors. Machara urged Cassie to sit next to her on a rock. Niall sat next to her as well and she knew without question Logan had somehow ordered them to protect her. Because though they might be with an ally, all of the MacLomains had their weapons not drawn but visible.

A small fire crackled in the center of the cave as the two chieftains remained standing and caught up on all that had happened. From what she could tell, everything Deargh had told Logan, everything he then shared with Cassie on the ride here, was the absolute truth. The MacLauchlin castle had been taken and a good majority of the clan murdered.

When the MacLauchlin Chieftain eventually plunked down on a rock, Logan sat beside him and at last made introductions.

"Laird Clyde MacLauchlin, this is my friend, Cassie," Logan said. "Cassie, meet one of the greatest Chieftains to grace the Northern edge of Argyll."

Cassie and Clyde nodded at one another, the MacLauchlin eying her with renewed interest as he took a long swig from his skin. Then he wiped his hand across his mouth and looked at Logan. "And who is she to ye?"

If she wasn't mistaken, Logan's eyes met Niall's and Machara's briefly before scanning his warriors. "Mayhap 'tis not the best time to tell ye, m'laird but I cannae in good conscience help save yer castle with lies betwixt us. 'Twould be wrong."

Clyde rubbed his meaty nose, braced his fist on his knee and eyed Logan. "So yer set to make my day more difficult, are ye?"

What was Logan doing? Was he actually going to tell this man what his daughter had done? Heck, just the pure size of Clyde made Cassie want to run in the opposite direction.

"'Twill be brief and 'twill be up to ye what ye make o' it," Logan said, his tone matter-of-fact as he held Clyde's eyes.

"Say it then, lad," Clyde huffed.

When Logan did, not batting a lash, she about hit the floor.

"I've love for another lass. I've betrayed yer daughter." Logan nodded Cassie's way, clenched his jaw then hung his head. "I cannae see through the promise my kin made to ye so long ago. But know this, as it has always been, ye've the support of the MacLomain clan. Our sword is yours and I pray ye might forgive me my weakness."

"Love for another lass?" Clyde whispered, his lower lip hanging as though he didn't quite know what to do with it. "Love for another *lass*," he repeated. "'Twas a pledge made long ago!"

Logan shrugged and stood. "And one that I cannae see through m'laird but still ye've my pledge that I will help retake yer castle."

"My c-castle?" Clyde sputtered as he stood, monstrous muscles bulging as he grabbed a sword tossed to him. Venom in his eyes, he roared, "No traitorous MacLomain will help *me* reclaim *my* castle."

Logan leapt away, barely escaping his blade. "Aye, but I will m'laird."

"Nay!" Clyde went after him. "Ye've always been like a son to me. Mayhap ye should have laid eyes on Aline sooner and this wouldnae have happened. But nay, that shouldnae have made a difference to an *honorable* lad." He shook his head, sword swinging. "I kept my daughter away from ye until the day ye wed because 'twas the right thing to do in God's eyes ye bloody bastard!"

"Not a bastard," Logan reminded, slamming a sword against Clyde's. "Born to two wonderful parents."

"Ye'll be a bloody bastard if I say ye are!" Clyde slashed again and again, muttering under his breath, "May God and yer good parents forgive me for my words but ken yer deserving of them."

Cassie screeched when Niall flung her over his shoulder and started running. Machara was right behind, sword fighting with warriors the whole time. What the *holy heck* was happening? It was hard to process anything until she was plunked on Athdara and the horse took off. Oh Lord, here she was again racing through the woods, ducking low and just waiting for the moment she fell off.

Except this time, there was no saddle.

"If ye but relax all will be well, lass."

"I am relaxing the best I can considering the screwed up circumstances," she yelled at Machara. The only problem? When she looked over her shoulder, the Scotswoman was nowhere to be seen. Instead, a MacLauchlin warrior was coming up fast on her right-hand side.

"Lean down further, grab my mane and hold on tight."

What. The. Hell.

When the man drew his sword, Cassie figured she better listen to the voice in her head. Good thing she did because the horse suddenly banked a hard left and the man's swipe missed her by inches.

Oh God, I'm gonna die, she said to herself.

"Nay lass, not if ye hold on tight."

Why was she thinking these thoughts? But it didn't much matter as Athdara banked around a rock ledge hidden by bushes then stopped. Hands clenched tight, Cassie kept her face pressed against the horse's mane. Heart hammering, she did not move, barely breathed. Everything went silent save the muffled sound of her heavy breathing. What was going on? Had Logan been killed by the behemoth Clyde? Because that would make sense. Seriously.

It was amazing how every second felt like a lifetime when you were frozen in fear, convinced death was right around the corner. So though it felt like an eternity, it was likely only a few minutes before she heard, "There you are, lass."

Not willing to look, she actually prayed that was Niall's voice behind her.

She opened one eye as he came alongside, chuckling. "Keep hold of your horse. 'Tis time to get you to safety."

Safety? Hadn't that been promised at the last stop?

Cassie kept her head against Athdara, not caring in the least if she looked like an idiot. Give her a Chevette any day of the week. At least she knew how to turn it right and left and hell, hit the brakes. The horse? Not at all it seemed. And heck, did she wish she had opted for pants today instead of a dress. Luckily, however, her skirts seemed to have stayed where they belonged.

She had no idea how far they traveled, her head plastered against Athdara's neck and hands wrapped desperately into her mane, before they stopped. Even then, she didn't move an inch, just stared at the never ending view of a sideways forest.

"Cassie," Logan said softly, having evidently joined them. He leaned over and turned his head sideways until their eyes met. "Are you ready to get down?"

"*Nope*," she said.

A small smile curled his lips. "Are you not going to save the future King of Scotland with me then?"

"*Yup*, and still will," she said against Athdara's neck. "From right here."

"Och, lass." He cupped her cheek. "'Twill be verra few that will fight you sideways such as you are."

"Then I have the advantage," she muttered.

"Nay, you misunderstand my meaning." Logan shook his head. "They'll make quick work of you at that angle as we Highlanders tend to fight best on our feet." He winked. "Right side up that is."

"I don't think there's anything right side up about you people," she whispered.

"Not at first," he murmured, pulling her off the horse into his arms. "But sooner or later, we level out."

Somewhere in the back of her mind she was yelling, "I promised you I wouldn't be a hindrance," while another part of her was arguing, "But I never anticipated how insane this would be. How insane *you* would be."

She was sort of prepared for violence, war, and even heartache.

Crazy Scotsmen and endless lies told in a cave?

Not at all.

"Put me down," she mumbled, feeling foolish as he carried her. "I can walk now that I'm off the horse."

"I know, lass." He didn't go all that much further before he set her down in another cave. Cassie looked around. It was fairly small with a low ceiling. A fire crackled and there were nothing but MacLomain clansmen around this time.

Her eyes went to his. "Are we safe?"

"Aye." He handed her a skin. "We're safe enough for now."

Logan's eyes scanned everyone. "Rest. Ye know what happens on the morn, aye?"

They nodded as several more men came in with fresh game tossed over their shoulders.

His eyes met Niall's. "Bring us some food once it's cooked, aye?"

"Aye." Niall nodded at her. "Rest well, lass."

Rest *well*? Was he out of his *mind*? But then she had agreed to come on this journey against Logan's wishes so she kept her mouth shut as the MacLomain Laird pulled her after him. They went back outside before he pulled her inside of...something. It was sort of a cave but not. One side consisted of a deep scoop in the rock and the other a wall of thick shrubbery. She would almost be inclined to call it an animal's den. That in mind, she peered around looking for evidence of bears or wolves.

Logan lit a fire in a small manmade circle of rocks and gave her peace of mind that humans had actually been here before. He removed a plaid from his satchel then laid it over a bed of pine needles before he sat and pulled her down beside him. Nodding at her skin of whisky, he said, "Drink, lass. Long and deep because God knows you need it."

Cassie nodded and took several long swallows before she licked her lips, shook her head and turned her eyes his way. Time to get some answers. "Okay, what the hell happened back there? Because it sounded like you took the fall for Aline MacLauchlin." Her eyes widened. "Did you? After that whole display with you fighting Baird at your castle, did you *actually* make yourself out to be the villain?"

Logan took a swig from his skin then urged her to do the same again. So she did. Several times.

"'Tis important," he finally began, "that some offenses not be punished too harshly."

Baffled, she shook her head and stared at him. "So you truly did cover for Aline, didn't you? At what expense? It seemed like her dad really cared about you." She kept shaking her head. Now that the sheer panic of swords clanging and Athdara racing through the forest was over, she could appreciate what he had done. "You protected a woman who betrayed you."

"I protected the relationship betwixt a father and his daughter," Logan said softly. "Nothing more."

Cassie brushed hair away from her face, rested her cheek in her hand and eyed him. "So you did. Holy shit."

"Why holy shit?"

"Because." She shook her head. "It's so selfless. So noble. Who *does* that?"

"Who wouldnae do that." He took another swig and eyed the fire. "My country is falling apart and my future king is in harm's way. Common decency needs to be protected and that means protecting the love betwixt family, betwixt clans."

"Sure, okay, I get that," she murmured. Wow. What a guy. She couldn't remember being so impressed with anyone. Then again, people like him were rare back home. "But what about the honor of your clan? Doesn't this look really bad for the MacLomains?"

"My clan knows the truth of it." His eyes went to hers. "They know of the battle betwixt Baird and me. *That* righted any wrong done. My people are forgiving. Besides, this isnae the first time something like this has happened betwixt clans and it willnae be the last."

Her eyes widened as the truth dawned on her. "So that battle between you two at the castle was all for show?"

"At least on my part." He grinned. "Not so much for Baird. 'Twas verra real for him."

"But you seemed so vicious."

"'Twas not so hard to seem that way." He gave her a knowing look. "After all, I wasnae in the best of moods."

Cassie took another sip, aware that she was starting to feel lightheaded from it. Or maybe it was because of the heat gathering in his eyes. A heat that had nothing to do with bad moods and fake battles. "I know I should be sorry for upsetting you, but the truth is I'm still not. Despite everything, I'm glad I'm here."

"Me too." His hand wrapped with hers. "Verra glad."

Uh oh. Things were definitely getting intimate fast. "Um," she started then trailed off, trying to think of something half bright to say. Come on, Cassie. It's not like you haven't been around men before. Just not ones this good looking.

"Um, what?"

She really had no clue.

"You could tell him of your conversation with me, lass."

Cassie rubbed her forehead. What was with her thoughts? The same sort she'd had when riding Athdara.

Logan frowned. "Are you okay?"

"'Tis Athdara, lass," floated through her mind. *"'Tis your horse speaking with ye."*

"That's impossible," she whispered.

"You finally hear her, aye?" Logan tilted her chin, forcing her eyes to his. "Do you hear Athdara in your mind?"

"Are you serious?" But he obviously was. "Oh my God. You mean to tell me..." She shook her head, not sure she wanted to finish her sentence.

"Is it really so hard to believe considering everything else you've learned since traveling back in time?" he said, eyes gentle. "'Tis because of your gift that you can hear her and 'tis nothing to be afraid of. She is your friend."

"Aye, I am," whispered through her mind.

Speechless, Cassie could only manage a heavy swallow. She couldn't believe this.

"Just picture me in your mind if ye wish to speak to me," Athdara said because it *had* to be the horse right? Or she was truly going *loco*. That was always a distinct possibility after everything she had witnessed lately.

"Try speaking directly to her within the mind," Logan said. "She can hear you no matter where she is." When she hesitated, he nodded and gave her a comforting smile. "Go ahead and try."

Cassie rubbed her lips together and nodded. She might as well. What harm could it do besides prove she was as insane as the rest of them.

Here goes nothing. She closed her eyes, pictured Athdara in her mind and spoke...telepathically. "Hi Athdara, it's me, Cassie. Can you hear me?"

"Aye, lass," Athdara responded. *"Verra clearly."*

A little thrill shot through her and she opened her eyes. "I think she responded." Excitement grew as she looked at Logan. "But how do I know for sure that I wasn't just responding to myself?"

"You weren't," Logan said. "I heard you when you spoke to her."

"Really?" She widened her eyes. "You heard my thoughts?"

"Just the ones directed at Athdara because I can hear her as well," he said. "I dinnae listen to your thoughts otherwise."

She frowned. "But you can if you want to?"

Logan nodded and squeezed her hand. "Dinnae worry, lass. I would never unless you wanted me to. But know this. If you ever wish to speak to me within the mind, simply do what you just did when speaking to Athdara."

"Okay," she murmured, still trying to process everything. Yet sitting here with him, calmed by the casual way he explained what should not exist, Cassie knew she would be all right. In an odd way, discovering all of this almost made her feel more normal. Where back home she kept her strange gift a secret, she didn't have to here. Instead, it made her feel special in a really good way versus a freak of nature.

Maybe Leslie was right after all.

Maybe she really was a witch.

"'Tis time for me to rest for the eve, lass, so I'll leave ye to yer lad," Athdara said.

Cassie was about to respond, mainly to tell her Logan was not her lad, but the horse spoke first. *"Now that we have connected, I've the power to keep our conversations from Logan as I'm doing now. I will have thoughts that only ye can hear. Always heed my call when it comes, aye?"*

"Of course," she responded. *"Is everything all right?"*

"Nay." Cassie swore she heard a touch of sadness in Athdara's voice. *"There are truly troubling times ahead for the Laird. Heartbreak of the verra worst kind."*

Chapter Ten

"ATHDARA SHUT ME off from her thoughts," Logan murmured. "'Tis good this. The bond forged between you two should be yours alone."

"Well, I don't mind you listening in." Cassie offered a little grin. "But it seems she's got all the control."

"Aye." Logan was happy that Athdara and Cassie had finally connected. The bond between the two would only strengthen now.

Logan brushed a lock of hair back from her face, enchanted by the way the firelight ignited sparkling streaks of strawberry red in her thick blond hair. He liked the shiver that rippled through her as her startled eyes met his. It was something she seemed to do whenever he touched her. Something he had made a habit of doing over the past few days.

If anything, his desire for her had only grown tenfold. Not just her beauty, but her personality captivated him. He enjoyed the way she often said things unintentionally. The way the tops of her cheeks and tip of her nose reddened slightly when she realized what she said. As a rule of thumb, most people tended to give him guarded words so he found her aloof bluntness refreshing.

For long hours, he had mulled over Niall's advice to simply take her and be done with it but the timing never seemed quite right. Besides, though his body entirely disagreed, he had wanted a chance to get to know her better. As far as he was concerned, he'd gone through life having less intimacy than most men so a few more days couldn't hurt. Or at least that's what he kept telling himself. The truth was he needed her to understand that he didn't just want her for sex. Because regardless of what Grant said about her being meant for one of his cousins, Logan meant to keep her.

"I've food for you, cousin," Niall said as he came around the corner. His eyes grew mischievous. "Unless you've decided on another way to satisfy your appetite."

He found the way Niall acted around Cassie interesting. While his cousin wasn't necessarily a brooder, he wasn't normally this…what? Lighthearted? But then battling and revenge was on the horizon and nothing gave Niall more pleasure.

Logan shook his head as Cassie took another hearty gulp of whisky. "Just bring us the food, Niall."

Niall grinned as he handed over some roasted game. "'Twas hard to know after the way you two have been looking at one another what you might be doing."

Cassie blushed, thanked him for the meat and took a bite. Logan figured she was determined to keep herself busy rather than be part of this conversation. "Many thanks for the food. Alert me when one of Laird MacLauchlin's men arrives."

Niall nodded, winked at Cassie then sauntered off.

Cassie frowned in confusion. "But I thought Clyde MacLauchlin wanted to kill you?"

"Likely he does but we both know he needs me and my warriors too much right now."

"And of course you'll help him because there's always the chance Robert's in that castle."

"Aye." Logan shrugged. "But I would've helped him anyway. I wouldnae abandon an allied clan in need of help."

"No, I can't imagine you would." She took a few bites and eyed the meat. "This is surprisingly good, considering there isn't any salt and pepper."

"Aye, there are plenty of herbs to be found if you know where to look," he said. "I'll teach you what to look for when we've time."

Cassie nodded and as they had done the past couple of nights, they settled into comfortable conversation. She was a pleasure to chat with. Though humble, she possessed a sharp wit. He suspected had she pursued any of her college majors, she would have excelled.

Yet the more he got to know her the more he sensed she lived her life a certain way…as if she already knew its outcome. Almost like someone planning to move to another country and preparing themselves for a different language and customs. Eventually, he intended to find out exactly what she was getting ready for. Whatever it was, it had her purposely changing subjects on a somewhat regular basis.

As he figured she would, Cassie eventually said, "Why are we eating separately from everyone else tonight?"

Though tempted to say it was unintentional, he would be lying. The truth was he wanted her all to himself. "'Twas a trying experience earlier. I thought you might want some privacy to relax."

She arched her brow and offered a lopsided grin. "Yet *you're* here."

"Well, you cannae be alone in these woods, lass." He polished off his meat and leaned back on his hands so that his shoulder was almost against hers. Voice lowered, he said, "And I'll admit to wanting to spend some time alone with you. 'Tis a luxury I rarely get."

"Ah." This time he didn't have to touch her to enjoy her becoming blush. His eyes dropped to her mouth when she licked her lips. He had never wanted to taste a lass so much in his life. When she cleared her throat, his eyes slowly returned to hers.

"You should probably stop looking at me like that," she said.

"Like what?"

"Like we're here alone for another reason altogether."

"Aye," he murmured, caught by how the firelight reflecting off the shrubbery behind her seemed to magnify the pale green in her eyes. Unable to stop himself, he brushed his thumb down her delicate jawline, eager for far more contact. "May I kiss ye, lass."

Her eyes widened slightly. "W-what?"

"Kiss ye." He ran the pad of his thumb over her lower lip and leaned even closer. "I've wanted to do it since I pulled ye onto my horse that first day."

"Oh," she whispered, not shying away.

Wrapping his hand in her hair, he didn't kiss her right away but brought his lips close to her ear and murmured, "I've never seen such a bonnie lass." He flicked his tongue beneath her dainty earlobe, relishing her quiver. "I've never wanted to touch and taste a lass so much that I cannae think straight."

"Oh," she whispered again, her head tilting to give him more access. God, she tasted warm and sweet and so bloody soft. He gently peppered kisses along her jaw, desperate to reach her lips but equally eager to sample everything along the way. Sharp arousal speared him when her breath hitched and she squeezed her thighs together. Hell, he had known the lass less than a week and he'd already imagined a hundred different ways he wanted to make love to her.

At last, his lips hovered over hers, savoring the heat of her breath, the ravenous anticipation before he finally...

"Och, m'laird, ye should have gotten to that sooner," Machara quipped as she came around the corner.

Cassie pulled back sharply and Logan scowled as he redirected his attention to his intrusive cousin. "What is it?"

"Ye said ye wanted to know when Laird MacLauchlin's man arrived, aye?"

"Aye." Logan stood and pulled Cassie up. "Is he here th—"

"Aye, I'm here ye bloody arse," Clyde MacLauchlin grumbled as he joined Machara. He scowled at the MacLomain men surrounding him with weapons. "Och, if ye mean to use the blades then ye should have done it before I got to yer laird." He held out his arms. "Besides, I've no weapons on me."

Logan sighed and told his men to stand down. "Many thanks but off with ye. I'll deal with the MacLauchlin."

"But m'laird," one warrior started. "He meant to kill ye!"

"I said I'll deal with him." Logan fingered the dagger at his waist. "See, I've the means to defend myself. Now off with ye."

His soldiers hesitated a few more moments before they reluctantly left. When Machara lingered, Logan said, "Ye too, lass."

"I dinnae think 'tis wise to leave ye." Her eyes narrowed on Clyde. Though Machara might have little use for Logan, he had to give her credit. She would always protect the Laird of the MacLomains despite what she thought of him.

"I'm fine, cousin." He nodded at her. "Now go, please."

Machara's eyes narrowed even further on Clyde. "If ye hurt m'laird I'll cut off yer ballocks and shove 'em up yer—"

"Now, Machara," Logan interrupted firmly.

She shook her head, sneered at the MacLauchlin, then left.

Clyde eyed Logan for a long moment before he plunked down on a rock, braced his fists on his knees and shook his head. "Yer a bloody good lad, Logan MacLomain." He nodded at the satchel. "Might ye have an extra skin of whisky in there for an old friend?"

Logan crossed his arms over his chest. "That depends on yer intentions."

"My intentions are to thank ye for protecting Aline's integrity." He ground his jaw as if angry before his brows shot up in resignation. "I know she married the Stewart and I know of their bairn." For the first time ever, he saw the man's eyes glisten as his voice grew rough. "And I know the wee one was murdered."

Cassie sat as Logan tossed a skin to Clyde. "I cannae tell ye how sorry I am."

Clyde gave a brief nod then downed half the skin in one long gulp. "'There is no help for the bairn now so 'tis best to set aside grief, aye?" Before Logan could respond, the Laird continued. "I owe ye a great debt for saying what ye did back there. 'Twas noble indeed."

Logan was about to respond, but Cassie spoke to Clyde first. "Like Logan I'm so sorry for your loss." Compassion met her eyes followed by curiosity. "But if you knew he was lying why'd you attack him?"

"What else should I have done? Shake his hand and pat him on the back?" Clyde cocked a brow at her and gestured at Logan. "The lad broke his vow. 'Twould have looked weak to handle his betrayal any other way."

Cassie shook her head and rolled her eyes. "You people are crazy."

"Aye." A wide grin split his face. "On occasion."

Logan sat next to Cassie and eyed Clyde. "How long have ye known of Aline and Baird then?"

The MacLauchlin sighed. "Longer than I would've liked." His eyes held Logan's. "I know I should've told ye of it sooner, but I needed my people to keep believing the marriage was on the horizon. That we would be strengthened more so with the power of the MacLomains behind us."

Despite the years taken from him when he could have been enjoying a loving wife, Logan understood. He might have done the same for his own clan. "Does Aline know that ye know?"

"Nay. Foolish lass. She thought me too old to recognize the lusty looks she and Baird exchanged when they were around one another." Clyde blinked away renewed moisture and downed the remainder of his skin. "She steered clear of the castle in her later months of pregnancy, but like her Ma, she carried small and hid it well beneath her dresses. After that, the bairn was kept in the village raised by another but I knew she visited the wee one often. As did I without anyone knowing."

Logan felt for the Laird. He really did. "Why not stop what ye saw developing betwixt Aline and Baird to begin with?"

Clyde almost appeared sheepish. "I meant to many times but…" He hesitated a long moment before continuing. "Did ye know my wife, God bless her soul, was intended for another lad?"

Everything became crystal clear. He empathized with his daughter's secret love affair. "So yer a bloody romantic after all, MacLauchlin."

"Aye, so it seems." Clyde peered at Cassie's skin of whisky. "Have ye a few drops left to share, lass?"

Cassie handed it over. "Sure, have at it."

"Many thanks." He took another long swig then belched. "'Twas never my intention to hurt ye, Logan, but 'twas just too heartbreaking to put an end to my Aline's happiness."

Logan repressed a sigh. At least Aline had found love over the long years leading up to their betrothal. His eyes slid to Cassie. Now that he'd met her he could only be grateful that everything worked out as it had. He wanted her so fiercely it would have been brutal had he been with another lass with her here.

"It seems, however, that my romantic nature paid off for both ye and my daughter though, aye?" Clyde's wise eyes flickered between Logan and Cassie. "Because I dinnae think 'twas so much a lie when ye said ye loved this lass."

Cassie's eyes rounded. "No way, buddy. Logan was *definitely* lying when he said that."

Logan wasn't so sure about that. Not at all. But right now, things needed to stay focused on why Clyde had come. "I take it ye've sought me out so soon not because your clan thinks ye capable of apologizing but because ye've a need to take back your castle."

Clyde took another swig and tapped his temple. "Yer always thinking, my lad. 'Tis what makes ye such a good Chieftain." He nodded. "Aye, I'm here because I think 'tis best to approach my castle under darkness. Sooner rather than later."

Logan rested his elbows on bent knees and considered Clyde's suggestion. As it did so often, the weather was shifting and another storm would be here within hours. Truth told it would be the perfect time to attempt to take the castle. "Have ye any idea how many of the enemy hold it under siege?"

"Maybe half yer current numbers but stealthy bastards." Clyde shook his head. "I didnae have the force to fight them. 'Tis half the reason a renewed affiliation with yer clan was so important."

"Ye should have said something," Logan muttered. "I would have sent ye extra warriors. You're not only the Da of the lass I was meant to marry but my friend."

"Aye, lad." Clyde shook his head. "'But my bloody pride got in the way."

Logan was about to reply when Cassie made an odd sound. She was holding her forehead, eyes squeezed shut. Concerned, he crouched in front of her and took her hand. "What is it, lass?"

When she removed her hand and opened her eyes, they seemed distant, unseeing. "I hear you, but I still can't see you." He moved back when she yanked her hand from his and held it out in another direction. "Is your name Robert?"

He realized she was having another vision and shook his head sharply when Clyde came alongside and started to speak.

"I can't hear you. Speak louder," she said, voice rising.

Logan scanned the forest, worried. Though tempted to silence her words to those who might be lurking close by, his magic might interfere with whatever she was experiencing.

"I heard you that time," she exclaimed, happy. "My name's Cassie and we're coming to get you. Do you know where you are?"

Considering how frightened she likely was, Logan was impressed with how gentle she kept her voice while asking exactly what they needed to know.

She dropped her arm and appeared to be listening. "So you hear running water? Like maybe a river or waterfall?"

Cassie paused then nodded. "All right. I'll let my friends know. They're great warriors and will save you really soon." Her brows drew together with concern. "Do what I'm doing and it will help keep you warm." She pulled her arms into her sleeves until they were wrapped over her chest beneath her dress. Nodding, she watched something only she could see. "There you go. That's it."

Then her eyes narrowed as if Robert was getting harder to see.

"Oh no, no, Robert, can you still see me?" She pulled her arms free and reached out again before her eyes drifted shut and she started to slump.

Logan scooped her up and sat on a rock. He went from curiosity while watching her speak with Robert to downright fear. Cupping her chin firmly, he said, "Cassie, are you well? Come on, lass, look at me."

She mumbled something then slowly cracked open her eyes and whispered, "Logan?"

"I'm here. I've got you," he said. "Can you see me?"

Her eyes again seemed distant and unseeing but unlike when having her vision he didn't sense any magic fluctuating around her. "Cassie?"

After several blinks, her gaze seemed to gradually clear but her words were weak. "Yeah, I see you."

Yet he got the sense she did not see him as clearly as she should. "Good." He stroked her cheek. Relief unlocked the tension in his shoulders as he brought a skin of whisky to her mouth. "Take a sip. 'Twill calm you."

Cassie did as asked then blinked a few more times before her eyes finally focused on his face. "I saw the boy again. It's definitely Robert."

"Aye, lass, I know."

"Ye gave us a good scare." Clyde eyed her with interest. "So ye've the gift of sight, aye?" His puzzled gaze went to Logan as he crossed his arms over his barrel chest. "It seems I'm not the only one keeping secrets."

Logan ignored him and remained focused on Cassie. "Where did Robert tell you he was? You said you heard running water."

Cassie nodded and tried to get off his lap, but Logan shook his head and kept her snuggly in place. "Nay. Not until you've regained your strength."

"And then there's that strange bite to yer accent every so often," Clyde muttered. "Not to mention the lass's accent in general."

Logan frowned at Clyde and again shook his head before meeting Cassie's eyes, his voice gentle. "Tell me everything Robert said."

She nodded and took another small sip of whisky. "Robert's not where he was the first time we spoke. They've been moving. He is, however, in another cave, this one colder than the last. It's very damp and he thinks the running water is a river because he heard the horse's hooves splashing through it before they stopped."

"Why couldn't he *see* the water?"

Cassie's sad eyes stayed with his. "Because they're keeping a sack over his head while they travel." Her eyes grew damp. "Who *does* that to a child?"

"Monsters," he muttered. "So he's not at the MacLauchlin castle then."

"Who's this Robert lad that's not at my castle?" Clyde's eyes narrowed. "And ye'd best give me an answer, MacLomain."

Logan's eyes met his. "Since he's not at yer castle 'tis not yer concern, m'laird."

Clyde's eyes widened and his brows slammed together. "If ye dinnae tell me then…"

"Then what?" Logan said as Clyde sputtered out, realizing there was nothing he could threaten Logan with. "Ye'll order me and my warriors away before we help ye try to take back yer castle?"

"Well, I'll be. Ye've a mean streak in ye after all," the MacLauchlin huffed and resumed draining his whisky.

Logan had just returned his attention to Cassie when a MacLauchlin warrior with Niall's blade to his back appeared.

"This one just joined us." Niall's eyes went from Clyde to Logan. "It seems our MacLauchlin Laird sent a few men ahead to scope out the castle."

That did not surprise Logan in the least. His gaze went to the drenched warrior. "And?"

Not responding to Logan, the man looked at Clyde.

Clyde nodded in Logan's direction. "Answer him. The MacLomain's our bloody ally."

"Aye." The warrior met Logan's eyes. "They've verra few men stationed on the battlements what with the rain and it seems they dinnae know ye've come because the vast lot of them are drunk."

Logan didn't trust that report. It seemed far too easy. He turned his attention Clyde's way. "How good is this man at scouting? Could he have been fooled by a ruse?"

Clyde leaned close to the warrior. "Let me smell yer breath, lad." The man complied. The Chieftain sniffed and shook his head. "'Tis no smell of whisky. As long as this one isnae in his cups, he's one of the best I have. So nay, 'tis doubtful 'tis a ruse."

Logan nodded, trusting Clyde's assessment. The MacLauchlin might have lied about Aline's betrothal but when it came to putting his friend's life at risk, he would give nothing less than the truth. He looked at Cassie. "How are you feeling? A bit better?"

"Much," she assured, renewed strength in her eyes.

"Okay." Logan stood and though it was the last thing he wanted to do, he carefully set her down. Hands still on her waist, he said, "Are you still well? Do you feel like you're going to fall?"

Cassie shook her head. "I'm good." Heat fluctuated between them and her breath hitched as their eyes held. Her voice sounded flustered. "Seriously."

Logan nodded and stepped away before he put this whole 'save the MacLauchlin castle thing' on hold, took her somewhere private and at last slaked his lust. He looked at Niall. "Remove your blade from the MacLauchlin and let's get our warriors rallied. 'Tis time to take back a castle."

When they joined the others, he looked at Machara. "Cassie will ride with you. I want five warriors with you at all times."

Though Machara's eyes flashed with defiance because she preferred being at the heart of battle, she nodded and urged Cassie to follow. He would much rather keep his lass with him, but he needed to lead his men.

His eyes met Cassie's. "'Twill be all right, lass. Machara will keep you safe."

"It's not me I'm worried about," she murmured, gaze lingering on him before she turned away. Startled, Logan realized she was referring to *his* safety. A surge of satisfaction blew through him as he prepared to leave. Hopefully, this would be a quick siege and they could resume where they'd left off before Clyde arrived.

Rain fell in heavy sheets, slicing through the thick canopy of trees as they traveled through the forest. The journey was short, perhaps half an hour before the MacLauchlin castle came into view. Save for a few torch-lit windows, it was shrouded in darkness. Not a large castle by any means, he had more than enough warriors to conquer it.

Clyde's horse came alongside, the Chieftain's eyes on his domain. "I'll see every last man beheaded."

Logan nodded his agreement. That was a damn good idea.

Clyde's son, Deargh, joined them, clearly ready to do whatever was asked of him. Though worried about the Chieftain's people,

Logan was glad Clyde had no immediate family in there. Aline was safe and his wife, God bless her soul, had passed on.

"I'm going in first to scout with the others," Logan said.

Clyde cocked a brow at him. "Ye always did like to get in on the battling first."

Logan gave no response but swung down from his horse and waved Niall and a few other MacLomain warriors after him. The beauty of this castle was the vast amount of trees surrounding three-quarters of it. No moat, no drawbridge, just a portcullis then a heavy gate. But none of that mattered because they were not going in the front.

He kept beneath the tree cover, signaling the others to fan out before he stopped at the last tree and squinted up. His superior vision allowed him to see better than most. When he saw nothing, he searched with magic. One man leaned against the backside of the wall walk above, head bent as he dozed.

Within minutes, Logan had managed a fairly thorough sweep of the castle via magic. Niall's voice entered his mind. *"I count only forty of the enemy, cousin. As was reported, most are drunk."*

The drunken men weren't faking it either which led Logan to believe this castle siege was a means to delay them as the real prize, Robert, was moved further away. No matter, the MacLauchlin needed his castle back and pursuing the future king on such a night would be unwise.

"I'll take care of the trees," Logan said. "Tell half the men to follow. The other half to remain hidden just beyond the front gate."

It may seem like an easy siege, but he preferred to err on the side of caution when it came to not only the safety of his men but the innocent people inside. Making a ruckus at the front would stir up a drunken slaughter. It was best to keep things quiet for as long as possible.

Logan put a hand against the closest tree and murmured, *"Terram clamavi ad te. Adiuvamus causa et crescere arboribus illis.* Mother Earth, I call to thee. Help our cause and grow these trees."

A rush spread through him as his body warmed and fingertips tingled. He watched as the trees' branches slowly grew out and up until they reached the battlements. Making sure his bow, arrows and sword were attached securely to his back, he began climbing. Before long, he dropped over the wall and crouched, eyeing his surroundings. The man he had sensed lounging made no movement. Silent, Logan crossed to him and sliced a dagger across his throat before he ever woke.

His men were dropping over the battlements and making their way around the wall walks, killing any of the enemy they might find before they alerted the others. It remained a fairly uneventful siege until he reached the courtyard.

Unfortunately, things went awry not because someone caught him unaware, but because of a drunken warrior who fell asleep leaning on his sword. Logan had just reached the last stair when the man toppled over and the sword clanged down. While the sound was by no means enough to wake the others through the driving rain, the fall was more than enough to awaken the man.

Logan got to him fast but not fast enough. He managed to unleash a bloody good roar before he was run through with a sword. Niall arrived behind him with a zealous grin on his face. No doubt his cousin had been finding the whole siege boring up until this point.

Drunk or not, the enemy started to awaken and like any Scotsman worth a grain of salt, they had no trouble swinging a sword despite their lack of sobriety. It soon became a muddy mess as swords clanged and arrows flew. Logan drove his fist into a man's face while whipping his dagger at another.

Niall, as always, embraced his berserker and made a verbal project out of fighting. "Bloody arse," this, "To hell with ye then," that, before he would swing his blade and be done with it. Yet Logan knew, like him, Niall was releasing some of the fury he had felt at the ravaged village.

Despite the unexpected skirmish, the MacLomains had the advantage and the battle was short. The gates were opened and the remaining warriors came through as the last of the enemy stumbled into the courtyard. His men had been told to keep the leader alive, but so far the man hadn't been found.

Logan knew full well that Clyde would want to torture at least a few of the remaining men. He didn't blame him in the least. So he motioned to his warriors with his hand. "The last of the enemy are the MacLauchlin's."

Clyde trotted in, his venomous eyes sweeping over the handful of stupefied warriors dragged forward. Every last one of them was shaking, eyes wide with terror as the behemoth MacLauchlin Laird swung down from his horse. "Where are my people?" he roared.

One man fell to his knees and traced the cross over his chest, his eyes barely able to meet Clyde's. "P-please m'laird, have mercy on me because I'm telling ye that they're safe and in yer dungeon."

Clyde's eyes narrowed to slits as he approached the man, voice dangerously soft. "*Mercy* on ye, aye? As ye had mercy on the lads, lasses and wee bairns of my village?"

The man lowered his forehead to the muddy ground, hands steepled in prayer, murmuring over and over, "Please dinnae kill me. Forgive me as the mighty Lord must surely."

A MacLauchlin warrior grabbed the man's hair and yanked him back to a kneeling position, then stepped away as Clyde roared, "Leave the Lord out of this ye bloody sinner. 'Tis ye and the Devil together now!"

Then his blade swiped and the enemy's head rolled from his torso.

Logan turned his attention from the MacLauchlin and his victims, concerned about Cassie. He did not want her to see this. But where was she? There was no sign of her, Machara, or the warriors assigned to stay with them.

He didn't need to communicate with Niall. His cousin felt his distress. The men swung onto the first horses they saw and flew through the front gates. Many of his men followed as they headed into the woods. They had not gone far before they came across a mini battle happening between his men and the remainder of the enemy. It seemed a few must have escaped down the trees.

Still no sign of Cassie and Machara.

When a scream pierced the air, he spurred his horse with Niall right behind. A minute later they came upon Machara. She was off her horse and sword fighting like a madwoman. Bigger than the others, her rival had an overly arrogant way of battling and a misplaced confidence when it came to fighting a female.

This was their man.

He was the leader of this miscreant group.

Renewed fear leapt in his chest as Logan scanned the woodline. Machara's horse was here, but there was no sign of Cassie.

"Niall, help Machara get this man back to Clyde." Logan spurred his horse and flew into the darkness with several of his men in pursuit.

"Cassie's with me, Logan," Athdara said. *"She would probably like ye to catch up with us soon, though. She doesnae seem happy in the least."*

"Is she all right?" He urged his horse to go even faster. *"Why is she no longer with Machara?"*

"Nay, she isnae quite all right." Was that humor in the horse's voice? *"But 'tis more of an emotional ailment than a physical one."*

Within seconds, Athdara came into view. She slowed to a stop as he approached. Now Logan understood what she meant. Flung belly down over the horse's back, Cassie was ranting mad as she clenched her hand in Athdara's mane the best she could. Logan made a motion for his warriors to fall back. Some would stay close but remain unseen.

Relieved that Cassie was well, Logan masked a small grin as he swung down and strode over to her. Words like 'raving lunatics' and 'damn Scots' were tumbling furiously from her mouth. Crouching, he tilted his head until their eyes met. He hoped to hell there wasn't a twinkle in his eyes. "'Tis a thing us meeting like this, aye? How fare ye, lass?"

A healthy stream of twenty-first century curses poured from her mouth before she spat, "Get me the hell down!"

"Of course." He stood and eyed her, almost wishing he could continue to admire her soaked backside thrust up in the air. But there was no questioning that she had to be uncomfortable so he pulled her into his arms. Though he allowed her feet to touch the ground, he didn't let her go.

"Do you know what your blasted cousin did?" Her wild eyes met his. "She just tossed me on Athdara then spurred the horse. Total crap. I didn't deserve that."

"Yer lass tried to help Machara fight the enemy and he almost ended her life. I knelt so that yer cousin could more easily get her onto me," Athdara said. *"Though I know ye've worked with her some, ye need to spend more time teaching Cassie how to use a dagger. 'Tis apparently something she doesnae take to naturally."*

Cassie frowned at the horse. "I *can* hear you. Remember?"

Athdara only neighed in response.

"It sounds like Machara might have saved your life, lass," Logan said carefully.

"Saved my life? I was doing just fine!" Soaked hair plastered against her head, Cassie's eyes shot fire. Cheeks flushed, her lips were rosy with passion. Logan had never seen anything so tempting. So when she started spewing another stream of disgruntled words, he decided there was only one thing left to do.

He kissed her.

Chapter Eleven

CASSIE DID NOT know what hit her.

One second she was rip-roaring mad, the next she was washed away in a deluge made of Logan's hungry, talented lips. She almost pulled away. Almost. But his warm lips were too tempting. Too persuasive. She vaguely prayed that he didn't realize how unpracticed she was at this. Yet he didn't seem too concerned as he groaned, wrapped an arm around her and pulled her tighter against him. When his tongue swung into her mouth, worry over her lack of experience faded away.

Cassie twisted her hand into his tunic and held on tight. He made being kissed so damn easy that she simply followed his lead. Their tongues danced, explored, roamed. At first, the kiss was slow and languid. But not for long. When he trailed his hand up the side of her neck then wrapped it into her hair; the kiss became far more passionate.

There was no telling how long they stood in the pouring rain kissing before Logan swung her up into his arms and started walking. When he set her down they were in yet another small cave. This one, however, was cozier than the others. His eyes never left hers as he flicked his wrist and a small fire sprang to life in the corner.

He cupped her cheek. "Dinnae be frightened by my magic, lass."

Strange thing to say. The fire hadn't bothered her in the least. Then he crouched and fisted some dirt while touching her dress. Eyes closed, he murmured, *"Tellus a totis nunc austerum.* Mother Earth from thy, might we now be dry."

Cassie gasped as tingles warmed her and her dress and hair dried in an instant. "Oh my God. How did you do that?"

"My element is Earth so with Mother Earth's permission I can manipulate anything that is of her." Logan removed a satchel from his shoulder that he must have grabbed off of his horse and pulled out a plaid. He laid it over a patch of grass she swore was not there before.

"Amazing," she murmured, completely enchanted. "Did you grow that grass as well?"

"Aye," he said.

She worked to ignore her thundering heart and the lust his kiss had invoked. Better to focus on his magic. "What about your cousins? Can they do the same thing?"

He shook his head as he sat. "Nay, we can only work with our element. Niall's is water, Rònan's, fire and Darach's air."

"Holy *wow*." What an astounding concept, one that would take some getting used to.

"Sit with me, lass," he said softly.

She had the distinct feeling they would be doing a lot more than sitting. Determined to stall him, she peered into the darkness. "Are we just going to leave the horses out in the rain?" They were nowhere to be seen. "Where are they anyway? Are they okay?"

"Aye." Logan pulled her down, eyes hungry. "Athdara will lead them to where 'tis warm and dry."

"And the castle? Is it safe to assume you got it back?"

"Aye." His eyes roamed her face with desire. She suspected the same was reflected in hers. That kiss had ignited all sorts of delicious feelings. Yet nervousness was once more flaring. Her cheeks heated and she tore her gaze from his.

"Why do you look away?" he murmured. "When you'd rather keep looking at me."

Way to lay it on the line. Cassie ignored her increased heartbeat and forced her eyes back to his, mumbling a flat out lie. "Actually, I was getting a little tired. Is this where we're sleeping tonight?"

That sounded good. Just make up an excuse.

"Aye," he said. "But there willnae be much sleeping."

Her mouth fell open at the carnal intent in his eyes.

"But, but…is that really such a good idea?" she blubbered, sounding *so* not sexy. Now she couldn't tear her eyes away from his.

"Och, 'tis a verra good idea, lass," he said, voice low and guttural.

Think quick, girl, because he's coming for you. "But Grant said you're not meant for…"

Logan cupped her cheeks and cut off another potential excuse with his lips. That was it. She was gone in an instant. Wrapped up in pure, heart-palpitating passion.

Adrift, completely immersed in the feel of him, she didn't realize he laid her back until he came over her. Then it was all little gasps as his lips wandered down her neck, his tongue flicking and tasting.

She should tell him to stop. Better yet, she should tell him *why* he should not take this any further. And it wasn't because Grant said not to but because he deserved to know what he was getting into with her. For years, she had prepared to face blindness on her own. It had never crossed her mind that she might meet a man beforehand. This was information he deserved to know before they got too invested. Wasn't it?

When he pulled down the front of her dress and latched onto her nipple, she arched and moaned. Oh, Christ. Maybe he really didn't need to know after all. For goodness sake, this wasn't a marriage proposal but sex.

Sex.

Oh, jeez, they were really heading in that direction weren't they? Cassie tried to speak, but she was too busy struggling for air as he made a feast out of her breasts. Should she stop this? Yes. No. Maybe. Sweet mother of God, why stop something that felt this amazing? When he tore off his tunic, every good intention went flying out the window...or little Highland cave in this case.

Cassie had half a second to admire his broad, muscular chest before he vanished down below. Her eyes popped when she realized what he was doing. He had her dress pushed up and thighs spread so fast, she barely had time to get a word out. "Maybe we should...this...is...not a good idea..."

"'Tis a verra good idea," he repeated his words from earlier, voice thick with arousal.

Then his mouth was on her.

Glory be, but there was a reason he could roll his r's so well!

"Oh, God, Oh, God, Oh God." She dug her fingers into his hair.

He was doing this. They were really doing this. Oh *hell*, yes they were.

Or he was.

Really, really well.

"Logan," she moaned, arching her pelvis against his welcoming mouth. His hands clamped over her hips, keeping her from wiggling away from his torturous tongue. Breathing became more and more difficult as he wrapped his arms around her thighs and ravished her. Nothing paralleled the pleasure tearing through her. It felt like a fissure had opened up deep inside and released hot, spearing heat through her weakened veins.

Even though she put a hand over her mouth to keep from groaning or likely even screaming, it didn't do much good. There was way too much feeling. Too much of something uncontrollable. Undeniable.

Most *definitely* unavoidable.

A climax didn't build, build, build but blasted through her. She arched sharply and a strangled cry broke from her lips. After that, she felt weightless and tingly, immersed in unfamiliar bliss.

Cassie was remotely aware of him making his way back up, vaguely aware of him once more laving his tongue over her breasts before kissing his way up her neck.

"So verra beautiful," he rasped. "I need to feel ye, lass." He murmured against her ear, "Can I feel ye?"

Feel me? Wasn't he doing that already? But she was all for *more* feeling.

Only when he whipped aside his plaid and settled between her legs did she realize what he was talking about. While she should probably say no considering how long they had known each other and her secret, she was suddenly feeling pretty selfish. Honestly, how much time was left to have sex while she could still see? Though it was safe to say that vision wasn't playing a big part right now, it still had its perks…especially when she got to look at *him*.

So instead of denying him, she murmured the last thing she probably should. "Just once. Sex that is." This wasn't coming out right at all. Then again, the feel of his lips, the nibbles and licks against the side of her neck, were turning her brain to mush.

"Just once," he whispered. "If that's what ye wish."

No, no. "I meant I've only had sex once. A while ago. A really long while ago."

Logan abandoned her neck and hovered over her, brows pulled together. He stroked her cheek, tender. "Are you nervous then? Should I stop?"

This was her chance to put on the brakes. Yet as she looked into his eyes and saw not only desire but genuine concern, Cassie knew she didn't want him to stop. Not even for a second. This felt too good, too right.

"No," she whispered, glad she had gotten the birth control shot. Call it wishful thinking that it would serve a purpose. Looks like wishful thinking paid off. Not to say she wasn't nervous. She was. The only other sexual experience she'd had was prom night and it was awful. Yup, she was *that* cliché.

When he kissed her again, it was just as arousing as before. Except this time, his hands wandered far more. Fueled by his stroking and caressing, she writhed against him as the ache between her thighs increased. A hollow, needy sensation that became more and more persistent. She felt the hot heaviness of his arousal against her stomach then lower before he spread her legs further apart, entwined their fingers and pressed her hand beside her head.

His eyes locked on hers before he slowly pressed forward. Cassie was unprepared for both the intimacy of his appraisal and slight burning pressure below. Heaven help her, she might as well still be a virgin. Or he was considerably larger than the last guy. Teeth clamped down hard on her lower lip, she started to tremble.

"'Tis okay, lass," he whispered, his lips brushing hers softly. "Just relax."

I thought I was. But apparently not. Then he kissed her again and again and she drowned. Lost in the sensations he invoked, she must have relaxed because he slowly pushed forward. Just a little bit at a time. His body shook and she knew it was hard for him to hold back. Lucky for them both he didn't have to wait much longer as the feel of him filling her had renewed the heat and sharp pleasure washing over her.

Cassie gasped when he at last gave one final thrust and filled her completely. Head hung beside hers; he released a ragged breath and whispered, "Ye feel as good as I knew ye would."

There was no chance to respond before his eyes found hers and he began to move. Caught by the emotion in his gaze, her discomfort vanished as an unbelievable well of pleasure grew with his increased thrusts. When he rolled his hips, she cried out and widened her legs. Nails dug into his forearm, low moans started to vibrate in her throat.

Heat didn't just warm her veins but blazed through them as the pace of his thrusts slowed. Ripples, almost microbursts, fluttered through her stomach, fanning up and out as he rolled his hips in the opposite direction. It was almost as if he was keeping her teetering on the edge of an orgasm. His tongue swung into her mouth again, mimicking the pattern of his hips.

If she wasn't lost before she certainly was now.

As his kiss intensified so did the movement of his hips. Then his lips pulled away and hovered against hers as he thrust sharply. She released more strangled moans as he clenched her hand tighter and moved faster. Sweat glistened on his skin as his vigorous momentum made her claw at his back with fervent anticipation.

"Logan," she pleaded, not sure what she was asking for.

"Let me feel all of ye, lass," he half whispered, half groaned by her ear. "Let go."

Something about his earnest words, the untampered need in them, made the microbursts spreading through her body become an astronomical swelling deep inside. Like a bunch of small waves becoming massive ones. She had never felt anything like it. Digging her nails in deeper, desperate to either escape or rush toward whatever was heading her way, she wrapped a leg around him and met his thrusts.

"Bloody hell," he said through clenched teeth as their movements turned almost frantic.

After that, everything became a blur as their sounds of pleasure and desperation mingled. Then, as if a huge wave of pure, unfiltered euphoria crashed over her, her body exploded into heart-stopping throbs. Cassie arched and cried out, trapped within the mind-numbing climax. At the same time, Logan locked up against her and roared with release.

There was no way to convey the intimate feeling of what she experienced. The way his deep pulses almost seemed to draw out her pinnacle. His forehead was pressed against the plaid beside her face, his breathing staggered and fast. Their hearts thundered. Heat and sweetness surrounded them as her body very slowly relaxed.

Desperate to keep him close, she wrapped an arm around his neck and allowed the other to fall beside her. A means to ground herself before her body drifted away. Thrown by the plush softness beneath her hand, she turned her head, still dazed, and whispered, "Oh, *wow*. Look at all of them."

Logan lifted his head, shock in his voice as he eyed the bed of flowers that had bloomed around them. "Purple petunias." He inhaled deeply. "Just like Ma used to grow in New Hampshire."

"Where did they come from?" she murmured, surprisingly bashful when her eyes met his. Lord, Cassie, you just made love to the man. You should be past this. But she imagined it might take a while to wrap her mind around the two of them…together?

"I dinnae know where the flowers came from. My magic I suppose." A warm smile blossomed on his face as he picked one then lay beside her, propped up on an elbow. He sniffed the flower, nostalgic, before he trailed the soft petal over her collarbone. "How fare ye, lass? Are ye well?"

Cassie fingered one of the tiny braids hanging in his hair before meeting his eyes, well aware she was blushing again. "*Very* well." Then, because it seemed like the thing to say. "You?"

"*Verra* well." He dragged the petal lightly up her neck sending little shivers through her. "Better than I can ever recall being actually."

Flattered, she arched her brows and found flirting far easier than she anticipated. "So I take it this is the first time you've magically grown a flower garden for a woman?"

"Aye." Logan chuckled, genuine happiness in his eyes. "My favorite flowers grown for my favorite lass."

"Am I then," she murmured, said less as a question but more as a means of humoring him.

He trailed the petal over her chin and along her jawline, eyes suddenly serious. "Aye, ye are."

Cassie truly didn't want to ruin the moment, but her mouth was stuck on 'spit it out' mode. "Back to what I was starting to say before. What about what Grant said? What about me being meant—"

Managing to keep the flower away, he pressed a finger to her lips and shook his head. "I dinnae care what the Hamilton said." His eyes almost seemed to flare a paler shade of blue with his passionate words. "I care about the way I feel toward ye. I care about the way ye feel toward me. Nothing else matters. Especially not my cousins because ye'd have to drive me through with a sword before I'd let one of them have ye."

Heat again flared beneath her skin at the possessiveness of his declaration. The truth was she liked it immensely. *But* there was a 'but'. She held up her hand and eyed the ring, stunned by how much she wished it reflected his eye color. "You might be willing to ignore Grant but what about this? I would think its actions override what either of us wants."

"So ye want the same," he murmured, eyes riveted on her face.

"That's not...I mean to say...the ring that is..."

Logan set aside the flower and tilted her chin until their eyes were aligned. "Do ye then? Do ye want me as I want ye?"

How could she *not*? Cassie swallowed, not sure what to say. What she would love to say is yes, like you wouldn't believe. But that niggling sense of self-awareness was gradually returning. The fact that she had not been truthful with him about what to expect from her. That she wasn't always going to be the woman she was today.

"I can see the worry in yer eyes, lass. And I know ye want me." His finger brushed lazily back and forth over her lower lip. "What holds ye back from putting voice to it?"

Again, she lied. "It's just that...won't I eventually go home? You guys obviously travel between here and there. So after I help you save Robert, I assume I'll be returning to the twenty-first century." Then she said something that she actually meant but wasn't so sure she wanted to hear the answer to. "Besides, even if I were to stay, would you really want to be with a woman from the future? One that doesn't even have that much Scottish in her? Especially considering you're the Laird and all."

Logan's expression had grown more and more troubled as she spoke. "I dinnae care what nationalities you are and I wouldnae care if you didnae have a drop of Scottish blood. I want you." His lips pulled down further. "And it doesnae matter in the least that I'm Laird. With God's blessing, I'm free of a betrothal I've stayed true to and He's given me the free will to follow my heart." He pressed her hand over his heart. "Now this belongs to you, lass."

Warmth uncurled inside. Never in her wildest dreams could she have imagined such an amazing man saying that. Her fingers rippled against the dusting of hair on his hard chest and she closed her eyes. She should just come out and tell him her secret. Why was it so hard? But she knew. She did not want to lose him. Selfish. He didn't deserve this. Not at all. Opening her eyes, she was about to spill everything when Logan shook his head sharply and yanked the plaid over them.

"I've given you plenty of time," Niall said with a grin as he ducked in out of the night.

Eyes wide, she yanked her dress back into position beneath the plaid as Niall shook the water from his hair and plunked down across from them.

"What the bloody hell are you doing here?" Logan muttered.

"Where else would I be?" Niall leaned back against the wall, crossed his legs and tossed Logan a skin. "You didnae think I'd leave the Laird unprotected all night, did you?"

"I know full well there are at least twenty men watching guard over me from those woods." Logan handed her the skin. "And I'd rather they be under cover and warm."

Oh, *fabulous*. Cassie took a swig, mortified to think of all the sounds she had made when she and Logan made love. Even more mortified to think one of those men might have very well been watching.

"'Tis not up to you when it comes to your protection, cousin." Niall shrugged. "Besides, they're taking shifts and have found shelter in several nearby caves."

"And why is it again that you've decided this is the cave for you?" Logan asked.

"Because no one can protect you better than I," Niall said with absolute conviction. "And *that* is best done from right here."

Logan muttered under his breath and took a swig of whisky when she handed it back. It looked like she wouldn't be sharing any truths with him tonight after all.

She eyed Niall's wet hair and kilt. "Logan, why don't you magically dry your cousin off?"

"Och, nay lass." Niall grinned. "I like being wet. It feels good."

Interesting. She cocked her head. "Is that because your element is water?"

Niall's brows arched in surprise before he shook his head and chuckled. "Nay. It just feels good after the battling is all. What little of it there was that is."

She had grown more comfortable with Niall but then he seemed far less intense when he wasn't hitting on her. Something he had not done since they left the MacLomain castle.

Like his cousins, he seemed to possess a rather consistent sense of humor. She had to wonder how they managed it considering the circumstances, better yet the current state of their country. But she speculated that perhaps the humor was an innate means of protecting themselves from how bad things really were. A means to keep things from growing too depressing at times. Or maybe even a means to keep their fellowmen's spirits up. In any case, she found it an interesting shared trait considering they were such fierce warriors.

"What of the leader you brought back to the MacLauchlin castle?" Logan said. "I assume Clyde's keeping busy with him."

"Aye." Niall's eyes landed briefly on Cassie before returning to Logan. "'Twas wise of you to keep the lass away for the night. The MacLauchlin Laird is making a bloody show of it for his people. And I cannae help but approve of his methods."

Ah, she had wondered why they hadn't gone back to the castle. Her eyes went to Logan, warmed by how thoughtful he had been. Yes, she loved history and knew she was going to see bad things while here but she was fine not watching torture for now. Then again, if she had seen what they had in that village, she might likely think otherwise.

"And what of his people?" Logan went on. "Were any hurt?"

A flare of anger crossed Niall's features. "None were killed, but the bastards had their share of the lasses available."

Cassie murmured a prayer and put a hand over her mouth. Those poor women.

"Bloody bastards, the lot o' them," Logan growled and took another long swig before handing the skin back to her. "Might the MacLauchlin release his wrath in full this eve."

"Aye." Niall nodded and took a long swig as well. "Clyde said you're to take some of his men wherever you might be heading next. It seems he suspects you've a journey ahead."

"Nay, he has too few to spare." Logan eyed the fire, troubled. "I've sent a message to our castle that extra men be dispatched to protect the MacLauchlins."

Niall nodded, yawned and leaned his head back against the rock, amused as he eyed the carpet of flowers surrounding them. "I never knew you were such a romantic, cousin."

Embarrassment flared once more and Cassie looked anywhere but at Niall.

"'Twas a thing this," Logan said, fingering one of the flowers. "I didnae think I used any magic."

Oh, he used magic all right. Just maybe not the sort he was talking about.

Niall chuckled. "'Tis good that. It says much about the exchange."

Exchange? Odd thing to call it. Then again, though Niall was certainly the lusty sort, she didn't get the impression that he was particularly romantic when it came to the actual art of lovemaking. He seemed more of a rash type which she could not really imagine when it came to sex. But then what did she know about sex and its variations. Pretty much nothing save what she had just experienced. She decided prom night didn't count because it sucked. Best just to erase that memory.

"'Twas far more than an *exchange*," Logan murmured, his hand sliding into hers. "I mean to make Cassie Lady of MacLomain castle."

Her eyes rounded. *Say what?*

Niall's grin slowly dropped and he spoke before she could. "'Tis a fine thing that ye got some lusting out with such a bonnie lass, but ye are not born of the Next Generation, cousin. Laird Grant said—"

"I *know* what Grant said," Logan cut him off. "But I willnae give up my lass."

"Um…" she started.

"Ye speak against the MacLomain arch-wizard then?" Niall interrupted with a frown. "That willnae go over well."

"Um…" she said again, trying to jump in but wondering what the hell would be the most effective thing to say.

"Grant will see things differently once he learns I am no longer betrothed," Logan said.

"I dinnae think it has much to do with yer betrothal but something that was meant to be by the Fates."

"Guys…" She scowled when Logan continued.

"Then tell me this. Why are there four Broun lasses and only three of you lads born of the Next Generation?"

Niall shrugged before the corner of his mouth shot up. "Mayhap one of us is meant for two of them. I know Rònan and I would be just fi—"

"Enough," Logan ground out.

159

But Niall kept going. "Well, I for one willnae go after yer lass but I cannae speak for the other two. Especially Darach. He seems quite taken with her."

Logan's eyes narrowed and Cassie finally managed to insert a whole sentence into the runaway conversation. "Hey, guys, I'm sitting right here ya know." Then she pushed out a few more sentences while she was on a roll. "First of all I can't be Lady of any castle without a proposal." She gestured back and forth between her and Logan, sort of amazed at how brazen she was being. "And no offense but you and I are nowhere close to that stage in the game." Then her eyes went from Logan to Niall. "Furthermore, I'll be with a guy because I *want* to be with him not because Grant or anyone else says I'm supposed to be."

Niall shrugged. "The best of luck with that, lass." He yawned again and closed his eyes. "'Tis time for me to rest." His lips quirked. "Dinnae let me keep you from your business." Then his lips hitched up just a bit further. "Mayhap this time try to keep it down a notch, though."

Cassie almost groaned. Unreal.

Logan's mood seemed to have soured as he muttered, "And here I thought ye were here to protect me."

Niall gave no response and within a few seconds his breathing slowed.

"Did he really fall asleep that fast?" she said.

"Aye, always after battling." Logan laid back. "Time to sleep, lass."

His discontent bothered her. "Sorry to be so blunt before but surely you understand that…well, you can't just declare I'm going to be your wife without asking first. Not to mention the fact that we just met. It's way too soon. We don't know each other nearly well enough."

Did he *seriously* want to marry her? Or was he just caught up in long repressed lust? While she contemplated continuing their conversation from earlier and telling him more about herself, she just couldn't do it with Niall here.

"Dinnae worry, lass." She rested her cheek on his chest when he wrapped his arm beneath her head. His deep voice rumbled softly against her ear. "'Twas just my desire for you speaking. When a lad's gone so long without the love of a lass, the length of time he's known her means verra little."

Understandable. In her own way, she could completely empathize. Save in her case, it had always been a complete lack of interested men. She was about to respond when his breathing slowed. A quick peek at his face proved that Niall was not the only one with the ability to zonk out fast. Probably for the better.

She could use some time to think.

That was the last thought she had before she dozed off.

"Cassie? Are ye there?" came a whisper. "Can ye hear me? Please say ye can hear me."

Startled, she shot up and looked around. Logan and Niall were gone. So was the cave. Instead, shadows rippled through a thick forest swathed in purple twilight. It almost seemed as if she hovered high in the trees as she looked down. A band of warriors traveled on horseback. She honed in on the child with a sack over his head riding in front of one of them.

"Robert, is that you?"

"Aye, 'tis me," he whispered so softly she had to strain to hear. He was clearly trying to keep his words from being heard. "Are ye still coming?"

"Of course. Are you doing all right?"

"Aye." But he sounded scared. "They mentioned that they were being followed so we're no longer in the cave."

Cassie nodded. "Have they said anything else? Do they know who is following or have they said where they're heading?"

"Nay, they didnae say who follows," Robert whispered. "They say that their Laird is eager for their arrival and that 'tis taking too long." His voice quivered with fear. "And they will suffer for it." Then his voice sounded stronger. "He waits for us at the oak tree ford."

The *oak tree ford*? Wasn't that the meaning of Athdara's name?

The man sitting behind Robert suddenly grunted and shook the child's shoulder roughly. "What are ye saying, ye little bastard?"

Trying to keep anger from her voice, Cassie said all she could think of to soothe him. "We *are* coming for you, Robert. Stay strong. It will be all right."

But it was too little too late.

Chapter Twelve

LOGAN CRADLED CASSIE against his chest as she murmured again and again that the man had just pulled Robert off the horse and was dragging him somewhere. "He's going to hit him, I know it."

Regrettably, she wasn't talking to him. There was no way to know *who* she spoke with now.

"How long did her vision last before?" Niall said, worried.

"Not this long," Logan replied as twilight crept through the trees. Grant, Darach, and Rònan had arrived a short while ago and crouched nearby, concern on their faces.

"And it wasnae like this before either." Logan looked at Grant. "She snapped right out of it. This time she seems caught in the vision."

Grant had already put a hand to her forehead in hopes of drawing her out but had no luck. "Keep speaking with her. If anything can pull her back, 'tis a voice she recognizes."

Logan nodded and kept murmuring in her ear, urging her to focus on his words. He never stopped stroking her hair in hopes that maybe physical connection might help as well. His eyes met Grant's and his frown grew heavier. The thought of her somehow getting caught wherever she was scared the bloody hell out of him. She might think they needed to know each other longer to feel so strongly, but he knew better. He had not been exaggerating in the least when he told her his heart was hers. But then wizards tended to have more insight than most.

Her mumbled words suddenly stopped and she whispered, "Logan?"

Thank God. "Aye, lass, I'm here." He tilted up her chin but like before her gaze seemed distant. "Can you see me, Cassie?"

She blinked several times and nodded. "I saw Robert again."

"I know." He rested her head against his chest. "Just take a few minutes to acclimate then you can share what happened, aye?"

"We don't have a few minutes." She pulled back. Strangely enough, when she spoke to him, she looked just to the right of his face though he knew she intended to look directly at it.

163

"They're on the move again with Robert and they know they're being followed. Robert didn't know if they knew by who, though."

Again Logan and Grant's eyes met. The Hamilton looked perplexed.

"Did they say where they were heading?" Rònan asked.

Cassie's head turned slightly, almost as if she was surprised that he was there. As they had with Logan, her eyes didn't quite focus on Rònan but more so on Darach, who crouched beside him. "Yeah, that's sort of the super strange part. They said their Laird was waiting for them at the oak tree ford." Her face turned back to Logan. "That's the meaning of Athdara's name right?"

Logan frowned, discomforted by the uncanny information. "Aye, but 'tis likely just a coincidence."

Darach looked at Grant. "We need to know who brought those horses to New Hampshire, Da. Was it you then?'"

"Nay," Grant murmured.

Cassie's brows perked and her eyes turned back in the general direction of Darach, clearly surprised he was there. Enough was enough. Something was wrong with her and he needed to know what. Logan looked at his cousins. "I need a moment alone with my lass. Make sure the men are ready to travel."

Grant's brows drew down sharply and he spoke within the mind. *"Your lass?"*

"Aye, until she wishes it otherwise."

Grant stood and sighed. *"We'll speak of this later, lad."*

Cassie remained silent as everyone walked away, her fingers clenching and unclenching ever so slightly on her lap as though she was nervous. Logan again tilted her chin until her eyes went to his. This time they seemed a bit better focused. "Are your visions starting to affect your eyesight, Cassie?"

She swallowed and shook her head a little too quickly. "No."

Frustrated by what he knew was a lie, he said, "'Tis understandable if they are. 'Tis also something I need to know as it puts you more at risk on this quest."

"I'm not worried about being more at risk," she murmured, her eyes now firmly locked on his. "I just want to get Robert back."

Logan caressed her cheek, his worry only growing. "I got the sense you wanted to tell me something last night before Niall arrived. What was it?"

Her eyes held his for a long moment before she shook her head. She was up and off his lap so quickly that he shot to his feet to steady her.

"I'm fine, Logan." Cassie started to walk away then stopped short, spun on her heel and put her hands on her hips. Her eyes were surprisingly confrontational when they met his. "No, that's not true." She shook her head. "I've been lying to you and it's time to come clean."

Logan remained still and nodded, his words gentle. "Okay, lass. Say what you will."

He thought for sure she would at last share that she *did*, in fact, have a love in the twenty-first century. For surely a lass this beautiful was pursued by many.

Cassie started to talk then stopped. She crossed her arms over her chest, then she uncrossed them. For a woman good at blurting things out, she was remarkably tongue-tied.

"There's something you should know about me," she finally said. "Something I should have been honest about from the start."

When he saw how uncomfortable she was, he could not help but go to her. He didn't pull her into his arms but took her hand and squeezed, words just above a whisper. "You can tell me anything. 'Tis all right."

If he was not mistaken, her eyes started to moisten before she blinked and straightened. Though her next words were firm and clearly spoken, he wasn't sure he heard her correctly.

"I'm going blind...and it has nothing to do with my ability to have visions."

The announcement hung between them as he tried to process what she had said. As if to fill in the blank space, she rambled, "I was diagnosed with something called Macular Degeneration. Usually, it happens when you're older and takes a long time." She shook her head, not quite meeting his eyes. "Not in my case. It started years ago and has been progressing pretty fast lately." Her shoulders pulled back and her eyes were at last strong when they met his. "I got laser surgery so that I could enjoy seeing clearly for awhile longer without my glasses, but it *is* a temporary solution."

When Cassie finished speaking, she released a deep breath and it occurred to him just how worried she had been about telling him. His heart broke for what she was facing, but he dared not show it...too much. So he reeled her closer and cupped the side of her neck, his brogue thickening with the emotions her revelation incited. "No doubt 'tis a difficult path ahead of ye, lass but ye are not alone." His voice deepened. "Never alone."

For the first time since Logan met her, he saw a flash of fear in her eyes before she clenched her jaw and the sentiment vanished. "I'm not sure you're hearing me. Pretty soon I'm gonna be totally blind. No blurry vision. No episodes that end up passing." She swallowed but plowed on. "Everything will be dark...black."

"Aye, lass, I heard ye." He cupped her cheeks. "And I meant what I said. Ye will never be alone. I'll face this with ye if ye'll let me."

Her brows drew together and she pulled away. "You can't possibly mean that. Do you have any idea how dependent I'm going to be on people for God knows how long?" This time her eyes *did* glisten before she turned away and adjusted clothing that didn't need to be adjusted. "I'm going to have an assistive care person live at my place for a while and learn how to adjust to a seeing-eye dog. Not to mention I'll have to figure out how to manage all the things most people take for granted. Preparing my own food, walking around in public, stuff like that. Good thing for audio books or..."

Cassie's mouth clamped shut when he turned her and clasped her shoulders firmly, eyes locked with hers. "When the time comes ye will excel at whatever ye set yer mind to but why not face this here with me? Ye dinnae need to go through this alone. I will help ye every step of the way." He gave her a comforting smile. "We'll go through this *together*."

A tear managed to escape and rolled slowly down her face. "That's sweet. Really. But not the least bit realistic. You're a chieftain in a day and age that keeps you extremely busy. There'll be no time for trying to deal with a disabled...friend. Besides, I wouldn't put that burden on you." She shook her head. "I just wouldn't."

His response was cut off when Grant returned. "We must go. The scouts have picked up tracks."

Cassie pulled away and nodded. "Grant's right. We do need to go. I'm really worried about Robert. I hope I'm wrong, but I think that guy was getting ready to beat on him."

Logan rolled his plaid and tucked it in his satchel. Then he strapped on his sword and bow and arrows before stepping close and murmuring in her ear. "Ye are not just my friend, lass. And seeing ye through what ye must face would not only be an honor but a privilege."

Grant's eyes flickered between them before he strode off. Logan swore for a moment he saw something more in the wizard's eyes. As if he knew something they did not. Almost as if things were going precisely as he wanted them to. But that would make no sense considering the Hamilton's insistence on Cassie being with one of his cousins. Then again, Grant was becoming more and more like Adlin by the day—meddlesome and evasive—so who knew.

Cassie insisted on riding Athdara. Though she had indeed improved at horseback riding, he presumed she felt more confident now because they communicated telepathically. Even so, he told Athdara to stay near him at all times.

Thankfully enough, the rain had let up again so traveling would be less slick. A handful of his men would remain at the MacLauchlin castle until the warriors from the MacLomain castle arrived. Then they would catch up with Logan.

He was glad his cousins and Grant were able to join him on this quest. They were far more formidable together than apart.

Once they settled into the journey and he knew Cassie and Athdara were doing well, he fell in behind her as Grant came alongside. The Hamilton's words were soft. "I dinnae think that those who have Robert know 'tis us who follow."

"Nay." Logan eyed Grant. They both knew two separate sets of tracks had been found. "But I wonder if they know who the others are that follow them. Have we any idea who *they* might be?"

Grant shook his head. "Mayhap 'tis the Bruce's men."

He'd thought of that but had to wonder. "The Duchess was vague about why she was in the MacLauchlin village to begin with and close-lipped entirely about whoever glamoured her to look like Aline." He arched a brow at Grant. "Did ye have a chance to speak with her alone?"

"Briefly," Grant said. "But she wouldnae share much. Just that she missed her wee bairn and 'twas not the first time she'd visited him in disguise."

"So 'twas simply fortunate timing then," Logan murmured, not a big believer in things that worked out so conveniently. If it could be said that being in a village the day it was ravaged convenient timing. Nonetheless, he strongly suspected that Marjorie was not there on a lucky happenstance. No, she was there to protect her son. Yet for whatever reason, it seemed she had not confessed to any of his kin which baffled him. Wouldn't it behoove her to share everything she possibly could to help those who were set to save her son?

Grant's voice entered his mind. *"So ye know of Cassie's plight with her sight now, aye?"*

Logan frowned at him. *"Ye knew?"*

"Of course I knew. The verra moment I touched her."

Sharp frustration rose. *"And why is it ye chose not to tell me?"*

"Because 'twas not my information to tell."

"So instead ye let the lass worry over telling me for days."

"Days, might I remind ye…" Grant's eyes narrowed on him. *"That ye were not supposed to woo the lass."*

"I didnae woo her." But he had. As often as possible. *"And in case ye somehow missed it, I'm no longer betrothed so my heart is free to do as it will."*

"How easily ye forget the ring she wears," Grant reminded. *"And mayhap the stories about how fickle it can be."*

"So now 'tis less about being born to the Next Generation and more about what the bloody ring has to say?"

"The rings are for those born of the Next Generation, lad." Grant sighed. *"And I love ye well so dinnae think I like reminding ye that the two are interconnected."*

"I willnae be sharing her." He made sure his words carried just enough threat without being too disrespectful. This was the MacLomain's arch-wizard after all. Still, he was willing to test boundaries when it came to Cassie. *"I willnae share her with my cousins. Not with anyone."*

"'Tis yer heart to do with as ye will." Grant's eyes met his. *"Just remember that 'tis not only your heart at stake, aye?"*

Logan knew Grant spoke of Cassie's heart, but he couldn't help but narrow his eyes on Darach as his horse fell in step beside hers. A smile broke over her face as the two started chatting. Having no desire to talk with the Hamilton about how his son might be a better fit for Cassie, he redirected the conversation. *"What make ye of the oak tree ford? 'Tis strange considering Athdara's arrival, is it not?"*

"Aye," Grant agreed, clearly contemplating his son and Cassie though he did not say it. *"'Tis a bloody difficult thing because there are far too many oak tree fords in Scotland."*

He mulled over how such a place might possibly relate to Cassie, him, Robert or even Athdara. While the trees were certainly kindred to Logan's magic, the water at a ford would be kindred to Niall's. Speaking of water, it wouldn't have hurt to have the wizard who was strongest with the element of water with them. *"Where is your brother? I thought for certain he would want to join us on this venture."*

Something troubling flashed through Grant's eyes so quickly he almost didn't catch it.

"Malcolm watches over my castle," Grant said. *"I wanted extra protection for my people and Sheila..."*

Horseshit. The Hamilton was lying. Something was wrong. *"Tell me what's happened."*

"Ye must stay focused on your mission." Grant's eyes were hard when they met his. *"Nothing else."*

Logan was about to tell him he wasn't a bairn anymore and could keep his wits about him regardless how dire the news but Grant spurred his horse and trotted ahead. What the hell was going on? Discontented, he frowned and pulled his horse up on the other side of Cassie.

The grin she had been aiming at Darach dropped when she looked at him. "Hey there. Everything okay?"

It would be better if his cousin stopped eying her with such avid appreciation. Then again, he didn't much blame him. She was lovelier than usual with her hair full and waving loosely down her back. Her cheeks were rosy from riding and her eyes sparkling from the endless chuckling the two of them seemed so good at when together. Though he could admit to being jealous, he would not put his bad mood on her. She didn't deserve it.

So he mustered up a small smile. "Aye, all is well." He couldn't think of a better way to cheer his spirits and soothe his jealousy than to say, "We soon travel over far hillier terrain and you're too unpracticed at riding for that." Cassie's eyes widened and she released a less then dainty grunt as he scooped her off her horse and plunked her down on his. "'Tis best that you ride with me for now."

Logan winked at Darach when his cousin's eyes narrowed.

The morning was balmier than usual, but he still tucked her cloak more securely around her. "Are ye hungry lass? I've some berries and dried meat."

"No, thanks." Her eyes met his over her shoulder. "Are you sure you're okay?" She grinned a little. "We don't always have to talk about *my* problems, you know."

He wondered if she realized that they had never talked about her problems until just this morning. And he certainly had no intentions of laying his troubled thoughts on her. "Nay, all is well enough, lass."

Cassie turned forward again, words soft. "Did it ever occur to you that I might want to help you through the stuff that's bugging you as much as you seem to want to help me?"

Logan considered her words. She made a good point. If he was going to convince her that he truly wanted to be there for her when she lost her sight, then it made sense that she felt she was there for him as well. "I worry about the behavior of my Da and uncles. Something is happening and they're determined to keep it from me."

Her eyes again met his. "It's something to do with my ring, isn't it?"

"Aye, I think so." He wrapped his arm more securely around her small waist, comforted by the feel of her.

Cassie turned forward again and he knew she was discreetly eying her ring. "I'd take it off if I could so it wouldn't stress everyone out so much."

"Nay." He rested his head next to hers and inhaled the scent of petunias in her hair. "'Tis meant for you and no other. Take pride in the wearing of it because 'twill only bring you the best of loves in the end."

God willing it be his love because there wasn't another lass on Earth he wanted to give it to. Having her in his arms and being inside her the night before had shot him straight to Heaven. He had never felt anything so astounding. Not just sexually but emotionally. Somehow it had felt like he had come home after being lost for so very long.

Immersed in honor and doing right by his clan, he had set aside his own needs for so long. Longer than he could remember. Indulging in laying with a woman without thinking once of his duties or obligations was not something he did. Ever. Or should he say lying with a lass period. That alone was a luxury that had not been his in far too long.

Thoughts of Cassie's moans and the way she had responded so readily to him made his groin tighten. Barely aware he was doing it; he ran his hand up her stomach and dusted the underside of her breast with the pad of his thumb. When she shivered, he murmured in her ear, "Would ye like me to share what I'm thinking now, lass?"

She adjusted her backside and he almost groaned. "No, I've got a pretty good idea."

Logan reached into his satchel and pulled out the petunia that he had dragged across her skin last night, whispering, "*Terrain venit a te, quia vibrant manere.* From Mother Earth came thee, stay vibrant for she." Then he tucked it into her hand and spoke, making sure the heat of his words dusted the shell of her ear. "'Twill forever look as it does now so that ye might remember our first night together. The first of many I hope."

"*Oh*," she whispered, emotion evident as she gazed at it. There was a slight curve to her lips and a dewy look in her eyes when they met his. "I think Niall's right. You're a romantic."

"He's right enough this time." He brushed his fingers over her cheekbone. "When it comes to you that is."

"M'laird."

Logan's attention snapped to the man veering in from the right. It was one of his scouts. "Aye, what is it?"

"We've located the band of warriors following the bairn. Ye willnae believe who—"

That's all he got out before a loud whooping sound was followed by a flourish of activity. MacLomain warriors surrounded him while others fanned out, weapons at the ready. When the whooping came again, Logan grinned. He knew that sound. It was one he had been forced to perfect when a wee bairn.

"Stand down. 'Tis any ally," he roared.

Darach chuckled as a female called out from somewhere unseen. "Are ye married yet then, Laird MacLomain?"

"Nay," he yelled back. "So ye best show yer face, aye?"

Logan patted Cassie's thigh and whispered, "Be right back," before he swung down. Moments later a horse came thundering out of the woods and a woman leapt off as it came to a stop a few feet away.

A wide smile broke over her bonnie face. "Och, lad, it has been far too long, has it not?"

"Aye, far too long indeed."

Then he hugged and swung around the woman he would have married had he been available a decade earlier.

Chapter Thirteen

CASSIE ABOUT FELL off the horse when she saw the woman fly into Logan's arms. Honest to God, she had never seen someone so beautiful. Ethereal almost. With silky, jet black hair and porcelain skin, her eyes were a vibrant cedar brown as they looked up at Logan fondly.

No, fondly wasn't the right word.

More like, 'Wow you look amazing and I want to pick up where we left off.'

Who *was* this chick? Because she obviously had a thing for Logan.

"Och, but where's yer wife then?" The woman eyed him up and down. "Did she forget she made a promise to ye?"

Logan wrapped an arm around her shoulders and squeezed affectionately. "It didnae work out."

Her brow perked. "Then ye be available for the taking?"

"Nay—" he started but was cut off when his cousins joined them, each overly affectionate as they pulled her into their arms.

Was he going to say nay because of Cassie? That was sort of hard to believe considering the Scotswoman who still had her eyes on him while greeting his cousins. They *definitely* had some serious history together.

Logan took Cassie's hand and waited until Niall finished borderline groping her before making introductions. "Brae, this is Cassie. Cassie, this is Brae Stewart, daughter to Laird Alan Stewart and his wife, Catriona." His eyes met Cassie's. "Like you, Brae's a time-traveler. She was originally born eighty years ago in 1201."

"Oh wow." She nodded at Brae. "Nice to meet you."

Brae's eyes flickered to their entwined hands and she quickly masked disappointment as she managed a too-bright smile. "Nice to meet ye as well, lass." She met Logan's eyes. "It seems ye've been busy since last we met."

"Aye." He squeezed Cassie's hand before he pulled away. "Is it safe to assume that yer the warriors following the wee Bruce?"

"'Tis." Brae put her fingers to her mouth and made a whistling sound. "For days now." A few more Stewart warriors trotted out of the woods and stopped behind her. "I figured 'twould only be a matter of time before ye caught up."

"Aye, lass," Rònan grunted, eyes roaming over her with flat-out lust. "I forgot what a feisty piece of—"

"Och, nay," Logan cut in. "We dinnae have time for yer sort of pleasantries, cousin." His eyes stayed with Brae's. "'Tis always good to see ye but I dinnae ken why yer here."

Brae swung onto her horse. "'Tis best I explain things once we catch up with the remainder of my warriors. We've kept the perfect distance behind the enemy and dinnae want to lose them."

Logan nodded and swung up behind Cassie, words soft in her ear. "We will be moving faster now. Just try to relax and adjust to the horse."

"Sure, no problem."

He wasn't kidding. The pace they set was much quicker despite the terrain. Though tempted to ask him more about Brae she did not. Furthermore, not only did the rough ride keep conversation to a minimum but she got the feeling he was deep in thought. Was it about the Scotswoman? Hard to know.

While she meant to tuck it in her pocket many times, Cassie still held the petunia. Too many times her eyes dropped to it and as Logan promised, she thought of the night before. The deep connection they had shared.

Then she thought of her confession that morning.

She had rallied the courage and finally came out with the truth. Most of it anyways. There were a few minor details she had not shared yet. But at least he had the most important facts about her now. Or just the main one. Because it was a zinger to be sure. His reaction, however, shocked her. While she didn't necessarily think he would shun her for going blind because he totally wasn't that sort of guy, she had not expected his words. Or the heartfelt look in his eyes when he said them.

"When the time comes ye will excel at whatever ye set yer mind to but why not face this here with me? Ye dinnae need to go through this alone. I will help ye every step of the way. We'll go through this together."

What made her so special that he would remain with her when she would become so dependent on him? Well, at least dependent at first. She ground her jaw. Hopefully not at all. For over a year now she had been buying self-help books to work on changing her way of thinking. Going blind was just another phase of life. One that she would face with courage and grace. She would stay strong and not be a hindrance to anyone. That in mind, she could imagine with confidence that she was a good catch by any man's standards.

Or so she kept trying to convince herself.

At some point, she must have dozed off because when her eyes snapped open, Logan's hand was wrapped around hers and the petunia as they slowed. Several other clansmen were mingled throughout; the color of their plaids different than the MacLomains.

Brae crouched in front of a small stream and splashed water on her face. "'Tis best if a few of us break off and have the bulk follow a ways behind." She looked over her shoulder at Logan. "'Twould also be best to keep Cassie with the majority of your soldiers. I dinnae like the feel of these warriors we seek."

Logan swung down and pulled Cassie after him, hands at her waist while she adjusted to standing.

"Nay, she must stay with me," Logan said. "She is too important to this quest."

"Quest," Brae murmured then stood, hands on her hips as she eyed them.

"Aye, quest." Logan urged Cassie to drink from the stream before he did the same then splashed water over his head.

Grant joined them and finally gave Brae a hug as well. "Good to see ye, lass. I thought it best to let ye greet the youngin's first."

The youngin's of course being Logan's cousins who now leaned against a nearby rock. Niall and Rònan were still ogling Brae for all they were worth. Darach, however, had his eyes trained on Cassie. She was sort of surprised he still seemed so interested despite Logan. Maybe he was not aware that she had slept with his cousin. Or maybe he didn't care.

"Yer aging well, ye are." Brae grinned broadly at Grant. "How fares Aunt Sheila?"

"Good, she'll be eager to see ye if ye'll be stopping by this visit, such as it is."

"Mayhap." Brae's eyes flickered over Logan. "'Twould be nice if I could call this home and stay amongst ye all."

"Ye can lass," Niall and Rònan said at the same time.

Brae waved their words away, eyes meeting Logan's when he stood. "Aye, only if the Laird sees through the promise he made me so long ago."

Promise?

"Och, lass." He chuckled, seemingly unaffected by the purposeful look in the Scotswoman's eyes. "What were we, six winters when we made that promise? Besides, ye dinnae want to marry the likes of me when ye've half of Scotland's lads for the taking."

"A promise is a promise, Logan MacLomain." Brae clucked her tongue. "And yers was that I'd be yer lass if ye didnae marry yer betrothed, aye?"

Oh, flipping wonderful. Cassie's eyes went to Logan. How many women was he supposed to marry?

"I couldnae handle the likes of ye, Brae Stewart." Logan didn't seem fazed in the least by her declaration as he offered a good-natured wink. "Considering I'd have to fight off my bloody cousins on a daily basis."

Brae quirked her lips at Niall and Rònan then shook her head. "See how hard ye make it for me to woo the laird, ye beasties."

They offered wide smiles in return.

"Besides," Logan continued, pulling Cassie against his side. "My heart's been taken by another."

Her face burned as everyone reacted to that. Brae's eyes narrowed slightly. Grant grunted and muttered something. Darach's usual happy demeanor fell flat. Rònan nudged Niall and cracked a grin. "So he's already had her then, aye?"

Niall smirked. "Aye, 'twas no quiet exchange either."

"Enough," Logan said, glowering at them.

She wished a sinkhole would open up and swallow her whole. The quicker, the better.

Apparently done with pursuing Logan for the moment, Brae asked anyone willing to answer, "How fares Uncle Bradon?" She pulled a healthy pink rose from her satchel. "When ye see him be sure to tell him his Brae still carries the rose he gave me when I was a wee bairn and he and Aunt Leslie visited the Stewart Castle."

"He's well," Darach said before he strode off.

That must have been part of Leslie and Bradon's adventure. Still so strange to realize they had been here before her. And it seemed preserving flowers was a MacLomain wizard trait.

Machara joined them and stretched before she crouched and splashed water on her face. Save being tossed over a horse by the woman, Cassie had barely seen her on the journey. She got the feeling Machara liked to do her own thing. Probably best considering the friction that could snap to life between her and Logan.

Machara stood and assuaged Brae's earlier concern. "I'll protect Cassie when we pursue the enemy so ye need not worry."

"Aye, 'tis good that," Brae said with humor. "Because last I remember ye wouldnae protect anything that made yer Laird happy."

Machara shrugged. "That hasnae changed any. But I *will* always protect the MacLomain chieftain and sometimes 'tis best to do that by protecting who he might worry over when battling."

"So now that we've established all that," Grant said, a less-than-impressed octave to his voice. "'Tis time to know why you're here, Brae."

"'Tis simple that," Brae responded. "Scotland's future king is in trouble, is he not?"

"Aye, but how did ye know that?"

"Ye forget that my Da's a wizard and my Ma's a mystic." Brae shrugged. "So it cannae be a big surprise that they knew of something so important happening."

"Eighty years in their future," Grant said. "Was it Adlin that told them then?"

"I dinnae think so." Brae swung onto her horse. "I havnae seen him in years."

"That means nothing." Grant's horse fell in beside Brae's as Logan pulled Cassie onto his and followed.

"So what precisely did yer parents tell ye?" Grant continued.

"Just that the future king o' Scotland was in jeopardy and I needed to help the MacLomains save him."

"So why was it ye didnae come straight away to the MacLomain castle?"

"'Twas just poor timing I suppose," she said. "By the time I got here he had already been taken. It made more sense to pursue him, aye?"

"Aye, mayhap," Grant murmured.

Cassie got the sense Brae was not being entirely truthful and suspected Grant felt the same way. Though the two continued to converse, their words were too soft to hear. After a while, Rònan fell in beside her and Logan. Any humor he'd entertained at the stream had vanished. Instead, there was a hard set to his jaw as he scanned the forest ahead. "I get an odd sense about all of this, cousin."

"Aye," Logan replied. "What does your dragon tell you?"

"That this kidnapping doesnae only have to do with Robert but with the MacLomains and mayhap even my MacLeods."

Cassie felt Logan tense. "But not the Hamilton's?"

"'Tis hard to say for sure but the dragon within is restless. That means its immediate kin is in harm's way." Rònan's brows lowered and his lips pulled down. "And I am half MacLeod and half MacLomain. Not Hamilton."

"What make you then of the mention of the oak ford?" Logan's tone shifted. "After all, 'tis an oak at the heart of your history. Two oaks at that. Though not technically at a ford, they were bloody close to a waterfall."

"I dinnae like it." Rònan shook his head. "Yet we are heading in the opposite direction of the baby oak's mother."

Though it probably wasn't the best timing, Cassie could not hold her tongue any longer as she looked at Rònan. "So we're heading away from the baby oak as well?"

He shook his head. "Nay, the baby oak is the tree you saw outside the MacLomain castle."

"So the baby oak and the mother oak obviously aren't near one another," she said. "So someone transplanted the small oak then?"

"Nay," Logan said. "'Twas magic that moved it."

Amazing. "Why?"

"Likely because my Ma wanted her kin well protected," Rònan said. "That oak was born of an acorn from the mother oak, a tree brought here from Ireland by the Celtic gods." He nodded at Brae, eyes flickering to Logan. "There is something more to her being here as well. Something to do with those rings."

"Aye," Logan murmured.

"What rings?" Cassie held up her hand. "This ring?"

"Aye," Logan said. "'Twas the coupling of Brae's parents beneath the mother oak with the help of the god Fionn Mac Cumhail that first ignited the power of the original Claddagh rings. Some have long speculated that Brae herself might have been conceived that verra day."

"And if that is the case then 'tis hard to know what gifts Brae might possess," Rònan said.

"That's incredible," Cassie said. "But wouldn't you guys, wizards..." She looked at Rònan. "And dragon shifters be able to sense what magic she has?" She nodded ahead. "If no one else can, Grant should be able to right?"

"Though he didnae take place in the intimate sense, a Celtic god was involved," Logan said. "Powers such as that lying dormant in a lass would be undetectable by even the most powerful of wizards and dragon-shifters alike. 'Tis verra likely that Brae herself wouldnae even know."

"I'll be damned," she murmured.

"Interesting that her twin brother, Cullen isnae along with Brae for something so important," Logan mentioned.

Rònan's eyes were on Brae's back. This time there was no lust in their brilliant green depths but a smidge of wariness. "The last I knew, the one sibling didnae do much without the other."

"Aye." Logan's arm tightened slightly around Cassie as though he needed her closer. "Nor has she mentioned him."

"You can be sure Grant's asking about him."

The men quieted after that, but Cassie felt the tension that settled over them. As far as she could tell only twenty or so men stayed with them as the rest fell behind. Yet if there was one thing she had learned it was that Logan's men always had an eye on him whether or not they could be seen.

Petunia tucked safely away in her satchel, she kept twisting the ring on her finger. It was hard to imagine how it had come into creation. This brought her mind back to the third ring that had been in the box at the Colonial in New Hampshire. She looked at Logan. "You spoke of a Celtic god being present when the three rings were created. What of the fourth? Was there a druidess there as well?"

"Nay, as the story is told and 'tis truly one I thought simply folklore, the ring was given to Chiomara the druidess after she and

King Erc gave up their unborn child, Adlin MacLomain, to the goddess Brigit. A bairn who was conceived beneath the mother oak when it was still in Ireland." Logan sounded troubled. "I cannae imagine the ring's power or why it has appeared alongside the others."

Absolutely baffling.

All of this.

From the gods to the rings to the magic.

She again eyed the ring, trying to quell anxiety. How was she part of all this? Sure, she could see and hear Robert but how did it relate to the ring? Why was she so privileged to be wearing it? Because that's how she felt. Though nervous about its meaning, she was definitely honored. But for what, she had no idea.

Did she want it to somehow proclaim she was supposed to be with Logan? Yes...and no. Yes, because she had never met another like him and would love to spend her life getting to know him better. No, because despite what he said and despite her determination to be otherwise, she still worried about being a burden after she went blind.

When Grant slowed his horse, Logan and his cousins joined the arch-wizard. All swung down from their mounts as Logan pulled her off his. Expressions stern, everyone started strapping on weapons.

Logan wrapped her hand around the hilt of a dagger, his eyes never more serious. "Niall and I have taught you how to use this but 'tis best that you try to stay near Machara and out of harm's way. If you have to use it, do so calmly. The enemy will take advantage of any weakness they see in your eyes." He wrapped his hand more firmly around hers and the hilt, eyes unwavering. "You think only of your need to set Robert free. Draw on that to see you through any strife that might arise. *He* is what you do this for, aye?"

"Yes," she said as firmly as she could manage, eyes dropping to the blade.

Logan tilted up her chin until their eyes locked again. "Do not let anything else distract you. Not me, Grant, Darach, nobody. We can take care of ourselves and most certainly you if we're able. Do you ken?" His thumb brushed over her chin. "Protect your own life first so that you might better protect the Bruce."

"Okay," she whispered but knew he needed to hear a stronger response so nodded and mustered all the courage she had. "I'll keep a level head."

Logan's eyes searched hers for a long moment before he nodded and pulled away. Machara joined them then everything after that became a quiet unit of men communicating not with words but gestures. The area of woods they were in was chopped up by numerous huge stones and fairly steep inclines. Her impression was that they weren't all that far away from a mountain but because of the tree cover it was hard to tell.

Machara gestured that Cassie stay close as they veered up onto a ledge that ran horizontally to a heavy row of shrubbery. Logan and his cousins ducked down the other side and vanished into the trees. The women only traveled for a few more minutes over rocky ground before Machara crouched and pulled Cassie to her side. She put a finger to her lips and pointed down.

A long trail of heavily armed men on horseback trudged through a shallow valley thick with golden pine needles and trees. Her eyes locked on the small boy with a sack over his head.

Robert.

Eager to get to him, she started to stand, but Machara pulled her down, fixed her with a deadly stare, and shook her head. Cassie nodded and eyed the group more closely. As far as she could tell, there were at least thirty men riding in pairs and possibly more ahead. She would swear that Robert was still on the man's horse she had seen in her vision. What she wouldn't do to be able to communicate with him now. To let him know that they were here and he would be all right.

The enemy appeared unaware that they were likely surrounded but then it seemed Logan and his cousins were very good at stealth. As much as she peered at the surrounding forest, she saw no one. All was quiet save the chirping of birds. So softly she barely heard her, Machara pulled free a bow and cocked an arrow, eyes narrowed on the enemy.

Heart hammering, Cassie barely drew a breath. What if Robert got hurt during the attack? Logan had told her to keep him in mind but had never mentioned who precisely would be focusing on the child when the shit hit the fan. Wouldn't the men be battling it out with the enemy? Wouldn't that leave Robert vulnerable?

There was little time to further contemplate before arrows whistled through the air. *Thump. Thump. Thump.* Three men fell. Then everything happened so fast she could barely take it in. Though caught unaware, the enemy was clearly experienced as they quickly took up formation and met Logan and his warriors in a clash of blades.

Meanwhile, Machara started to unleash arrows. Cassie realized she was hitting anyone who came too close to Logan without him being aware. Yet there seemed to be few of those. Like his cousins, he was ferocious as he swung his sword and cut down several. However, unlike his cousins, he had an almost calm, methodical way of killing. It was as if he thought about exactly how he intended to kill the next man while still fighting his current prey.

As she had figured might be the case, there were a whole lot more of the enemy than could initially be seen. Rònan and Niall seemed to work as a pair, slicing and dicing too many warriors to count. Out of all of them, Darach appeared to have the most finesse. If that word could be applied to such brutal battling. His method almost seemed like a dance as he ducked and swiped his leg, knocking a man off his feet while running his dagger through another.

She had never seen so much blood and death as cries rang out. Palms slick, she tried to follow everything that was happening, but there was too much activity. This was unlike anything she had seen on television. You didn't hear the gurgles of men with slashed throats or smell the tang of blood and the pungent odor of loosened feces wafting on the wind. You didn't hear the murmurs to God before men's eyes glazed over or hear the crack of bones when someone was crushed beneath a horse.

Heart in her throat, body shaking, Cassie's eyes were not on the other men long. No, they were inevitably drawn back to Logan. Stark fear for him had her mouth dry and heart nearly beating out of her chest. Yet she had assured him she would remain calm and focused.

And she would.

Had to.

So she set aside concern for Logan and kept her eyes locked on little Robert. The warrior he was riding with was well protected by his fellowmen as he spurred his horse and raced into the forest. At the same time, an onslaught of the enemy raced in from where Robert's captor had vanished.

Hundreds of them.

"Bloody hell," Machara muttered under her breath as she shot arrow after arrow. "'Tis an ambush on an ambush."

The MacLomain warriors who had been following at a distance finally arrived, rushing down into the maelstrom of war. But God, were there enough? Machara was about to shoot off another arrow when there was a flurry of activity behind them.

The Scotswoman spun fast, narrowed her eyes and shot. Arrow lodged in his gut, a man fell to his knees but not before he whipped a dagger at Cassie. She barely processed what was happening until Machara pushed her out of the way and took the blade in her shoulder.

More of the enemy rushed forward. Believe it or not, the Scotswoman was by no means defeated by the dagger. Pulling it free with a grunt, she tossed it aside and started clashing swords with a man, all the while standing in front of Cassie.

"He wants the one with the sight," the enemy spat to his fellow warriors as he and Machara went at it.

The one with the sight? He couldn't possibly be talking about her could he?

Where they currently stood, Cassie was nearing the edge of a small cliff with about a fifteen-foot drop. She peered over and knew going that way would mean a few broken bones. Her eyes swept over the area before she spied a small path. It was steep, but definitely a means out of here. Not that she intended to take it. No way. Not if it meant leaving Machara alone to fight one, two, three, nope, here came a fourth. *Too* many men.

Dagger at the ready, Cassie positioned herself next to Machara and prepared to fight.

"Nay, ye bloody fool," Machara said to her as she whipped a dagger at one of the men, catching him in the thigh while she kept fighting another. Though blood poured from her wound, her jaw was set and a severe glint shone in her eyes. She made a come-hither motion at the other men while shooting a few direct words at Cassie. "Ye know what ye need to do, lass. Take the path. Now."

Machara wanted her to go after Robert.

Or she knew she would die if she stayed here.

"Absolutely not," Cassie said. "There are too many of them."

Machara swung her blade on Cassie, ducking as a warrior's sword swooped over her head. Eyes narrowed to slits, she ground out, "I'll run ye through now if ye dinnae go." Then she sneered, as ferocious as her MacLomain male counterparts. "And dinnae think I willnae, lass."

Cassie stumbled back a few steps when Machara simultaneously drove the sword at her while side-kicking a man in the groin. Holy warrior woman!

Well aware that there was nothing but destruction in the Scotswoman's eyes, she listened. Half sliding, half scrambling, she ignored the scrape of pebbles on her hands and shins and made it down quickly. When she glanced up, she wasn't able to see anything but she still heard the clash of blades and Machara's endless cursing.

Time to focus on what Machara had seemingly sacrificed herself for and it was not Cassie. It was Robert. She rubbed slick palms over her dress and grasped her blade tighter as she crouched and kept moving along a line of thick brush. Heavy fighting could be heard everywhere but by pure luck she managed to stay on an empty path.

An odd haze of calm settled over her even though she should be scared to death. She was surprised she wasn't frozen with fear. Instead, she managed to put one foot in front of the other until she was running in the general direction Robert had gone.

Cassie kept repeating the same words in her mind, hoping that he might somehow hear them. *"I'm coming, Robert. I'm right behind you."*

"Cassie," whispered through her mind. *"Where are ye, my lass."*

Was that Logan? Was he talking to her within the mind like Athdara did? No sooner did she think it her horse appeared. When her voice entered Cassie's mind, she knew for certain Athdara had *not* spoken to her before.

"Get on," Athdara said.

Cassie swung up. *"Thanks for coming."*

"Aye, where else would I be?" Athdara launched forward, swerving around random warriors as they entered the heart of the fighting. *"Stay low and hold on tight."*

Unlike the last time they had done this 'mad race through the woods thing' together, Cassie felt no fear. Her entire focus was on catching up with Robert. Nothing else mattered. She concentrated not on the death and destruction around her but kept her eyes locked on the path ahead. Thin, spindly branches rushed by her, but she ignored their sting as she relaxed into the flow of the horse.

Within minutes, they broke from the forest and raced across a sprawling hill. Part of a band of about fifteen men, Robert was nearly on the other side. Maybe it was her imagination but though the sound of battle was fading into the distance, Cassie thought she heard several horses in pursuit.

Long grass blew in the wind but did not slow Athdara down as she flew after Robert. *"They flee toward great magic, lass. Either they will continue or turn and confront ye soon. Either way, stay brave and know that I am here as is Logan. Ye are not alone."*

Strange how Athdara's words seemed to echo Logan's, how they gave her the same sense of comfort and security. Because truly, how much could a horse really do when it came to fighting men? They had just topped the hill when the enemy did as Athdara suspected they might. They stopped and swung back. She could not help but notice that they were back-dropped by two towering oaks with a wide river running behind them.

An oak tree ford.

As it turned out, it had not been her imagination when she thought she heard hooves behind her. Logan, his cousins, Brae and Grant stopped beside her as Athdara came to a sudden halt. Though she thought at first it was because the enemy was heading back in their direction she could not have been more wrong.

No, a woman had just staggered onto the field between them and the enemy.

Baffled, terrified, her disbelieving eyes met Nicole's.

Chapter Fourteen

EYES NARROWED, LOGAN tried to make sense of what he was seeing. He knew based on her clothing and Cassie's reaction that the woman staggering onto the field had to be her friend from the future.

"Something is wrong here," Grant said softly. "And I dinnae refer to the lass."

Short, dark red hair blowing in her face, the woman cried out, "Cassie?"

"Nicole?" When Cassie swung down, Logan did the same, grabbing her arm before she got too far.

His cousins remained on their horses, but he knew they were as torn between curiosity and distrust as he was. For all intents and purposes, the battle they'd just fought had been well orchestrated by the enemy. Planned. It had been a war that intended to slow down the MacLomain's or anyone who dared to get in their way. Just like the siege of the MacLauchlin castle. Everything was a detour meant to get them to this moment.

Brae and Grant swung off their horses and joined them.

"Tread carefully with yer friend, lass," Brae murmured. "There is something unnatural at work here."

Logan kept a firm hand on Cassie's wrist and focused on the approaching enemy then further on to the oak tree ford.

"My friend is out there." Cassie's worried eyes shot to his. "You need to go get her before the other guys do!"

Grant looked at him and shook his head.

The air felt different. Not gusty and warm as it had been moments before but with a bite of chill and thickness. Great magic was at work here. A darkness he did not recognize.

True evil.

Regrettably, Nicole never looked around but strode a little off center in their general direction. If he wasn't mistaken, she was intoxicated.

Bloody hell. Bradon and his whisky.

"Does the lass have no sense about her then?" Rònan grumbled, his horse restless as he shifted, clearly undecided whether or not he should head her way.

"It doesnae seem it," Niall responded, a touch of incredulousness in his tone.

Cassie shook her head. It seemed she finally understood the gravity of the situation because she yelled, "Stop, Nics."

Strangely enough, this made the lass stop short, a disgruntled expression on her face as she mouthed, "Nics?"

Cassie pointed at the enemy. Though she wobbled and hiccupped, Nicole's slightly glazed eyes turned and she froze as much as one could when in their cups.

"You can't just leave her out there like that," Cassie whispered. "Especially not in her current state."

No, he could not. But what the hell was he supposed to do when he sensed the enemy had a trick up their sleeve? Though the man with Robert on his horse held back, the others fanned out in front of them. Weapons drawn, they drew closer and closer. Logan knew without a doubt that these men were the best the enemy had to offer. They had to be to have survived the hellfire he and his cousins brought down on them. That made the mission even more dangerous if their Laird was willing to sacrifice some of his best men to get what he wanted. Trained, hardened warriors, their eyes were filled with death and emptiness. They had *nothing* to lose.

"They've the power of the gods behind them," Brae warned, voice low. "A darkness in the divine ye never could have imagined existed."

"And yer just telling us this now?" Logan ground out, pulling Cassie closer.

"I wasnae sure until just now," Brae whispered. Her eyes were trained not on the warriors but on the oak tree ford Robert's captor was slowly backing toward.

"Something needs to happen," Cassie said. "You can't let Nicole get hurt or the guy with Robert get away."

"Nay," Athdara's words whispered through his mind. *"Ye cannae, lad."*

Logan had half a second to understand what the horse intended before she reared up, released a mighty neigh and took off toward the enemy. After that, everything happened fast. When Athdara went plowing ahead, the enemy assumed they were on the move.

Eyes wide with terror, Nicole started running toward Cassie.

"After Robert," Logan roared.

Grant grabbed his arm and shook his head sharply. "Let yer cousins go. Ye stay here with yer lass where I can best protect ye."

Logan was about to argue but stopped when the Hamilton's eyes glowed blue and his expression grew fierce. Even if he wanted to, he could not get around the arch-wizard's magic right now. Meanwhile, Darach, Rònan, and Brae were already rushing ahead and slamming their blades against the enemy's.

Niall, muttering the whole way about foolish, drunken lasses, raced in Nicole's direction. Eyes round as saucers, she stumbled back as his horse thundered toward her. He had nearly reached her when a man cut him off and they started crossing blades. The enemy was skilled, but regrettably he was meeting Niall not when his cousin felt battle lust but was plain old grumpy. And when Niall grew especially moody—a trait he had inherited from his Da, Malcolm—men went down very quickly beneath his sword.

As Logan knew would be the case, Niall's blade made a clean stab through the center of the man's neck in under thirty seconds. Nicole wasn't just stumbling back anymore but had plunked down on her arse as Niall swung down and strode in her direction.

"Shoot, I hope she realizes he's the good guy," Cassie muttered, upset.

"I dinnae think there's much good about him right now," Logan said.

True to form, Niall growled as he caught Nicole by her ankle before she could squirm away. Grabbing her around the waist, he swung her up into his arms. Cassie winced when he then proceeded to fling her squealing friend over his shoulder and strode for his horse.

"Who the *fuuuuckkkk* do you think you are? Put me down you jackass," Nicole slurred, trying to pound on his back and hold on at the same time.

Logan shook his head, eyes torn between their fiasco and the battle his remaining cousins were warring. Meantime, Nicole must have done something to Niall because he grunted with pain and stumbled. At the same moment, an enemy warrior came swinging at him. In his attempt to hold onto a flailing Nicole and swing back at the man, Niall dropped to his knee and Nicole went flying. Cassie and Logan flinched as she thumped down on her back in front of him.

Under different circumstances, the scene would have been almost comical.

"Bloody hell, I'm not the enemy, lass. On my honor, I will protect ye," Niall roared, fighting the man from the ground as he partially covered Nicole.

"I'll bet you anything she can't hear a word he's saying," Cassie murmured.

"Why is that?"

"Because on occasion she runs hard of hearing."

Crash. Crash. Niall's blade was criss-crossing back and forth as he simultaneously tried to keep Nicole from squirming away while fighting the enemy. The twenty-first century woman seemed to have sobered up fast as she half screamed, half sputtered.

"This is insane," Cassie cried at Grant. "Let us go help them!"

Grant shook his head. The wizard wasn't going to budge an inch.

"But we need to save Robert," she argued. "Isn't his life more important than ours?"

"'Tis far too dangerous right now." Caught within his magic, Grant's response sounded far away. "I dinnae ken the magic being used. Ye, Logan and the ring willnae be put at risk."

Nicole appeared both furious and horrified as she clawed the ground then leapt to her feet. It was then that Logan saw it. "She wears a ring as well."

"Oh my God," Cassie whispered.

Grant's eyes narrowed on Nicole's finger. "Bloody *hell*."

Niall had just downed his man, cursing about foolish lasses that don't know when they're being protected, when Nicole was scooped up by another warrior. Rònan flung out his hand and a wide swath of fire lit a long line of grass, blocking the man from retreating.

Or so they had hoped.

The enemy chanted something and jumped the flames. When Niall started chanting, clouds formed quickly and rain gushed down, dousing the flames so that they could pursue. Darach was summoning wind in hopes to slow the enemy, but it didn't seem to be working.

The man with Nicole had nearly caught up with the man who had Robert. They were only a few feet away from the oak tree ford.

Grant narrowed his eyes on Logan and Cassie. "If either of ye move it'll be the death of ye by *my* hand. Do ye ken?"

Though frustrated, Logan nodded his consent. He had never seen this particular look in Grant's eyes and was not about to test it. Arm wrapped tightly around Cassie, he pulled her back a few steps as the Hamilton strode across the field, flung his arms in the air and started chanting.

The enemy had been defeated save the two who had just made it to the ford. Robert was struggling and Nicole was being just as defiant with the man who held her now as she had been with Niall.

Something strange was happening between the two trees that had nothing to do with Grant's magic. And it was not in their favor. The air seemed to be compressing, blurring everything beyond it. Almost like a hot summer mirage but a hundred times more intense.

"Athdara, get back," Logan said into the horse's mind when she got far too close.

She did not respond.

"What's Athdara *doing*?" Cassie said, voice trembling.

"It seems she's trying to help," he murmured, rubbing Cassie's arms in an attempt to soothe her.

The horse was in the thick of the turbulent magic as she tried to spook the enemy's horses to run in the opposite direction. However, it didn't seem to be working. Then several things started to happen at once. Just as the enemy's magic grew more intense, Nicole managed to fling herself from the horse. Athdara tried to protect her but the other horse reared up and she had no choice but to back away.

Cassie started talking, eyes glazed. "I hear you, Robert. It's okay. We're going to save you."

Logan didn't like her telepathically communicating with the bairn with so much foreign magic around him but had no way of severing the bond.

"The woman you hear is Nicole," Cassie explained. "She's a friend."

The magic surrounding Robert and Nicole had ripped them from sight.

"You got the sack off your head? That's really good," Cassie said to Robert. "What do you see?"

She went silent as she listened to his response.

Grant seemed to be losing the battle against whoever was taking them as heavy wind not of Darach's making started to whip harshly. The oaks swayed, their branches vanishing then reappearing as they bent in and out of the maelstrom between them.

Then, as quickly as it began, it ended and Cassie slumped.

Logan swept her into his arms and narrowed his eyes on the oak ford. It was as it had been before, trees swaying gently in the breeze. Head hung, Athdara stood alone. Everyone else and their horses had vanished.

Grant's words entered Logan's mind. *"Is Cassie all right?"*

Cassie's eyes remained glazed over. *"'Tis too soon to tell."*

Grant nodded then cursed as they headed for the ford. Whatever magic had been here was completely gone. Vanished. Still, the Hamilton halted everyone before they got there and double checked. When satisfied that it was safe, he waved them over. Crouching in front of Athdara, Grant placed his hand against her forehead.

Logan was surprised when Cassie stirred, eyes a little less unfocused as she murmured, "I can hear you, Athdara."

"As far as I can tell, Athdara sleeps." Grant's eyes went to Cassie then Logan. "I cannae hear her. Can ye?"

"Nay." Logan shook his head. "It seems only my lass can."

Almost as if she was responding to his words, Cassie blinked a few times. Her eyes cleared then she peered around almost frantically until her gaze locked on the horse. "Something's wrong with Athdara."

"Aye." Logan carefully set her down and made sure she was steady before letting her go. She crouched next to Grant. "She's stuck sleeping." Cassie stroked her muzzle. "She doesn't want us to worry about her. And she's fairly certain Nicole made it back to the twenty-first century."

"Well, at least that part of my magic worked," Grant grumbled. "Did she say anything else?"

"Just to keep an eye on my lad."

Logan frowned. Odd thing for the horse to say.

Grant stood and pulled Cassie up. "We will stay here for the night in hopes that she awakens soon."

Cassie nodded, concern in her eyes as they lingered on Athdara before she looked around with alarm. "So Robert's not here." She shook her head, more and more worried. "I was hoping somehow he would be."

Logan took her hand. "You spoke with him. He'd managed to get the sack off his head. What did he say?"

Her eyes met his. "That he was at another oak inside a cave."

Brae made an indiscernible sound and Grant's eyes shot to her. "What know ye, lass? What is this evil of the gods that ye spoke of before? Because I only know of one oak that grows inside a cave."

The mother oak.

Brae leaned back against a tree, eyes sadder than before as they flickered over him and his cousins before landing on Grant. "I know the evil is somehow harnessed from the gods because 'tis Cullen at the heart of it. 'Tis my brother."

"Nay." Grant shook his head. "That cannae be. He would never…" His words trailed off at the defeated look in Brae's eyes. "I dinnae ken. He was such a good lad."

"We dinnae know what happened," Brae murmured. "All we know is that he tapped into a power that even Ma and Da cannae harness. Whatever was in it changed him."

"Yet ye knew he was coming here," Grant said. "How?"

"And what does he want with the rings," Rònan added. "Because I know they're part of this."

"Like me, he's connected to the rings via my parent's role in their creation. We dinnae ken why he wants them save mayhap because of the power they possess." Her eyes stayed with Grant. "Cullen has become verra powerful. The magic he's tapped into has made him a visionary amongst other things. That's how he knew about Robert the Bruce and what he would do for this country. He became fascinated at first by the King's timeline, but something turned fascination to obsession. He started having episodes, trances almost, where he would speak of the Bruce when he was a wee bairn. How he'd been given an opportunity to see Scotland's future changed."

Logan frowned heavily, eyes on Grant. "Is this from the same source in which ye learned of the wee Bruce?"

The Hamilton shook his head. "There is no way to know. 'Tis doubtful."

"Did ye learn of Robert from the gods then, Da?" Darach said.

"Nay." Grant's eyes swept over them before landing on Brae. "Only one man knew what was to come and as far as I know I am the only one he told."

"Adlin MacLomain," Brae murmured.

"Aye," Grant said. "But then 'tis likely his information came from the Celtic gods." His eyes narrowed on Brae. "Why did ye not share all of this with us sooner?"

"Because I had hoped my parents were wrong when they sent me." Intense pain shimmered in her eyes. "Cullen is my twin brother. My best friend. Ye cannae begin to ken how I feel right now." Her hand went to her chest. "'Tis torture hating and loving someone so much. To feel so betrayed." Her eyes met Logan's. "I cannae tell ye how sorry I am for his actions…and for not telling ye sooner."

"Och, lass, ye were but following yer heart. Me and mine dinnae hold that against ye."

Her eyes went to his cousins and as he knew they would, all gave her reassuring nods. Yet, like him, he knew they were hurting. Though they had not seen him as much as they would have liked over the years, Cullen had been family to them all. It was baffling to think of him as the enemy.

"'Tis a sad thing for ye and yer parents." Grant sighed. "Hopefully we will see this through to a good outcome and have our Cullen returned to us from wherever his muddled mind has gone."

Logan looked at Cassie. "Did you actually *see* where Robert was?"

"Not this time." She shook her head. "All he said was that a big oak grew inside the cave from outside and that there was a man there." Cassie shivered. "He was upset that they didn't have the lass with sight with them. It was the same thing the guy said back there…" Her brows lowered and her eyes widened as she looked back the way they had come. "Oh no, Machara. She was hurt!"

When she started walking that way he stopped her. "Machara is well enough. I can sense her. She knows how to take care of herself."

"You're sure?" Cassie said, heart in her eyes. "Because she saved my life."

Logan nodded. "I'm sure. You will see her soon enough."

"What exactly was said back there about a lass with sight?" Grant asked Cassie.

"Just that they were supposed to grab her." She bit her bottom lip as her eyes met Logan's. "They were talking about me, weren't they?"

"It seems likely," he murmured, upset but unwilling to show her as much. "But they willnae get you as long as I draw breath."

Her body trembled as he wrapped a comforting arm around her shoulders.

"As I said before, we will make camp here this eve. There is nothing left of the enemy in these parts," Grant said. "If my magic worked enough to get Nicole back to the twenty-first century then 'tis likely the other bit o' magic worked as well. 'Twas a binding spell that they will have to muddle through before they can leave wherever they ended up. That will give us some time to get to the oak."

"Though a silly lass, are ye sure Nicole is safely in the twenty-first century?" Niall asked. "Because I'm honor bound to see the crazy little thing safe." He rubbed his lower back, grumbling, "Never have I felt a pinch like that. Bloody nails like daggers."

"'Twas a pinch that brought ye down then?" Rònan said, mirth in his eyes.

"Did ye see how bloody—"

"That's enough," Cassie cut in. Pulling away from Logan, she crossed her arms over her chest. "While I'm thankful you tried to save Nicole, Niall, you better not say another damn word against her. For your information, she was probably loaded because she was stressed about me going missing and I'm sure Bradon made sure she calmed down with whisky. And you might as well know now that there's a good chance she didn't hear anything you said to her." Cassie's voice grew softer. "Because she occasionally has trouble with her hearing."

This caught Grant's attention, but he made no comment.

Niall frowned. "Her hearing?"

"Yes." Cassie's eyes went to Logan before she sighed and looked at his cousins. "There's a reason I connected with Nicole, Erin, and Jaqueline." She took a deep breath as she rallied her courage. "Like me, they're all facing something life-changing.

Where I'm going blind, Nicole might be going deaf. Erin and Jaqueline are also dealing with potential disabilities."

Quickly masked surprise flickered across their faces and silence fell as his cousins digested the information. Rònan, of all people, was the first to speak, reminding him why he loved these men so much. "Well, know this, lass. We will help ye every step of the way. Ye willnae go through yer battles alone."

"I've heard it said that when one sense goes the others grow much stronger," Darach volunteered. "Some say 'tis a powerful experience."

"Most dinnae know it about me but I've a way with words," Niall added. "I can describe things around ye in great detail when the time comes."

"A way with words?" Rònan winked at Cassie as he spoke to Niall. "Ye've barely a way with a sword without a lass's pinch bringing ye to yer knees."

Cassie's eyes grew moist and she offered a wobbly smile. "Thanks, guys. You're sweet." She shook her head. "Sorry I didn't tell you about this stuff sooner. Honestly, I wasn't totally convinced about my friends being meant for," she gestured at them, "any of you, but now that Nicole's been here it seems it might be true. And while perhaps it's not my information to give I'd rather you have your facts up front before they travel back in time."

"Aye, 'twill be helpful," Niall agreed. "We will be gentler with them."

Cassie shook her head. "Oh, I wouldn't go that far. My friends are pretty independent and don't like being coddled. Hell, Nicole alone has dumped three guys in the past year for getting too mushy about her affliction.

Niall's brows perked. "Dumped?"

"Makes sense." Rònan chuckled. "She dumped ye with a good pinch, aye?"

"Not literally dumped." Cassie snorted. "Just stopped their involvement."

"She was bonnie enough to be sure, but 'twas probably best the lads got away from her," Niall muttered. "The lass is too wild by half."

Rònan grinned. "Aye, I'd like nothing better than to ride—"

Logan shook his head sharply and stopped the offensive words about to come from the MacLeod's mouth. "Nay, cousin."

"Och." Rònan snickered. "I was going to say that I'd take the bonnie lass for a ride on my *horse*." He shot Niall a crooked grin. "As many times as I could."

Niall shrugged, but Logan didn't miss the flicker of uneasiness in his eyes when he murmured, "She's all yours."

The remainder of the MacLomain and Stewart warriors were starting to arrive. Though leaving Cassie's side was the last thing he wanted to do, Logan had to attend to Lairdly duties. Cupping her cheek, he connected eyes with her. "I have to see to my men. Stay with either Grant or my cousins, okay? Dinnae wander off."

She nodded. "Sure, no worries."

Though tempted to ask Cassie how her vision was doing, he decided against it. He would have to feel her out as time passed. What was and was not acceptable when it came to her condition. He understood her need to not feel like a burden but at the same time he wanted her to open up to him and accept his assistance. It would be a delicate balance between her not feeling coddled and him being able to care for her the way he hoped to. *Needed* to.

So even as he mingled with his warriors, she was never far from his thoughts.

Thankfully, they had lost very few lives in the battle. His men had fought well and he could not be prouder. He made a point of speaking with every warrior, thanking them and offering words of encouragement. All the while, he kept his eyes open for Machara. Eventually, he came across her caring for a wounded man who had seemingly dozed off.

Though it was clear she tried to hide it, her hands shook slightly as she wiped a wet cloth across his forehead. Logan crouched beside her and frowned at the stain of blood blossoming beneath the makeshift tourniquet on her shoulder.

"Let him rest, lass." Logan took her elbow. "Come with me so that I can see to that wound."

When she scowled at him, he said. "That's an order."

Though she muttered under her breath the whole time, he managed to get her to sit on a rock. Logan scowled just as fiercely as he removed the tourniquet. "Ye didnae care for yerself properly, cousin." He waved at a nearby warrior then nodded at the stream that ran down to the larger river. "Bring me both a wet and dry cloth and a skin of whisky."

"'Tis fine," Machara bit off. "A minor wound if that."

Logan shook his head. "Ye'd get yer arm cut off and call it a scratch." After he received what he had asked for he was thorough about cleaning out the wound. Machara—stalwart warrior—barely flinched even when he poured whisky over it.

"I want to thank ye for protecting Cassie so well," he murmured as he wrapped a fresh cloth over her wound. "None could have protected her better."

"Aye, 'tis true enough," she mumbled, eyes avoiding his. "I assume she fares well then."

Logan nodded. Machara did not realize how appreciative he really was. How fearful he had been for Cassie's life during the battle. His cousin was his hero though she would never believe it if he told her. So instead he filled her in on everything that had happened. Every last detail. Because she was amongst his closest circle of warriors, the very best the MacLomain clan had to offer.

"So yer lass is going blind." Machara sighed, troubled. "'Tis a hard thing that." Her eyes at last met his and she shocked the hell out of him. "Well, if any can help a lass through such 'tis ye."

Logan knew if he thanked her for the compliment it would likely frustrate her and she would find a scathing comment to mask it with. So he simply said, "Aye, ye've the right o' it," before he stood and handed the remainder of the whisky to her. "Drink lass. 'Tis well deserved."

Machara grunted her agreement before he left. While he would have preferred to stay with her and mayhap talk for a bit, she wouldn't want it. At one time, they'd been friends, as close as he and his other cousins, but becoming Laird had ended that. He could only hope that someday she would forgive him.

The men who had lost their lives were buried and prayers murmured before everyone set up camp in the woods edging the field. Though he knew all would prefer to sleep beneath the open sky, it was always best to remain in a well-protected area. Especially considering the new threat they faced.

Not surprisingly, Cassie had stayed with Darach. They were sitting on the shore of the river when he joined them with a few skins of whisky. The sun had nearly set and deep crimson swaths swept over the water, rippling away as clouds started to roll overhead.

"Now I know you're safe enough, I'll leave you two be." Darach squeezed Cassie's hand, gaze affectionate and a smidge sad. "'Twas a good talk, lass. 'Twill be an equally good friendship betwixt us, aye?"

She smiled. "Definitely."

After he left, Logan handed her a skin. As always, he could not tear his eyes from her face. She had tied her hair back with a swath of plaid, but a few wisps blew around her neck, brushing her delicate collarbone. Her eyes shimmered a darker green, caught in the shadows of dusk.

Though he knew it was none of his business, he could not help but murmur, "That sounded serious."

Cassie took a sip and eyed him. "Actually, it sort of was."

Logan arched a brow. "Aye?"

She nodded. "Yup. I figured it was time to tell him that I wasn't interested in more than friendship with him."

He had never heard more satisfying words. "'Tis good that." His hand slid into hers. "Because I didnae want to have to battle him over you."

"I wouldn't have let it get that far." She shook her head. "It was just strange is all."

"Why?"

Cassie shrugged. "I dunno. I guess I'm not used to dealing with one guy interested in me let alone two."

"I dinnae ken." He cocked his head, accent thickening of its own accord. "Yer the loveliest lass I've ever laid eyes on. 'Tis no surprise that Darach feels the same."

"I appreciate the compliment but trust me, that hasn't been the general consensus with the guys back home." She pressed the tips of her forefingers to the back of her thumbs and formed circles around her eyes. "I've always worn these thick glasses that made my eyes look huge. Total turn off."

He grinned at the goofy expression on her face. "I can think of nothing better than magnifying those bonnie eyes."

Cassie chuckled. "You might think otherwise if you saw me wearing them."

"Did Darach see you wearing them?"

She nodded. "He did."

"It seems he thought you just as beautiful then as he does now."

"Yeah, I guess." She gave a little shrug. "But I get the feeling he's just into modern day women in general."

"So did he desire Nicole as well?"

"Hard to know," she murmured but he got the impression she *did* know and that Darach's interest was solely for Cassie.

Either way, he was glad she had been honest with his cousin. Darach deserved nothing less. And truth be told, he was glad that any potential competition was out of the way. He and Cassie might have slept together, but that by no means meant she had committed to him. That was something he would have to continue to work toward because she *would* be his.

"I wanted to thank you for sharing what you did with my cousins," he said. "About your friends that is. You didnae have to do that and I imagine it wasnae easy for you."

"No, it wasn't." She sighed. "But they deserved to know and whether or not the girls initially appreciate it, I don't want them to stress over telling whoever they might have to tell like I did with you. Erin and Jaqueline can share their specifics later, but at least the guys know something's up."

"I ken that." He eyed her, words soft. "This is half the reason you created your ancestry website, isn't it? To find those with not only a shared bloodline but a life changing event ahead of them."

Cassie nodded. "Yeah." She looked at him, bemused. "I always thought it was so strange how quickly they seemed to find me. Sure, I'd been having some visions but still. Then we all hit it off so well. Soon after we started planning weekly online chats and formed a little support group to help us get ready for what lay ahead."

A small smile blossomed on her face as she gazed at the water. "We'd watch a movie, listen to songs, try different foods, read or listen to books then share our thoughts. Really what we were doing was building a network of shared things we'd be able to chat about after we faced whatever we had to face. Sort of a bond where you knew that you had three best friends in the world that could remind you what so and so sounded like when they sang. Or how hot we thought this or that actor was."

Logan had never heard anything so amazing. "So this was your idea...because of the visions you had?"

200

"Yes. Ones that always seemed to have to do with Scotland, or should I say my Broun ancestry. Nothing definitive but a general sense that I would find the support I needed by seeking out more Brouns." Her eyes again met his. "I probably should have told you all of this sooner, but things have been a little overwhelming since I arrived. Yet coming here and having the visions I've had with Robert are starting to make me think maybe we four were always meant to come together." She eyed the ring. "Now more so than ever."

Logan brought the back of her hand to his lips, kissing the area just above her ring before he murmured, "Ye are here for a reason, lass and I can only hope that part of the reason is for me."

Cassie's breathing switched and her eyes glazed with desire for a moment. Apparently needing to switch the subject, she said, "How are the warriors doing? Machara especially?"

"Everyone is well including Machara. Game has been hunted and is roasting. I've set up a tent for us." He stood and pulled her up. "Come, night's nearly fallen. Let's head back in that direction."

Cassie nodded, a somewhat hesitant expression on her face as they walked along the river. "Since I was so straightforward about the conversation I had with Darach, mind if I ask you something?"

"Aye." He led her into the forest. "Anything."

"It's about Brae." Her eyes met his. "What is she to you exactly? Because it sort of sounds like you two had something going...or intended to."

Of course, she would have been wondering about the Stewart lass.

"Brae has always been like a sister to me." He chose his words carefully. "As you probably gathered, we spent a lot of time together as bairns. She knew of my pre-arranged marriage and always felt bad for me. Making the promise we did was really just her way of soothing a young lad's restlessness."

"Ah." Cassie pursed her lips and nodded. "You do realize that she's totally serious about fulfilling that promise." She hesitated a moment before continuing. "And you know that she's totally into you, right?"

He knew. Brae had not hesitated to let him know just how much upon greeting. Within the mind of course. But Logan had been clear about where he stood and it wasn't with Brae.

"The feeling isnae mutual." Determined that she understood how serious he was, Logan backed Cassie up against a thick tree and cupped her cheeks. "You need to ken that when I told you I wanted you, I had never said more truthful words. I didnae lay with you to slake my lust, lass. I laid with you because I'm in love with you."

Chapter Fifteen

CASSIE COULD BARELY see Logan it had grown so dark but she most certainly heard his words. *I'm in love with you.* While it was a serious declaration, her mind was saturated with insecurity and disbelief. Irritated with her lack of confidence that a man could love her she wished she murmured something like, "You have great taste. Makes sense." Instead, she whispered, "I find that hard to believe."

"Then find it hard to believe but 'tis true." His rough hands were achingly tender as he smoothed the pads of his thumbs over her cheekbones. "Did you hear me when you were riding Athdara through the battling? Did you know that we are far more mentally connected now than before?"

"What?" Her heart pounded into her throat. "Why?"

"Because we've lain together," he said softly. "'Tis a thing that happens with wizards."

Cassie tried to recall all her thoughts since last night, but it was hard remembering that sort of thing. Lord, that probably meant he knew how jealous she was of Brae. Then there was the constant stream of thoughts about having had sex with him. Super lusty ones that had no business in anyone's head but hers. *So* not good. "Have you been listening to all my thoughts then?"

Logan shook his head. "Nay, I would never do that unless you asked it of me." He cleared his throat and a smidge of desire met his words. "Though some slip through when they're especially intense."

Oh, God. She had been having tons of those. Rather than speculate, she blurted, "So are we talking about my fear during battle or maybe Nicole getting hurt or maybe even my concern about Athdara?"

"Nay," he murmured, one hand abandoning her cheek to drift down the side of her neck, his fingers splaying over her sensitive skin. "More like the way you can't catch your breath when I do this." Then a finger trailed down her chest, skimming so softly over her cleavage that gooseflesh radiated over her. "Or the way this sends shivers through you before everything starts to burn."

"I see," she managed, voice raspy as she tried to stay focused on…what exactly?

"Love," whispered through her mind.

Love. Right. She closed her eyes and shook her head. Impossible. Yet her mind was fluttering after the word like a bird taking flight. Eager. Curious. Free. *His* word. Entrenched within her mind.

Unlike Athdara's voice, Logan's seemed to wrap deep into her soul, giving her a glimpse of his own. It was made of honor and loyalty, of deep, rich feelings that he did not shy away from but embraced. As she surmised from the start, Logan knew his own heart and could never, not for a moment, be persuaded by anyone not to follow and believe in it. Though she had no idea how she knew, he absolutely meant what he said.

He *was* in love with her.

Warm, embracing, his love showed her flickers of all the moments they had shared. The way he could not get enough of the light that entered her eyes when she laughed. The way her oftentimes blunt words stirred his emotions and kept him enthralled. How beautiful he found her inside and out.

Those were the sensations swirling at the surface of his feelings.

The deeper he took her, the more she saw. How proud he was of her courage and commitment to Robert. How impressed he was by her willingness to travel on such a difficult journey and learn how to wield weapons. Her endless concern for those around her when her own life was constantly at risk.

It was one of the final emotions he had that brought tears to her eyes.

How incredibly courageous he found her strength in facing her number one fear. Blindness. He did not see her upcoming disability as a hindrance to himself in the least. Rather he saw it as an opportunity to help someone he respected conquer and succeed at what they had to face. He viewed it not as a potential weakness but something that would only make her stronger. It didn't matter in the least how long he had known her, he wanted to be an intimate, loving part of her life.

"You really do love me," she whispered.

"Aye, verra much," he murmured by her ear.

The incline of the root structure gave her a height advantage and put him only three or four inches taller than her rather than just under a foot. Still, it had become so dark that she could barely make him out. Rather she was forced to rely on her other senses. Something she would soon have to do all the time.

"'Tis good this," he whispered. "The darkness embraces us both." Her breath caught when his tongue flicked just beneath her ear. "Now there is nothing but you and me, lass."

No truer words were ever spoken. Her eyes slid shut as he kissed his way along her jawline. He fondled and explored her breasts before grasping then massaging her backside.

Their passion and need grew so quickly and with such intensity that their lips trembled against one another's before they at last sank into a ravenous kiss. Where she had been deeply aroused but tentative the night before, now it felt like a dam broke open. Their tongues twisted and stroked, desperate to get closer. He tasted faintly of one-eighths whisky and seven-eighths hot masculine need.

Sizzling pleasure speared between her thighs and she moaned when his knee wedged between her legs. Running her hands beneath his tunic, she explored the rock-hard ridges of his abdominal muscles then higher to his chiseled chest.

Logan tore his lips from hers, muttering, "Och, lass, I need ye something fierce." He braced his hand over her head, words so soft she barely heard them. *"Tellus clamavi ad te, ut de veste carere possumus.* Mother Earth I call to thee, from clothes might we be free."

Tingles spread through her, then it was almost as if a gentle wind blew over them before she realized they were both completely nude.

"Why not just rip off my clothes," she joked before her words were cut off by the feel of his hands sweeping over her body.

"Not fast enough," he growled before kissing her almost savagely.

Then she could not stop *feeling* for the life of her. The intensity of his mouth owning hers. The hard edges of his strong body as he pressed close. The pulsing, searing heat of his thick arousal against her stomach. The feel of her nipples tightening to painful points against his broad chest.

There was no need to *see* him when a picture of his body so clearly formed in her mind. She ran her fingers over the width of his biceps then the chords of his forearms. Then she trailed her hands down his side, tracing the shallow dips above his hipbones and below the last ridge of his abs. That wonderful V that pointed straight down at...

He released a hiss of pleasure when she wrapped a hand around as much of his arousal as she could and squeezed. Caught by the feel of satin over steel, she barely heard him grunt out more words. *"Tellus mitescere, parva quid temporis non cortice quid esse.* Mother Earth soften thee, for little time might no bark there be."

For a second she thought he was asking to lose his erection but *oh* was she wrong. Cassie gasped, legs widening when Logan clenched her backside and lifted her further up what was now not abrasive bark at her back but smooth softness. Her eyes rolled back in her head when he thrust up and filled her with one, long deep stroke.

Her senses burst to life as her body rippled around him and an impatient climax roared up and hovered just out of reach. He shuddered against her in pleasure but didn't move. Not at first. Instead, he murmured soft words against her ear. The things *he* felt while shrouded in the darkness around them.

The way he would see her if he was to lose *his* sight.

His brogue was thick and husky as he pressed closer, caging her in heat and lust with his arms, hips and thigh muscles. While one hand held her backside firmly in place, the other explored her face, fingertips dusting lovingly over every inch of her. "Such soft eyebrows, furrowed as ye fight to find yer release."

Logan's finger trailed down her nose, slowing at the tip. "Turned up ever so slightly to suit your occasional defiance. A defiance I will push past and turn to pleasure every time I take ye." Then he traced her cheekbones and chin. "So well formed. The perfect fit for my palm."

His fingertip lazily outlined her lips before he thrust his hips and her mouth fell open on a sharp inhale. "Plush lips that will always open for me when I wish it." Logan thrust again and her head fell back. He skimmed her neck before his tongue flicked, teeth nibbled and his words whispered downward. "A slender, soft neck that I cannae get enough of."

He palmed her breast, testing its weight before he ran his tongue around her nipple then sucked it into his mouth. She released a strangled cry and dug her hands into his hair as a piercing climax ripped through her.

Lodged deep, he abandoned her breast and slammed his hand against the tree as his hoarse words rumbled through his chest. "And this feeling," he panted. "This bloody feeling of ye drawing me into your body. 'Tis incomparable. 'Tis something I want ye to give me again and again."

Give *him*? Heck, he was *so* giving *her* everything right now.

His body was tight and locked up against her, as though it was taking all he had to remain still and let her enjoy the orgasm rocketing through her. Yet it was clear he could only take so much because the minute her body floated down out of the clouds and spasms stopped raking her, he started moving. Hoisted against the tree, he grabbed her backside with both hands as he thrust deep and hard.

Thunder rumbled across the sky as he vigorously lost himself within her. She felt not only the rebuilding pressure in her own body but the churning depths of his unadulterated and near violent physical need to possess her. Feeding into his desire, wanting to merge with him just as thoroughly, she wrapped her legs around his waist.

Lightning flickered behind her eyelids as their bodies synchronized and became wild, as abandoned as the wind whipping the leaves above. She couldn't stop her sounds of pleasure as her entire being centered on the feel of him moving within her. Up. Down. In. Out. Around. His astounding energy soon had her varied sounds turning into cries of immeasurable gratification.

Digging her heels into his ass, she arched against him as he drove her toward a peak that he alone controlled. She dug her nails into his shoulder while simultaneously flattening her other palm against the tree, clawing for escape from overwhelming need.

Desperate, writhing, they all but devoured each other before catapulting into the deepest reaches of passion. Thunder cracked as not only lightning flashed across her vision, but a vast spectrum of colors detonated around her. It felt like she shot right out of her body her release was so strong. When his thoughts, ones entirely immersed in lust and love, flickered rapidly through her mind, another explosion raked her.

This time, she took him with her.

The thunder was loud, but his roar was louder as he locked up against her, his body a powerhouse frozen in time. Their release was so ferocious that neither could move for several long moments. Then tremors started to rock them. He quaked against her and she knew he struggled to keep them afoot. Though her legs had started to slowly slide down his thighs, her feet were still off the ground. Good thing because she was pretty sure there weren't any working muscles left in them.

Their hearts pounded as he breathed harshly against her ear. She got the sense he was trying to form words but could not. Rain had started to fall but protected by the tree it only glazed their skin in a breezy mist. Though her eyes were open, the thick darkness was only broken by occasional flashes of lightning.

Until something else caught her attention.

A glow.

Faint at first, she thought maybe she saw a fire flicker through the forest but no. Squinting, it took a moment for her eyes to adjust. The light wasn't coming from the distance but up close.

"Logan," she whispered, not completely sure what she was looking at.

"Aye?" he murmured, face still buried against her neck.

"Am I seeing what I think I'm seeing?"

He pulled back enough that she could put her hand between them. "Do you see it?"

"I do." He peered at her ring. "There's a flicker of light within."

A response died on her lips when Athdara's weak voice whispered through her mind. *"I need ye to come to me, lass. Logan soon suffers great loss and I dinnae want him to be without ye."*

Her eyes went to Logan's face. He was still studying the ring with curiosity. Keeping anxiety from her voice, she said, "Athdara's awake. She needs us."

"Aye, 'tis good." Pulling away, hand still on the tree, he murmured another one of his Mother Earth chants and they were once more clothed. Though she tried to keep it from him, she knew Logan sensed her distress as they headed back.

The storm had been quick moving—almost as if it had swept through as a mirror to the intensity of their lovemaking—and now a light drizzle fell. A glow lit the shore at the oak ford and Cassie's heart caught in her throat when they left the forest behind.

Athdara lay on her side with Grant kneeling beside her. Logan's cousins stood nearby, expressions somber. Cassie rushed over and fell to her knees on the other side of the horse. Grant's sad eyes met hers. "Ye'll want to make room for yer lad. 'Tis best that he's close to her now."

"Of course," she murmured and moved over so that Logan could crouch next to Athdara's head.

He looked at Grant, confused. "I can barely hear her." Like Cassie, he was stroking the horse, trying to offer comfort. "I dinnae ken."

"'Tis hard, this," Athdara whispered into her mind. *"'Tis so verra hard."*

"What's hard?" Cassie said. *"Why can't Logan seem to hear you?"*

The horse's nostrils flared and though her eyes fluttered, they did not open. *"Because his heart isnae ready."*

Grant hung his head and started murmuring prayers.

"What ails Athdara?" Increasingly alarmed, Logan shook his head. "What's happening here?"

Cassie jolted when fire flared nearby and Ferchar appeared on the shore. Grant immediately stood and stepped away as Logan's father, face ravaged with grief, fell to his knees where Grant had been.

"Nay, my lass, dinnae leave me." Tears rolled down the Scotsman's face as he pulled the horse's head into his lap. Body tense, brows lowered sharply, Logan shook his head. "What is it, Da?"

Not sure what else to do, Cassie wrapped her hand in Logan's and held tight. Good thing because what happened next made her mouth fall open in disbelief. Air started to shimmer and fluctuate around Athdara, warping everything until the horse vanished...

And a woman remained.

She looked familiar.

Older but remarkably beautiful, her golden eyes fluttered open and locked with Ferchar's. Though her voice was Athdara's, her brogue faded away as she spoke. "Husband, my love, it's almost time for me to go."

A strangled sound broke from Logan's chest and his eyes widened in anguished disbelief as he clasped the woman's hand with both of his. "Ma?"

Oh dear God no.

Athdara had been his mother all along?

This was Caitlin Seavey from the twenty-first century?

But of course she was. Though aged, this was the woman Cassie had seen in the picture on the mantle.

Caitlin's eyes lingered on Ferchar's face for a long moment and Cassie couldn't stop the tears if she wanted to. There was no way to describe all the unsaid words, all the shared moments, all the complete and thorough love that passed between them in that one look. A lifetime of memories that would remain theirs through eternity.

Ferchar pressed his cheek against Caitlin's palm as she turned tired eyes to Logan. Though it was clearly hard to do, she managed a small smile. "You've made me so proud, son. Now isn't the time to be sad but strong. Your dad's going to need you."

"Och, nay." A tear streamed down Logan's cheek and he shook his head. "Nay, Ma. Dinnae leave us. It cannae be your time yet."

Though they kept a respectable distance, his cousins including Machara drifted closer, pain in their eyes. As if she sensed them, Caitlin murmured, "Never abandon the bond you've forged with your cousins. You are always stronger together."

Logan nodded then shook his head, bringing the back of her hand to his lips, words pained. "I willnae fail ye, Ma. I'll live my life as ye raised me to live it."

"Not once from the moment I knew you were in my belly have you failed me, Logan MacLomain." Her skin grew more ashen. "But I think maybe it's time for me to go back to New Hampshire for a bit. In one form or another." Caitlin's wise eyes drifted between them and her words entered Cassie's mind, brogue thick once more. *"Might ye take his hand and mine, lass?"*

While uncomfortable interrupting a family moment, she did as asked. Shaky, Caitlin's hand wrapped around theirs, voice weaker and weaker as her eyes went to Logan's. "Know the kind of love I did, son, and cherish it always."

Logan nodded and squeezed their hands, more tears trickling down his cheeks as Caitlin's eyes struggled to swing back to Ferchar. Logan's father cupped her cheeks and pressed his forehead to hers, whispering words only meant for her ears, words shared between best friends and lovers who were saying goodbye for the final time.

Caitlin's hand gradually went slack.

Grant made a cross over her chest and spoke softly. "The Lord is my shepherd; I shall not want. He maketh me to lie down in green pastures: he leadeth me beside the still waters. He restoreth my soul: he leadeth me in the paths of righteousness for his name's sake. Yea, though I walk through the valley of the shadow of death, I will fear no evil: for thou art with me; thy rod and thy staff they comfort me…"

Though he finished the prayer, Cassie's attention was soon ensnared by something far beyond her comprehension. The glow around them grew brighter and something shifted. Changed.

"I've been waiting for you, my beautiful granddaughter."

Cassie's mouth dropped when she looked over her shoulder. Ethereal but clearly visible, an elderly woman with twinkling blue eyes and a cane was smiling. An old man stood beside her, a wide, mischievous grin on his face.

"Gram? Adlin?"

Her head whipped around and she leaned back as a younger version of Caitlin stood. Ethereal as well, she stepped away from the woman lying at her feet. Her eyes swept between Ferchar and Logan, words a whisper. "I love you both so much." While there was incredible sadness, there was also peace in her eyes. "I will see you again someday."

Neither had a chance to respond before she drifted away from her body. When Cassie turned again, the couple waiting was no longer old but young. Adlin nodded at everyone in greeting but said nothing.

His sole focus now was Caitlin's…ghost.

"Come, lass." Adlin took Caitlin's hand as the woman who could only be his one true love, Mildred took her other. "We've missed you."

After that, their words were muffled and the bright light faded along with the apparitions. Ferchar wrapped his arms around Caitlin's shoulders, burying his face in her neck, body wracked by silent sobs. Logan's body was just as tense as before, eyes unseeing and lost as he stared at his mother's prone body.

Sickened with sadness, Cassie did not know what else to do but wrap her arms around him. For several long moments, he didn't respond. He was nothing but rock, unbending and shell-shocked.

Then, though it might have been her imagination, she felt a push against her mind. It was a flailing of the subconscious, the unconscious, the living soul trying to comprehend the departure of a soul in transition…to understand death. It almost felt like a repressed thought, much like her denying for so long that she would eventually go blind. Panicky, flittering, she tried to focus on it, calm it, to help it embrace the inevitable.

Only when Logan jerked, blindly wrapped his arms around her and yanked her against him did she realize that the thought had been *his*. Holding on tight she said nothing but kept thinking calming thoughts. Anything to ground him. Anything to help him not fight but embrace his intense grief. Because pain like this, a pain she readily felt through him, was crippling, life-altering.

Cassie had no idea how long she held him, no idea of anything save the heavy weight of his strong arms around her. His mind was adrift in shock, separated from itself.

Logan's memories became hers.

His mother when she was young rocking him on the swing hanging from the oak in front of the Colonial in New Hampshire. The smell of petunia's wafting on the wind. Then he was maybe eight or nine and she was scowling as Ferchar taught him how to swing a blade in the courtyard of the MacLomain castle. Then it wasn't his father but his mother standing behind him when he looked to be in his pre-teens. She was showing him how to shoot a bow and arrow. They were so happy, her laughing as he shot the first arrow straight up into the air. More and more memories washed over her and his grief became so very much hers, as if she was soaking it up and giving him some relief.

Tears poured down her cheeks as she became immersed in his pain.

Only the feel of a warm, firm hand in hers started to pull her back from wherever Logan had taken them. Bleary eyed, her vision swam as she tried to focus. When at last she could somewhat see, she realized that Ferchar held her hand and that Caitlin's body was no longer there. She was tucked on Logan's lap, sitting on a rock, his worried eyes on her. Dim light dulled the stars. It was already pre-dawn.

Cassie shook her head, eyes flickering between them, confused. "I'm so sorry for your loss. Are you okay?"

"Aye," Logan murmured, brushing his thumb over her cheek, voice thick with emotion. "Ye shared my pain lass...ye eased it so verra much. How are ye?"

Her eyes felt dry and her chest tight, but the world was a brighter place with Logan no longer in the stupor he had been in before. "I'm good...I think."

"We waited for you to awaken before we said goodbye," Ferchar said softly. He squeezed her hand. "Caitlin would have wanted it. After all, she gave you her ring."

Grant was there, as were Logan's cousins and every last MacLomain warrior. Their stoic and proud faces were on the shore as Ferchar nodded and a small, makeshift boat was pushed into the water.

"'Twas the magic of our Viking ancestors that allowed her to merge with the horse," Logan murmured. "And 'tis a Viking warrior's burial she will have."

"I must stand." He looked at her, eyes far calmer and more accepting than they had been the night before. "Do me the honor of sitting with my Da?"

She nodded, speechless.

Logan set her down then eyed his bow for a long moment before he lifted it. Cassie pressed her lips together when she realized it was the one she had seen in his memory. The one Caitlin first taught him to shoot with.

"Here, lad, she'd want you to wear this," Ferchar said, holding out a black glove.

Eyes moist, Logan nodded as he took it, words fond. "She couldnae let go of some parts of the twenty-first century, aye?"

"Och, she worried over yer soft hands," Ferchar said, brogue thickening with his emotions.

Chuckle low and forced, Logan slid on the glove. Bare-chested, hair tied back, plaid low on his waist, he took a few steps, turned to the river and lifted his wooden bow.

Ferchar squeezed her hand as the horizon almost seemed to honor the moment. Wind driven, black-bellied clouds somersaulted across the sky, warring with the sun as it crested. A wicked explosion of violent purple and rash blue fought against a splash of deep orangey yellow. All the while, Logan held his bow and arrow, cocked and ready as he eyed the water...as he eyed his mother floating away. His pain was hers and she felt the soul-deep tremble of his fear of hurting Caitlin, his fear of saying goodbye.

"We only let her go for now, son," Ferchar said. "'Tis not her soul but a shell ye see out there."

A long moment stretched and a slight shudder rippled through Logan before he whispered, "Aye, Da."

Ferchar, head held high, proud, murmured, "My truest love, my wife, forever ye be, might the heart of my fire now set ye free. *Meum amorem collimant, uxori aeternum ye be, cerneres cor domini mei ignis ite solutae iam sollicitas.*"

The end of Logan's arrow ignited with fire and his eyes met Ferchar's. Their heartbroken but strong gazes held before Ferchar finally gave a firm nod. "Let her go."

Logan turned, aimed, whispered how much he loved his mother and released the arrow. His cousins, who had been edging closer, now formed a supportive wall behind him as the arrow met its mark. The wind caught the flame and within seconds fire engulfed the raft.

Arms limp, eyes unwavering, the bow fell from Logan's hand as he silently watched. Niall put a firm hand on his right shoulder, Darach on his left. Rònan and Machara's hands landed beside the others as they stood close. The moment was intense, one made of tears and barely inhaled breaths, one made of family letting go of family.

"Farewell, my love," Ferchar whispered, never releasing Cassie's hand as his eyes stayed locked on the flames. "I will see ye again someday."

Wanting to go to Logan but understanding he needed his cousins right now, she remained silent and watched the burning boat as it drifted.

"Aye, but then my lass had a plan all along," Ferchar murmured, awe and love in his voice.

Cassie's eyes turned to him, confused.

Ferchar nodded at her ring. "It had always been hers. A symbol of our love." His eyes met Cassie's. "Now 'tis yours, lass."

Her eyes dropped to the Claddagh ring. The stone nestled between the hands was no longer clear but pale blue with tiny flecks of gold.

A sapphire.

The exact color of Logan's eyes.

Chapter Sixteen

THOUGH HIS GRIEF had lessened some because of what Cassie had done for him, his heart lifted when he turned and saw the ring. Nodding his thanks to his cousins for their support, he strode over and dropped to his knees in front of her. He had never seen a more welcoming sight than the sapphire. Eyes never leaving hers, he kissed the ring then pulled her into his arms. "Thank God."

Logan wasn't kidding himself. He knew this didn't mean she would stay with him, but it did mean that there was a man meant for her. That *he* was meant for her.

Not tentative in the least, her arms wrapped around him and she pressed her cheek against his chest, whispering, "Again, I'm so incredibly sorry for your loss."

A loss that she had so selflessly shared with him. Cassie might not know how she managed it, but he did. She loved him. Simple as that. Had her feelings not run so deep she never would have been able to take on so many of his memories. So much heartache. Her mind, her very soul, had soaked up so much of his grief that he could love his mother and say goodbye without the shock and emotional blindness that such a loss could cause. She offered him sight past a pain that could have kept him in self-induced darkness for a very long time.

Logan held her for several moments wishing they could stay that way forever but knew that there was revenge to be had. On Cullen Stewart. Because as he had learned from his Da and Grant while Cassie was in her healing haze, his mother had sacrificed herself. Connected to the MacLomains via her ring, she was able to utilize the magic of their Viking ancestry. A magic that allowed a wizard, or witch in this case, to merge with a horse and in turn eventually be resurrected.

But not this time.

The evil she had been thrust into was far too powerful.

Yet, as Ferchar sadly shared, his mother had gone into this with her eyes wide open. Apparently, without his father's knowledge, she had willingly put herself into the death slumber at the Hamilton castle, merging with Athdara. That's why her ring ended up on Cassie's finger. His mother had somehow made sure the ring found its way to Logan's one true love. When Ferchar saw the ring on Cassie's finger, he sought out Caitlin. Then when her body eventually vanished from the Hamilton's, he came here.

What truly broke Logan's heart was that his mother *had* to know she would eventually die. Why else would she ensure the ring ended up on Cassie's finger never to return to hers? This, naturally, meant that she knew Robert would soon be taken and what her role in saving him would be. And as Grant soon shared, it had been Caitlin's magic that helped the Hamilton cast the binding spell that kept Cullen from getting too far. He suspected that's why the horse's name was Athdara to begin with.

It was the location that his mother would meet her end.

Grant met his eyes as Logan and Cassie stood. "I was wrong, lad. There can be no doubt now that not all of the rings were meant for those born of the Next Generation. Only the gods know why but we willnae question it, aye?"

"Nay, never," Logan agreed.

Grant nodded and redirected the conversation. "We willnae stay on here much longer. There is vengeance to be had and a king to be saved."

Logan nodded and cupped Cassie's cheeks. "How do you feel? Strong enough to continue the journey?"

"You better believe it," she said, a determined look in her eyes.

God, he was so impressed with this woman. He might lust after her something fierce, but he knew his attraction had as much to do with unequivocal admiration. Without question, she would make a perfect Lady of MacLomain castle.

And damn would he be proud to call her his wife.

Logan turned to his men. "As many of ye already know, this ford is a place of great power. A place that can be harnessed by those of us with magic. Like many across Scotland, 'tis a portal to another location in our country. This time, we will use it to travel to the Mother Oak."

He connected eyes with as many men as possible. "There is no way to know what will greet us when we travel there, but I can tell ye this with certainty, 'twill be extremely dangerous. Because 'tis so incredibly unpredictable and could verra well mean certain death, I am giving any who wish to remain here the option."

There was a moment of hesitation before men shook their heads and cried out.

"We go where ye go, m'laird!"

"We will avenge yer Ma!"

"We will avenge the poor souls lost in the MacLauchlin village!"

Logan nodded. Proud. He was about to respond when several warriors crested the hill and a mighty roar came from the man leading the way. "Ye'll go nowhere without me, ye bunch of bloody bastards!"

Clyde MacLauchlin.

His son Deargh and his daughter's husband, Baird Stewart were with him.

Cassie released a small chuckle, undoubtedly amused by the gigantic chieftain's wild appearance. Skinny braids were tangled in his unkempt hair and his tunic didn't quite contain his belly.

Logan shook his head and clasped arms, hand to elbow, when Clyde reached him. "Ye should be at your castle, m'laird."

"Och, nay. Not when there's battling to be done and more revenge to be had. I owe ye, my friend." Clyde had a devilish twinkle in his eyes as he rubbed his reddened nose. As usual, there was the faintest whiff of whisky on his breath. "Besides, I slaughtered those whoreson cowards ye left at my castle and now the MacLomain warriors ye so kindly sent are protecting my people and helping to rebuild."

Logan knew there would be no talking him out of it so he grinned. "Have it yer way then."

Clyde leaned close, a co-conspirator gleam in his eyes. "So will ye be telling me who yer settin' to save?"

"Nay and 'tis truly a dangerous quest. Are ye sure yer up for it?"

"Up?" Clyde huffed, winking at Cassie. "There's never been a lass or a battle that I havnae been *up* for."

Naturally, Niall and Rònan chuckled.

Logan nodded at Baird, acknowledging that the man had stayed true to his word. "How fares Aline?"

"Down half an arm but she will keep her life," Baird said. "Never was there a stronger lass."

"'Tis good news this." Logan clasped his shoulder. "Ye both can stay on at the MacLomain castle as long as ye need to."

"Thank ye, m'laird." Baird nodded, chin firm as he warred with emotions. "I couldnae be prouder to fight for ye this day."

Logan nodded and his attention turned to Clyde when the chieftain's eyes drifted to the burning boat sinking into the water downstream. "I dinnae like the looks of that," he said softly before his gaze returned to Logan in question.

Unable to push the words past his lips, he was grateful when his Da joined them and shook Clyde's hand. "It has been too long, my old friend. I cannae tell ye how sorry I am about the pain inflicted upon yer clan." Ferchar's eyes went to the boat, his gaze sad but strong. "'Tis my wife, Caitlin we say farewell to."

"Nay," Clyde whispered. His lips slashed down and deep grooves formed between his eyes. "I'm so verra sorry to ye both. Never was there a finer lass."

Ferchar and Logan only nodded.

A silent moment stretched before Clyde unsheathed a dagger and gripped it like he was ready to kill someone. "Something tells me saying farewell to such a bonnie lass is all the more reason to skewer the bloody swines we're after, aye?"

Ferchar's eyes narrowed. "Ye couldnae be more right about that, lad."

Though he disliked putting the MacLauchlin Laird in danger, very few were as savage in battle as Clyde. With arms the size of tree trunks, he could down three men with one mighty swipe.

Grant came alongside. "'Tis nearly time."

Logan nodded and turned to his men. "Once those of us with magic open the portal betwixt these trees, 'twill be a jarring transition from here to there. Have yer weapons at the ready and yer eyes open. Dinnae fret if the sun has moved across the sky in an instant as traveling this way can sometimes steal a few hours from ye." His gaze swept over them, again pausing on as many as possible. "I thank ye for fighting alongside me. 'Tis always an honor. Now go into this battle with nothing but vengeance in yer heart, aye?"

"Aye!" they cheered.

Logan thrust up his blade and roared the MacLomain's war cry, *"Ne Parcus nec Spernas!"*

"Ne Parcus nec Spernas!" everyone roared.

He just prayed it would be a battle of weapons and not a slaughter by magic.

"Fortis et Fidus!" Clyde and his men roared the MacLauchlin's war cry.

His cousins nodded at Logan, battle lust already in their eyes as he turned his attention back to Grant and his Da. He had never seen the Hamilton look so serious.

"Ye, yer Da and I will stay close to Cassie," Grant said. "She and the ring must be protected at all costs." His eyes went to Machara, Rònan and Niall before landing on Darach. "Ye four go after the Bruce. Be prepared for anything and protect one another well."

"Aye," they said with determined, eager, looks on their faces.

Logan squeezed Cassie's hand and met her eyes one final time. "Keep that dagger at the ready, lass." His voice lowered. "I willnae leave your side."

"You will if you need to," she said softly, strength in her eyes. "Robert comes first."

While his head knew she was right, his heart did not agree in the least. Yet he kept his thoughts from his face and nodded. "Aye, lass."

When Grant and Ferchar started chanting, he and his cousins joined in. This was exceedingly dangerous considering someone so powerful had recently used this portal, but there was no other choice. The Mother Oak was too far away and they didn't have time.

Logan pulled Cassie against his side, sword ready, as the wind started to whip. Pressure intensified as colors swirled around him. For several long moments, he could make out no one save his lass. Though tempted to wrap his arms around her, he could not afford to take his eyes off of their surroundings.

When things started to come into focus again, they had but a blink to react before they were hit hard and fast. While some of it was magic, a great deal was what he had hoped it would be.

Plain old fighting.

The cave that housed the majority of the Mother Oak's limbs was high above the ground. Her trunk grew down the side of the mountain. It was not an overly large space so fighting was tight as swords crashed against swords. Many rival warriors were flooding down from the area above where the baby oak used to grow. However, his men were pushing back rapidly and the battling was spreading out in that direction giving them more room to move.

Logan stayed in front of Cassie, running his blade through anyone who came too close. Grant and Ferchar were fighting and chanting, their magic buffering against the enemy's. His cousins had stayed in the cave, fighting like madmen, livid hatred on their faces as they carried out justice.

Niall was as verbal as ever when he thrust his sword into a man's gut then stabbed him in the groin with a dagger. "Ye'll not be using yer bloody cock to take a lass against her will again, aye?"

Rònan roared with crazed laughter as he swung a mace and fell two warriors at once. Other men stumbled back at the mad look in his eyes as he chased after them.

Darach and Machara fought side by side. Of the lot of them, Darach was the fastest on his feet and often managed maneuver's that won him plenty of praise after battle. This time Logan knew he stuck close to Machara because though she would never admit it, she was weakened by her wound.

Brae was silent, a dark, venomous look in her eyes as she fought. Clyde and his men had made their way up onto the mountain and his bellows of rage were so loud they could be heard over everything.

Yet all the while, Logan kept searching for Cullen Stewart.

"Oh no, ya don't," Cassie muttered, up to something he couldn't see.

Logan sideswiped a man with his blade then sliced the back of his thigh open before he cast a quick look over his shoulder and quirked his lips. She had managed to thrust her dagger into the stomach of a man who was sneaking up behind them. He nodded at her with approval but her eyes had locked on the tree. When he swung back, he saw why.

Cullen Stewart.

As tall and muscled as the MacLomain wizards, he was a formidable opponent. Whatever binding magic Grant and Caitlin had used was weakening as the Stewart became visible. But was it their magic holding him? It didn't quite feel like it. Ensnared by the Mother Oak's limbs, it almost for a moment seemed as if the tree helped cloak him as his body shimmered in and out of the leaves.

When their eyes met, Logan felt it like a punch in the gut. Gone was the good natured lad from his youth. Now there was only a villainous darkness churning in Cullen's eyes and swamping his aura.

"I see you, Robert," Cassie said. "Can you see me?"

Logan frowned and looked back and forth between Cassie and Cullen. Who was she talking too? Obviously Robert but where *was* he? Grant and Ferchar's eyes were narrowed on Cullen as well, their chants unending as they battled the Stewart's magic.

"Nay," Cullen said. Though his words were soft they were enhanced so that all MacLomain wizards could hear him. His cousins kept battling, but their eyes continually flickered to the tree as the Stewart spoke. "'Tis time for the future to change." His eyes fell to Cassie's ring. "Mayhap 'tis time as well for the past to change."

Nearly all the enemy had fallen at this point, more lambs simply led to slaughter by the monster Cullen had become. Great power was building and Logan couldn't for the life of him figure out where it was coming from. It wasn't evil but different. Unknown.

Suddenly, everything went very, very silent as the last of the enemy fell and the branches started to fluctuate and bend. A tall, muscled Celtic warrior appeared, his sole focus Cullen. "Ye never should have taken matters into your own hands, laddie."

"Fionn Mac Cumhail," Grant murmured.

The god who had overseen the coupling of Alan and Caitriona Stewart within this very tree. The god who oversaw the creation of the original Claddagh rings.

"Och, but we do for kin, do we not?" Brae said, strolling in her brother's direction, a sly look on her face.

Cullen's expression was flat as the last of his cloaking magic evaporated. Only then did Logan see his clipped wings and realized the shocking truth. Not only was the Stewart a warlock but…a fallen angel?

"How the bloody hell..." Logan whispered.

Grant shook his head, eyes slits as he watched Brae closely. His damning words sent chills down Logan's spine. "Bless the all Mighty, it doesnae get worse than this."

Brae chuckled as she stood between Cullen and them, arms crossed over her chest as she cast Grant a bemused look. "It worked out verra well that ye didnae hear that my brother died a while back."

When Grant frowned, her brows shot up. "Aye, we were battling with another clan and he just happened to trip into my dagger. An unfortunate thing, that." She snorted and shook her head. "Always with a love for God over the rightful pagan gods, the imposter went and gave him wings." Then she rolled her eyes. "Apparently he'd been enough of a do-gooder in life. I tend to think the rival God just wanted more soldiers to fight against those gods who were here first."

Before Grant could respond, Brae shook her head. "It doesnae matter now. When he learned of my new Laird and our plans for the wee Bruce, our plans to see a different future for Scotland, Cullen saw the good sense in it. Yet the only way he could join us was to embrace evil." She shrugged. "The false God didnae like that so cast him down..." A twinkle met her eyes as she pouted at Cullen's back. "But left those dreadful half-wings. Use your magic and put them away, brother. They're appalling."

Both Cullen and Brae were their enemies?

"Nay, sister, I dinnae think I will just yet," Cullen growled.

Her eyes narrowed.

"Do ye really think I would have turned from God and become a warlock for a lass who killed me to begin with?" He shook his head. "Nay, I but fooled ye, Brae." Wrath turned the varied prisms of Cullen's blue eyes to a piercing glow and the last of his magic fell away to reveal a young boy standing by his side. "I did what I had to do to stop ye from getting yer hands on the wee Bruce."

"Robert," Cassie cried, but Logan stopped her when she tried to go to him. Though shaking, the Bruce had his little shoulders back and was trying his best to stay strong.

"Och, nay, ye bloody traitor," Brae seethed at Cullen. "We've the future at our disposal now." Her eyes shot to Cassie then back. "And one o' the rings. So much power!"

Logan shook his head and kept Cassie tucked behind him as he glared at Brae. All along they had been chasing the enemy *with* the enemy. A rather cunning plan to get ahold of the ring and Robert all at the same time. But it seemed Cullen had outsmarted his sister by leading her into a trap. Or so he hoped.

"Ye'll get Cassie over my dead body," Logan growled.

"So it seems," Brae said with disgust. "Yet mayhap not as easily as I had hoped."

"She's partnered up with a dark demi-god," Cullen said to Grant before his eyes again narrowed on Brae, his warlock aura crackling black. "Ye almost managed to make it through the oak ford with not only Robert but another ring, but ye didnae expect Athdara doing what she did, aye?"

Brae bristled and cursed when she understood his meaning. "Yer visionary abilities." She shook her head. "So 'twas ye who contacted Caitlin and set her fate in motion."

Cullen's steady eyes went to Ferchar. "A fate she agreed to willingly if it meant helping Robert." Then his gaze went to Logan. "And making sure ye found yer lass."

Dumbfounded, Logan could barely believe what he was hearing. It had been such a whirlwind during the battle yesterday that it never occurred to him to question why Brae had been so close to the ford in those final moments. It made sense at the time. She was trying to save Robert.

But no.

She was trying to join him thinking that her brother, her ally, waited on the other side. And she would have made it.

Had Athdara not stopped her.

The horse, Caitlin, wanted Brae to remain with the MacLomains. To arrive here with them. That sacrifice cost her life. A life she was more than willing to give up to protect the future king.

And see her son find his true love.

Cullen looked at Logan. "Brae and her dark Laird somehow yanked Nicole back in time because their hope of taking Cassie while under the protection of Grant's magic was dwindling." He sneered at his sister, their dark power testing one another. "That plan didnae work out so well for ye either, aye?"

Grant's eyes stayed on Cullen. "Why not contact me, lad? I would have helped ye."

"Because he has always been a rebel who tends to take matters into his own hands." Fionn Mac Cumhail glowed golden as his discontent grew. "'Tis both a gift and a curse being such a powerful visionary. Cullen ultimately followed the course of action that saw the least amount of MacLomains killed and still put ye wizards in Brae's way at the end."

Fionn's disgruntled eyes went to Cullen. "Still, ye gave up too much for this, warrior."

"*See*, the Celtic gods have no use for you either, brother," Brae spat, expression exceptionally upbeat considering how sorely outnumbered she was. Then magic began to hiss and spit around her as something started to change in the air and Logan realized she wasn't defeated by any means.

"No god matters when it comes to the safety of the future King of Scotland," Cullen responded to her taunt, the undercut of his tone fierce. "A king that doesnae belong in the hands of evil."

"But ye *are* evil now, ye bloody fool!" Brae threw back her head and laughed as the air started to bubble around her. Whoever she was in league with was fueling her own intense magic. A dank smell started to saturate their surroundings.

Fionn's eyes widened as his magic pushed against hers. "Ye harness the power of the *Genii Cucullati*, the hooded spirits. 'Tis ill that." His gaze blazed with gold and he seethed, "Flesh eaters."

Grant's lethal eyes swept over Logan and his cousins in a flash. "None of ye get involved in this. The magi is far too strong."

Wind started to roar around them as not only Fionn but Grant, Ferchar, and even Cullen started to fight her with magic. Black and murky wind mixed with gold and blue as Brae shook her head and kept laughing.

"What the *heck*?" Cassie muttered.

Momentarily distracted by the immense power being unleashed, Logan loosened his grip on Cassie just enough that she took advantage. Hell, if the woman didn't barrel straight toward Robert. Heart in his throat, he watched the horrific scene unfold. Her eyes never having left the little boy, Cassie saw something nobody else had.

Three shadows, inky and dark, were heading right for him.

Cassie, not thinking of her own welfare, bolted through the storm of magic fluctuating between his kin, Cullen, and Brae. Magic so great and with such a mix of good and evil, he was surprised she wasn't ripped to shreds in an instant. When Logan flew after her, he slammed into a wall of Fionn Mac Cumhail's making. Furious, he roared at the Celtic god, but it made no difference. Cassie might have slipped past, but he was not letting anyone else.

Each step difficult, she had her head down as she struggled toward Robert. Trembling, eyes wet, the boy shook his head as the shadows edged closer.

"I'm coming, Robert," Cassie cried, her words garbled and warped in the whipping magical cyclone.

When the Bruce started running toward her, he was scooped up by the shadows. Cassie broke from the storm and ran after him. Terrified, Logan watched as she dove straight off the cliff and grabbed Robert's ankles. So fast the eye barely caught it, Cullen spun and grabbed her calves. The creatures, Robert, and Cassie swung down as if they were falling, but the Stewart still held on over the edge.

Though infuriated at first, there was a tinge of triumph in Brae's eyes when she roared, "Get me out of here. The ring from that screaming banshee of a lass is nearly ours. 'Twill be more than enough to get the Bruce later."

Fionn Mac Cumhail, Grant, and Ferchar threw everything they had at Brae, but it was too late. The three shadows released a blood-curdling scream and swooped around her until her form mangled, twisted then trailed away in a thin stream of dust.

Free of the god's magical grip, he raced to the edge of the cliff as Cullen hauled Cassie and Robert up. Logan pulled them into his arms, shot the Stewart a grateful look then buried his face in her hair and held on tight. He didn't let them go as Robert snuggled close and cried.

Logan didn't miss what was happening nearby.

Fionn spoke softly to Cullen. "Ye always were a good lad." He shook his head. "But 'tis a wicked life ye embraced to stop Brae. Ye cannae stay here now. Ye cannae be of further use to your sister because ye will be whether or not ye know it. Somehow she will manage to use ye to get the wee King through yer blood connection. 'Tis the only way it can be with twins conceived beneath this tree.

Twins who embraced evil. Her Laird willnae be tricked again by yer ability to see bits of the future. Celtic demi-gods never make the same mistake twice."

Cullen had a stony look on his face but as Logan suspected he had done several times before, the Stewart wasn't shying away from his fate but looking it dead in the eye. "What will ye have of me then?"

"If it could be any other way 'twould be but I cannae risk ye being here any longer." Fionn sighed. "I'm banishing ye to the twenty-first century. When there seek out the *Worldwide Paranormal Society*. They're warlocks born of a man named Calum. He was of a Celtic lineage related to the Broun clan. They will be able to keep ye well hidden from your sister."

"He doesn't deserve that," Cassie broke in, lifting her head. "He just saved us!"

"Shh." Logan pulled her head back against his chest. "Fionn means to keep him safe, lass. There is no other choice."

"Och, the bloody future," Cullen muttered. "For how long?"

"'Tis hard to know," Fionn said. "Mayhap indefinitely."

Cullen wiped a hand over his face and shook his head. He didn't look at Logan or even his cousins, men who had cared so much about him. No, the decisions he made, even if for the right reasons, had caused him to fall from grace. Even before accepting the essential darkness of a newly made warlock, a man like the Stewart wouldn't think he deserved the kinship or forgiveness of his brethren if God Himself had cast him out.

He would go it alone.

Jaw set, eyes hard, Cullen said, "If it will help keep the Bruce safe." His eyes dropped to the boy in Cassie and Logan's arms and his gaze softened before the sentiment vanished and he looked at the god. "Just do it."

"Wait," Niall and Rònan said at the same time but it was too late. Fionn whipped out his hands and bright white light flashed. When it faded, Cullen was gone. Logan closed his eyes and murmured a prayer for the Stewart's soul. Might he find redemption wherever he ended up.

"Bloody hell," Rònan murmured.

Niall swore under his breath, plunked down on a thick branch and held his head. Machara and Darach had equally disturbed looks on their faces as they started to wipe the blood from their weapons.

Fionn turned to Grant and Ferchar. "Ye and yers stay here for the eve. 'Tis well protected by my magic now that I've a better idea of what we are up against. The *Genii Cucullati* willnae return here anytime soon nor will any Celtic god save myself."

"The *Genii Cucullati*," Grant murmured. "Not only do they eat the flesh of the soul..." He shot Fionn a concerned look. "But 'tis said they have a tendency to hover around births. Though not a birthing, could they have done such when Brae and Cullen were conceived here?"

"I would have known," Fionn replied but there was a perturbed look on his face and Logan wondered if he truly believed his words.

"'Twas ye who helped Robert's mother, Marjorie visit her son all along, wasn't it?" Grant said, evidently trying to piece together several things at once. "'Twas yer glamour that enabled her to look like Aline."

"Aye, as it was me who told Adlin MacLomain of Robert's destiny so that ye could make sure Logan saw him safely into this world." Fionn gave them all a pointed look. "And so that ye could keep the King safe through this difficult period."

Logan remained curious about something. "Why disguise the Countess to look like Aline? 'Twas risky considering Aline herself was in the village."

"That is where the story grows more interesting," Fionn said. "As it turns out Robert was not just visiting the MacLauchlin village the day of the raid but lived there. 'Twas where he received his fostering." A twinkle lit his eyes. "And 'twas Aline herself who often helped foster the lad."

"Och, I always did wonder about that," Clyde MacLauchlin mumbled somewhere in the background before he chuckled. "My wee lass fostering someone so important. Well how about that."

"So Aline knew you glamoured the Countess to look like her when she visited the village and I assume she made herself scarce on such occasions," Logan said.

"Aye," Fionn said, sadness flickering over his face. "But not nearly scarce enough that dreadful day."

Logan was curious why the god did not just protect the Bruce himself but supposed there was likely a good reason. Perhaps because of the love of the couples the rings were meant to bring together. Or perhaps even the relationships they would all likely forge with Robert before everything was said and done.

"What of this demi-god Laird that Brae has involved herself with?" Ferchar asked. "Do ye know who he is?"

"Nay. Nor did Cullen it seems. Though he knew of him they never actually met." Fionn frowned. "But whoever he is, he has access to our otherworld and keeps Brae safe there for now."

"What did she mean when she said that the screaming banshee lass's ring was nearly hers?" Cassie asked. Though she had lifted her head, Logan realized her eyes remained unfocused.

"I think I can answer that," Grant said. "It means that Brae and her counterpart must have somehow locked onto Nicole's essence when she traveled at the oak ford."

"Oh no," Cassie said, alarmed. "Then did she make it to the twenty-first century or not?"

"Aye, the magic Grant and Caitlin used to get her home was strong but 'tis hard to say how long 'twill hold for. Now that we know the *Genii Cucullati* or at least a darker variation of them are involved, what Brae can harness in the mystical realm is truly unknown," Fionn said. "The *Genii Cucullati* are spirit gods that first made themselves known with the Romans and have since dwelt with the Celts. With their help 'tis always possible that Brae might try to take Nicole again."

Cassie's frown only deepened. "When that happens, *if* it happens, will we know and if so, how do we save her?"

"I swore on my honor that I would protect her, lass," Niall said, anger and—interestingly enough—genuine worry in his voice. "And I will. I will save her if she is taken. Ye dinnae have to worry, ye ken?"

Cassie gave a small nod, concern still etched on her face.

"Only one person will be able to track Nicole's whereabouts if she's taken by Brae and whatever dark magic was at work at the oak ford," Fionn murmured. "But that isnae something to worry over yet if at all."

Logan's eyes narrowed as the truth dawned on him. If he understood the god's implication correctly, then it could only be someone who had experienced the same magic as Nicole. Someone taken against their will as she had been.

Robert the Bruce.

So he well understood the god's desire to be vague right now. There was no need to broach something that might not happen.

"I'm gonna worry about Nicole regardless." Cassie sighed. "I know she's meant to travel back in time but the idea that she could end up in the enemy's hands seriously stinks."

Yet she kept her voice soft as she stroked Robert's hair, wholly aware that he had been through more than the lot of them. Fionn's eyes went to her and softened considerably. He gestured at Machara to follow him.

Air shimmered around the god as he strode Cassie's way. By the time he crouched beside them he was no longer a massive golden warrior but a little old woman with kind eyes. It was the visage he used when trying to comfort.

She met the boy's eyes. "How fare ye, laddie? It has been a frightening journey but ye have been verra brave and soon ye will reunite with your Ma and yer fosterer, Aline aye?"

Robert's eyes were moist when they met Fionn's. "Aye, but I think mayhap I was brave because of my friend, Cassie."

"Aye, 'tis verra good. Our true friends can often give us courage when the way is dark. They make ye a better person for knowing them. Always remember the bond ye forged with Cassie so that when ye someday rule this great country ye will better recognize friend from foe." The old woman's gaze grew wise. "Because it can sometimes be difficult to recognize the difference."

"Aye, mistress," he whispered. "Cassie saw me when nobody else could and never gave up on me. I will look for friends that can see me better than anyone else and never, ever give up on me."

"Aye, my lad." Fionn cupped his cheek. "And always remember to treat your friends the same way."

Robert nodded. "Aye."

"So now I ask ye to treat your friend, Cassie with a kindness. Let her spend some time with her love for she faces something just as frightening as ye did." Fionn introduced Machara. "She will keep ye safe for the eve, all right?"

Logan's heart clenched when he looked at Cassie. God, no. Not yet.

Robert's brows furrowed and he took Cassie's hand. "Are ye well, my friend?"

Though she clearly meant to, Cassie didn't quite look at him when she replied. "I'm fine. Don't worry about me, okay?"

But the Bruce had every right to be concerned. As did they all.

The magic she had forged through to save Robert had sped up the inevitable.

Cassie was blind.

Chapter Seventeen

WHEN ROBERT'S LITTLE arms wrapped around her and he murmured, "'Tis all right. Be brave as I was and we will get through this, aye?" Cassie bit back tears.

Fionn had explained to Robert about her eyesight. Regrettably, she could no longer see the child's response. Until now. Or should she say hear and feel it. With a thick swallow, she hugged him and whispered, "You got it. I'll try to be as brave as you were."

When Robert stood and walked away, she knew he was safe with Machara. Soon after, Logan picked her up and started walking. "Everyone is spending the night in the cave below so that we might have the mountaintop to ourselves."

Cassie kept her eyes squeezed shut and head buried against his chest. Maybe, just maybe, when she opened them again the blurriness would return...anything other than complete darkness.

The faint metallic scent of blood from battling faded as Logan climbed something and fresh air met her nostrils. "There have to be so many dead bodies around us."

"Nay," he said. "Fionn got rid of them with magic."

"Ah," she whispered. "Did you lose many men?"

"Not one." He sat with her on his lap and pulled her cheek against his chest, voice soft. "Dinnae worry over anyone, lass. The harm is behind us for now."

For now. Key words. But the gentle way he stroked her hair and held her tight allowed her to at last relax. Something Cassie realized she had been terrified to do. Opening her eyes, she tilted her head and looked up. It was completely dark. Nothing. But perhaps it was like last night against the tree? Rallying her courage, she murmured, "Is the moon out...or stars?"

She felt the increased thud of his heart and the slight tension of his body as a long silent moment stretched.

"Just tell me," she whispered, closing her eyes. "I need to know."

He again paused before he inhaled deeply then spoke. "The moon is nearly full and the rock around us is shining silver from its

231

glow." When he cupped the back of her head, his response husky with emotion, she realized he was trying to create a picture with words. "There are a thousand stars covering the sky. They speckle the glistening rocks off to our left, damp from the wind blowing spray from the waterfall below."

Cassie tried to nod but couldn't. Grasping his tunic, she squeezed her eyes tighter then opened them again. Nothing. Only darkness. Had the day truly come? Though incredibly frightened, she knew she had to ask. She could only be grateful that she was questioning not only a wizard but a man who loved her. Trying to keep fear from her voice, trying to be strong, she cursed the shakiness of her words.

"I'm blind, aren't I?"

His body stiffened further, but it seemed he preferred honesty versus sugar coating the truth. Still, his voice was pained when he said, "Aye, lass. You are blind."

"Officially blind, for-sure-no-turning-back-blind?" Cassie would be kidding herself if she said she hadn't wondered since learning magic existed that perhaps...just maybe...it could cure her.

"No turning back blind," he whispered so softly she barely heard him.

Eyes shut again, she rested her cheek against his chest and tried to focus on deep, steady breaths. Logan said nothing, only held her. She was never more grateful. This was the day she had dreaded for so long. This was the day that she said goodbye to the woman she had been and hello to the woman she would be. A day she had long prepared for and swore to her friends she would face with bravery and courage.

Yet as she twisted her hand further into his tunic it occurred to her that nobody, not a single soul, could ever really prepare themselves for something like this. Indescribably lonely in its own way, it almost felt like she had been separated from the rest of the world. She was her own entity floating in this deep, dark space now made entirely of her mind and thoughts. Sure, technically it was that way for everyone but losing your sight sharpened it a thousand times over.

Strong.

Stay strong.

Do not give into the fear.

Logan never stopped stroking her hair and she swore his words dusted her mind. *"There is strength found in grief. There is also strength in letting go. Ye taught me that so verra well last night, lass. Dinnae be afraid to embrace the fear."*

Was there truly? Because it felt weak. Yet the more firmly he held her against him, the more her emotions started to make their way to the surface. It almost felt as if he anchored her while they washed over her. Wrapping her arm around his waist, she choked back a sob. Dear God, she was going to cry. She didn't want to do that...had promised herself she would not. Then another sob wracked her, this one more violent.

"I don't want to," she choked against his chest. "I don't...I can't...I'm so scared..."

Logan engulfed her in his strong arms and braced his feet on the ground so that she was cocooned against him. "Ye can and ye will. There isnae any weakness in letting go, lass."

But there was...wasn't there?

Whether or not there was, her body, her very soul, followed the unexpected freedom his soft declaration allowed. Face buried into the alcove beneath his chin and collarbone, she faced the darkness and completely fell apart. All the years of worrying and fear reared up. All the years of uncertainty and bracing herself to face something life-altering.

The limitless emotional battle that lay ahead of her.

Tears ran down her face as she cried but for the life of her she could not brush them away. All she could do was hold on tight and pray the grief didn't ravage her. There was no way to know how much time passed. No way to know if after all the years of preparing herself for this she wouldn't end up becoming the exact opposite of the courageous woman she hoped to be.

Cassie had no clue when the heavy wracks of pain in her tight chest started to loosen or when the relentless tears finally abated. What she *did* know was that Logan never let go, his silent support profound and so much more meaningful because he said nothing. Letting her sift through her thoughts and find herself through the darkness was a personal battle that seemed to almost build the foundation for what? The next breath? The ability to lift her head and be aware that *yes* she was blind, but unlike so many, she still had her health, her very *life*.

She remembered the long conversations she'd had with Nicole, Jaqueline, and Erin. Though she intended to keep her thoughts inside, they poured out. "My friends and I chatted about what it would be like afterward." Cassie sniffled and rubbed her lips together, damp cheek still resting against his tunic. "The one thing we all agreed on was that we were gonna be having a lot of selfish thoughts. Woe is me sort of stuff. And when we did we should focus on one thing. Do you know what that was?"

"Nay, lass," Logan murmured, kissing the top of her head. "What?"

"That somebody always has it worse. Everybody's going through something. That we all face struggles and remembering that we're simply human and vulnerable is part of living. No one is perfect in body or spirit. That we'd be better people if we remember that absolutely everyone faces difficult things in life. What we take from it, how we grow, is *everything*."

"Aye," he breathed. His arms tightened a fraction as his emotions became hers. "'Tis the verra best way to look at life."

Cassie continued resting her head against his chest for a long time as she recalled all the long conversations she'd had with her friends. Yes, they had become a support group to help her prepare for what was happening right now but they had *no idea* how helpful they really were. She could only hope that when their time came they were able to draw on her support just as much.

Yet her emotions continued to fluctuate.

On occasion, she was convinced she felt Logan's mind brush hers, his strength and support lifting her up when she thought she would drown in misery. Then she would refocus on what she had told him about the way she was determined to look at life, and the fear would lessen. It was truly the most emotional roller coaster ride of her life and she sensed he was there every step of the way. As she slowly but surely came to grips with being blind, she must have dozed off because her eyes snapped open when Logan moved.

"All is well, lass," he whispered. "I but moved us a bit so that I could lean against a log."

"Oh, sorry," she murmured, groggy. "We can lie down if you want."

"Nay, I'm content here. The sun sits just below the horizon. Within hours, the rest will awaken."

"What?" Startled, she sat up and tried to suppress the gripping terror of darkness still surrounding her.

Logan pulled her back against him and murmured soft, reassuring words in her ear as he cupped her cheek. "'Tis okay. Rest."

Though still fearful, she relaxed beneath his touch and stared in what she hoped was the direction of his face. Oh, that face. She would miss it so much. But her concern lay more in what he had said. "You moved us so that you could lean back? Does that mean you've been sitting up all night?"

"I've been holding you all night," he said. "'Twas no hardship."

No hardship? That had to have totally sucked. Sure, he was muscular but sitting up without leaning against something for that long took perseverance. Curious, she asked, "So where are we now?"

There was a touch of nostalgia in his response. "Actually, 'tis the verra spot the Baby Oak once grew."

"Oh," she murmured, privileged but wary. "It's sort of a sacred spot then, eh? Should we really be sitting here?"

"It is as sacred to the MacLomain clan as you are, Cassie." He cupped both cheeks. "So, aye, we should be sitting here and I know for certain that the Mother Oak agrees."

"How would you know that," she started but stopped. His magic. Mother Earth. "Wow…really?"

"Really," he murmured. "How are you feeling now? Any less frightened?"

Cassie considered his question. How *was* she feeling now? Scared? Yes, somewhat. But she realized it wasn't quite as terrible as before. Not entirely sure how she knew it, she whispered, "You absorbed some of my fear, didn't you?"

"Of course I did," he murmured. "As you did for me when Ma died."

Cassie fought a wave of emotion. "You didn't have to do that."

"I would *always* do that for you." His words grew huskier. "As I said before, I will always be there for you whether or not you're fighting difficult times."

With a small nod, she realized that though she might have lost her sight, few were so lucky.

Logan stroked her cheeks and while he had always invoked immediate feelings with his touch, this time she nearly jumped out of her skin. Intense. Profound. Every miniscule slide of his weapon-roughened fingers made her flesh come alive. She shivered, lips trembling in sudden anticipation when she felt the whisper of his hot breath close to her mouth. The heat of his words. "I'm going to kiss ye now, lass."

"Okay," she whispered with an unexpected thrill of anticipation. It was different knowing she was going to be kissed without seeing it coming, to be both vulnerable and eager at once.

When his lips closed over hers, it almost felt like she was being kissed for the first time. Delicate, searching, he pressed and molded and shaped, allowing her to feel the contours of his lips.

As he might have intended, she didn't picture his lips as she had seen them even a day ago. No, he was creating a new visual of them with his actions. The way their fullness worked against hers. The way the bristle of his unshaven facial hair created a delicious friction against her skin. Not enough to be abrasive but enough to let her feel his masculinity, the difference between his hardness and her softness.

Her hands went to his face, eager to search out the rest of the picture. She traced her fingers along the slight arch of his slashed eyebrows. They almost seemed to mimic what she had learned about him. That he was a stern man with a heart eager for humor, something to lighten his way in a homeland fraught with unrest.

Then she trailed her finger down his straight nose as he had done to her. When she came to a slight bump, a miniscule ridge, she smiled. God, the smile felt good. *So* good. "You've broken your nose."

"Several times in battle." She heard the smile in his voice. "You're only just noticing?"

Her smile widened and she murmured, "Yeah, I guess so."

Amazing how she seemed to be opening her eyes now that they were permanently closed to sight. Cassie continued exploring the strong edge of his jaw. Not quite square but by no means weak....then the alcoves of his cheeks before she skimmed his lips, feeling their curvature. "I knew you were hot as hell but had no idea how much so until now."

A low chuckle rumbled in his chest, spreading up through her inner thighs, belly, and breasts until the vibration ran up her neck and made her lips throb. The hitch of his breath and the twitch of his steely erection sparked a brash rush of desire. Cupping his cheeks again, she made sure she knew where his lips were and kissed him.

The taste of him nearly made her come undone. Warm, male, scrumptious, there was no more tentative exploring, but the blazing hot heat of tongues twisting. Starved, determined, his hands cupped her cheeks even as hers cupped his and they struggled to get closer, to become one.

He yanked up her dress and pulled her until she straddled him. Cassie groaned and thrust her hips against the abrasiveness of his wool plaid. Forget focusing on being blind, there were far better ways to push past the unknown and relieve stress.

"Use your magic," she rasped. "Lose the clothes."

"Och, nay, no magic, just the feel of us getting closer the old fashioned way," he muttered tearing his lips from hers. He released a frustrated grunt as he arched and yanked off his plaid. The scratch of the fabric between her thighs made her yelp with pleasure.

Totally lost in passion, their lips were about to lock again when shadows started to form and she saw the outline of his face. "I thought you said no magic."

"I did." He hauled her tight against him, his throbbing arousal eager. "I do."

"But, but..." When his lips crashed against hers, Cassie didn't care what the hell she thought she saw. Their tongues began to dance again, so eager she honestly wasn't worried about coming up for air ever again. Only when he tugged impatiently at her dress, apparently wanting it off, did they separate long enough for her to clearly see what had been flickering in her vision before.

Vision!

But not the normal sense by any means. He almost appeared ghost-like as a light blue light flickered over his face. His *face*. In and out of shadows and darkness but somehow there. Though beyond desperate to have him inside her, Cassie shook her head and put a hand to his chest, panting, "I don't get it. What's going on?"

Logan shook his head, brows drawn together, lips open, breath harsh as his eyes devoured her face. Everything she could make out, no, somewhat see was glowing blue... "Holy *shit*."

His eyes dropped to what she was staring at and a slow smile blossomed on his face, brogue as thick as the magic she must be witnessing. "Yer ring glows for me, aye?"

Blazing, a shining light within her darkness, the stone nestled between the hands on her Claddagh ring glowed the color of Logan's eyes. A beautiful pale blue with gossamer threads of gold that lit him up.

And her.

She could see her body when close to him.

Tears didn't just come to her eyes but overflowed as she looked at him... as she again saw his face, all the more handsome for having seen it when blind. While somehow she knew— whether by the magic of the ring or by her own special vision—that though her sight was gone she had been gifted with this.

The ability to see him.

Logan MacLomain.

As she stared at him, her mind went back to the moment she had pulled into the Colonial's driveway back in New Hampshire. The intent look in his eyes when he rode Athdara. Someone, somewhere, either a god or a wizard or maybe even a motherly witch had given Cassie an amazing gift.

Him.

This Highlander with his heart in his eyes.

A man she never would have imagined she was good enough for. But she realized as he gazed at her so lovingly that not only was she lucky to have found him but he was just as lucky to have found *her.*

Yes, his strength and support gave her courage but something about this moment, knowing that she was willing to *accept* his support and that she was stronger for it, was eye-opening. It was almost as if he lit the spark beneath a strength she had been working toward for years but only now acknowledged.

Not his strength but *hers.*

A strength found because she was finally willing to see that it was there.

That it had *always* been there.

"Do you see the glow as well?" she asked, voice not wobbly in the least. No, she was done with insecurity. In fact, she was done with being blind to what mattered most.

The woman she had become.

The woman she intended to live her life being.

"Aye, I see it," he whispered, such pride in his eyes as he gazed at her.

"Good." Cassie tore off her dress. Then she didn't use the ring's glow to guide her way but tucked it between them, flicked her tongue over his lips and sank into him. When he groaned in pleasure and clasped her waist, she let her head drop back and reveled in the feel of him. She rolled her hips and trembled at the undulating flutters shooting through her.

"Och, I love ye, lass," he whispered as he trailed kisses everywhere.

Hips rolling and grinding, she gave into being a desired woman. A loved woman. Things that had never been hers. Within not only the newfound confidence but the deep-seated pleasure, there was a complete lack of fear.

Yes, some might say she wasn't completely blind as long as she was with Logan. She would always see him. But there was still such closure. No more sunrises or sunsets. No more gazing at the ocean off the coast of Maine. No more eying her little Chevette and patting her on the hood.

That was all behind her.

Cell phones, television, technology, modern day…*that* was all behind her. Now it was something entirely different. Logan. Medieval Scotland. A king to keep safe. A friend to possibly save.

A new life.

Just not the one she planned for.

When Logan grabbed her backside and thrust especially deep, she cried out and pressed close. Any thoughts after that became null and void as they moved against one another. Frantic, heaving, they thrust again and again, painfully desperate to not just climax but be one. They nearly climbed one another they were so impatient, so out of control.

There was no darkness here but pure feeling, pure passion.

Pure love.

When her body seized and movement became impossible, he pulled her so tightly against him that she gasped. Apparently it didn't matter if she was blind or not, a rainbow of colors burst across her vision as she quivered almost violently.

"Bloody hell," he murmured over and over right before her sharp climax ripped him along for the ride. With one hand gripping her shoulder, he pressed his cheek to the top of her head and groaned, "Cassie," with so much possessive passion another intense orgasm lashed through her.

They held one another for a long time, completely absorbed in how good they made each other feel. Time was completely lost. What was not lost to her were his words whispered against her ear, "Be my wif. Marry me, lass. 'Twould make me the happiest Laird in all of Scotland."

She smiled against his neck. "Wif?"

There was a definite grin in his response. "*Wife*."

Finally able to muster the muscles to move, she pulled back enough to cup his cheeks. Though she felt the first rays of sunlight warm her back, she saw only the blue glow of his face as she gave him her heart. "By truly realizing how much I love myself, I can now easily recognize and tell you without a shred of doubt that I love you, Logan MacLomain."

Then she braced herself, wondering if she should be honest. Because the old 'her', who she was prior to coming to Scotland, might have agreed to marry him in a heartbeat. After all, a girl like her wasn't about to get many more offers, especially from a guy like this. Yet she wasn't the old her anymore. Not in the least. It didn't matter if the revelation had happened in such a short time...it *happened*.

So she went with honesty. "But I won't marry you."

Cassie didn't miss the pain that flickered in his eyes but as was Logan's way he nodded and kissed the back of her hand. The man truly was unendingly noble. So she finished her sentence. "Yet. I won't marry you *yet*."

"Yet?" he murmured, lips lingering on the back of her hand.

She nodded, trying not to drown in the adoring way he looked at her so she could say what needed to be said. "I'll be staying here. Based on what I've seen, the shit's not nearly done hitting the fan and my friends are likely heading this way."

Cassie licked her lips and stuttered, "A-and I should b-be here when they go through that," when he shifted his hips, apparently springing back faster than most men.

"And?" he whispered, trailing his lips up the underside of her arm.

"And I...um..." Cassie closed her eyes and pulled her arm away from his distracting lips. When she opened them, that same look of pride had returned to his eyes.

A small smile came to his face. "Go on, lass."

Right. Go on. Cassie caught her breath and nodded. "I need to learn how to live my life blind. I thought it was going to be in the twenty-first century, but I was wrong."

"Aye?" He quirked the corner of his lip. "So ye'll be staying but not marrying me then?"

Cassie nodded then shook her head when he shifted just enough to remind her how intimate their position still was. But what she meant to say was important so she cupped his cheeks and narrowed her eyes. "You are without question the most incredible man I've ever met and I can say with all honesty that I don't want another. But I need to learn about the new me for a little bit."

"The new you?"

"The blind me."

Logan nodded.

"I need to acclimate and learn my way around your castle," she said. "I don't want to be the twenty-first century girl 'saved' by the Highland Laird. I don't want to be the 'oh poor her' story."

Logan said nothing, but that same look of pride was still on his face as he nodded for her to continue.

So she did. "I want to learn my way around and earn your clan's respect not because I'm Lady of the Castle but because I'm me."

"And who are you?" he murmured, watching her closely.

Cassie thought about it. Who *was* she? Was she the twenty-first century girl who needed to learn the ropes in medieval Scotland? Was she the girl who might've helped save Robert the Bruce?

Or was she the blind girl?

Their eyes held and she realized that while she was a little bit of all of those things she wasn't really any of them. No, at the root of her, broken down into this singular moment, she was someone entirely different.

Someone she would enjoy getting to know better.

Leaning close, she whispered exactly who she was before kissing him. "I'm just a girl who believes that a woman can find

'Happily Ever After' by embracing and loving who she's become."
She deepened the kiss then murmured against his lips, "And I
suppose I have you to thank for that."

He whispered, "Nay, lass. I couldnae have loved ye so
thoroughly if ye were not exactly who ye were from the verra start."
His hands wrapped into her hair. "'Tis good though that ye can
finally see what I've seen all along.

What an absolute sweetheart.

"I really do love you," she murmured, so astoundingly glad that
they had made it to this moment. That she had found such an
incredible man to share her life with. She was never more hopeful
and eager for what lay ahead.

Though the enemy was not defeated, Logan and Cassie *did* get
what they set out for.

The wee king was safe and the future of Scotland secure enough
for now.

As it turned out, the quest of her Scottish Warrior had never
been entirely about saving a young boy or even protecting his
country but finding a love he deserved.

A love they *both* deserved.

So when their lips locked and the world faded away, they
reveled in the end of a successful journey. After all, their ending, one
built on acceptance, respect and true love, was by far the very best
beginning.

The End

With two evil enemies lurking in the Celtic Otherworld, little Robert
the Bruce's life remains at risk. Who better to protect him then
spunky Nicole and the exasperated Highlander honor-bound to keep
her safe? Continue the series with Niall and his 21st-century lass in
Honor of a Scottish Warrior.

Previous Releases

~The MacLomain Series- Early Years~

Highland Defiance- Book One
Highland Persuasion- Book Two
Highland Mystic- Book Three

~The MacLomain Series~

The King's Druidess- Prelude
Fate's Monolith- Book One
Destiny's Denial- Book Two
Sylvan Mist- Book Three

~The MacLomain Series- Next Generation~

Mark of the Highlander- Book One
Vow of the Highlander- Book Two
Wrath of the Highlander- Book Three
Faith of the Highlander- Book Four
Plight of the Highlander- Book Five

~The MacLomain Series- Viking Ancestors~

Viking King- Book One
Viking Claim- Book Two
Viking Heart- Book Three

~The MacLomain Series- Later Years~

Quest of a Scottish Warrior- Book One
Honor of a Scottish Warrior- Book Two
Oath of a Scottish Warrior- Book Three
Passion of a Scottish Warrior- Book Four

~Calum's Curse Series~

The Victorian Lure- Book One

The Georgian Embrace- Book Two
The Tudor Revival- Book Three

~Forsaken Brethren Series~

Darkest Memory- Book One
Heart of Vesuvius- Book Two

Also available in the Forsaken Brethren Series Twinpack.

~Holiday Tales~

Yule's Fallen Angel

~Song of the Muses Series~

Highland Muse

About the Author

Sky Purington is the best-selling author of seventeen novels and several novellas. A New Englander born and bred, Sky was raised hearing stories of folklore, myth and legend. When combined with a love for nature, romance and time-travel, elements from the stories of her youth found release in her books.

Purington loves to hear from readers and can be contacted at Sky@SkyPurington.com. Interested in keeping up with Sky's latest news and releases? Visit Sky's website, www.skypurington.com to download her free App on iTunes and Android or sign up for her quarterly newsletter. Love social networking? Find Sky on Facebook and Twitter.

Made in the USA
Las Vegas, NV
20 November 2022